lost

on

purpose

women in the city

edited by **Amy Prior**

SEAL PRESS

Published by
Seal Press
An Imprint of Avalon Publishing Group, Incorporated
1400 65th Street, Suite 250
AVALON
publishing group incorporated
Emeryville, CA 94608

Library of Congress Cataloging-in-Publication Data

Lost on purpose : women in the city / [edited] by Amy Prior.-- 1st ed.
    p. cm.
  ISBN 1-58005-120-0 (pbk.)
  1. Women--Fiction. 2. City and town life--Fiction. 3. Short stories, American--Women authors. I. Prior, Amy.

PS648.W6 L
813'.0108321732'082--dc22

                                                    2004028005

ISBN 1-58005-120-0

9 8 7 6 5 4 3 2 1

Design by Amber Pirker
Printed in Canada by Transcontinental
Distributed by Publishers Group West

contents

Introduction

W e are in love with the city the way others love the country: the mountains, the hills, the fields, the plains, the prairies. We romanticize its streets and buildings and parks and wastelands and bars and clubs and movie theaters with remembrances of things past, our histories recalled in a kind of fragmentary collage of glimpsed image and sound and chatter when we turn this corner or that, a kind of personal psychogeography. *See that house, that one there with the front porch, you remember I lived there with Jo and Lou after college, that crazy time when we all had jobs in copy shops.* We tell new stories, make our own myths, rival the old tales.

A new city can be a dreamy, Oz-like land waiting to be discovered, and we trail the yellow brick road to seek exile from other places—towns, countries, villages, fields—experiencing the intensity of newness once we arrive. We discover new urban districts in the same way: We move around the city and it becomes cities, each neighborhood another mini-empire. In twelve years, I've lived with elderly Jewish people in a 1930s apartment block; in an eighteenth-century house that hosts historical walking tours; on the thirty-third floor of a high-rise; in a big shared house by a huge green heathland; with artists and musicians in an old factory space; with European curators in an old squatted shop ; in a flat the size of a cupboard next to a crack house. I've stayed in one city, but it seems like I've lived in many.

We go from work to record shop to supermarket to gallery to theme bar to pizzeria to glittery warehouse party, and somehow through the fog of the faceless, we find our neighbors, friends, love. We connect in strange ways, indecipherable networks. Sometimes we disconnect—we get lost and alone by mistake: We get wrapped up in our heads and the city becomes a blurry background on which to project our moods; we get scarred by experience and take the difficult way round. Sometimes we get lost on purpose: We lose ourselves in the crowds and turn into someone new.

In *Lost on Purpose*, we are making sense of these things, telling new fictional stories, reinterpreting the old. We are viewing a detail—a house, a street—under a magnifying lens, and calming the background noise so the city begins to unravel, collapsing into focus. We are crossing international borders, finding common patterns in female urban experience. We, too, can embrace the unfamiliar, the edgy, the random, the risky, the extraordinary, the isolation, the connection in the urban. Our experiences are unique; our experiences are universal.

—Amy Prior

Glory B. and the Gentle Art

by Emily Carter

All right, maybe I do. Maybe I do talk first and think later. Yes, it's true, I admit it freely. It's because I'm from the city. Now, you can say to me, Glory B., it's no crime to think about what you're going to say before you say it, to figure out how it relates to the topic being discussed, or if it does at all, or if what you're going to say has the slightest factual basis whatsoever. I've got that argument down cold, because listen, words are my music. When I talk, I improvise. It's not so much what I'm saying as how it sounds. Take jazz, all right, let's use jazz as an analogy, parallels are always good. Now, what I mean is, what—do you think every time Bird sat down to blow, he had the whole musical score right in front of him? Did he have the whole thing thought out? He did not. Well, he probably did not, I'm not entirely familiar with the man's work, but probably, most likely he improvised is what I'm saying.

Now some people, people from Someplace, say, like Minnesota, they think about what they're going to say before they say it. They're not attuned to the sound of words, because they probably grew up sitting on their porches after dinner and homework, listening to crickets, which just make one sound, over and over again, and put you in a trance so you can just sit there not moving and think, think, think, until you go inside and watch television or make fruit jellies. That's where all those types with the master's in philosophy come from: Minnesota, Wisconsin, North Dakota, like that. Brooding and musing all the time. Very, very Swedish, if you catch my drift. Trust them, why should I?

Never go to the movies with someone from Minnesota. Here's what I mean:

I have this friend, we used to go out in high school, about six hundred years ago, but he went to college and grad school while I kept forgetting to get up in the morning, and now he's my friend and he lives in Inwood, which is way far north, where the subway stations have elevators in them to get you back up to street level because you're so far underground, and when you come up you're on top of a hill and all around you are miles and miles of nothing that looks like the city you grew up in, wide boulevards with vague glittering lights from fast-food restaurants and body shops. So you see what I mean—my friend has chosen an untrendy existence in an unfashionable part of town. So when he calls me up to tell me he has fallen in love with this amazing girl who's not only beautiful, but also brilliant, where does she come from? Well, a hint, it's a lot farther west than Fort Lee, New Jersey, and there's plenty of wheat out there. And what's she doing here? Getting her degree in Kierkegaard, another Nordic goodtime boy. He tells me her name is Lara Kjellaan and he wants me to meet her, for some reason he thinks it's very important that we meet. So all right, they'll come down from the north pole and we'll go to the movies.

When I meet them outside the theater and we all shake hands, I'm thinking that I probably really am an alcoholic because one of the questions they ask you is, "When you're in social situations where alcohol is not present, do you feel uncomfortable?" Answer: Yes, absolutely. Let's face it, the only thing I like to do is sit around a bar and drink alcoholic beverages. This meeting people I don't know, this going to the movies, it's not for me, really it's not. But I shake this Lara person's hand and smile warmly at her, a smile that communicates nothing so much as the fact that I have no plans to try to sleep with her boyfriend, because if we don't start from there, forget it, I won't be able to hack this evening at all, and I'm already wishing that I could just spend my whole life talking to strangers who love the sound of my voice, buy me shots of the local spirits, some kind of potent potato liquor brewed in the mountains by peasant women who mix it all up with their saliva. What's so bad about people's saliva? I think we should all share each other's saliva, why not? Saliva, of course, is something I'm thinking a lot about when I meet my old friend and his new girl, because she's very small, has sparrow-boned shoulders and ivory fingers delicate as a tree frog's knobbly feet. Her hair is the color of straw and her face is washed with a faint dusting of freckles. The whole deal makes me nervous, and when I'm nervous I tend to spit when I talk. Not much, just a little, a little mist.

When I calm down enough to hear what's going on around me, I hear my friend reeling off a list of Lara's academic credits—University X, Foundation Grant Y—because he thinks given half a chance, I will dismiss this sweetie as a generic love interest, which really isn't giving me any credit at all. We're all standing in this long line and just as he gets to the part about applying to some writer's colony the line starts to move. I hover over Lara, ready to confide, this must be awkward for her, too? She's hardly had the chance to say one single word, what with her boyfriend doing her advance PR work. I remember in high school we almost never got around, me and this guy, to making out, because he talked so much, and half the time we'd end up in an argument about who was the biggest hypocrite and not speak to each other for a week. We broke up by midterms, if I remember correctly.

So I'm hovering over this Lara, and like always with really small women, I feel like Alice after she took the one pill that makes you larger, big and—here's the word—galumphing. Galumphing, good word, and that of course makes me feel this heady sensation of protectiveness toward the smaller woman, and then the usual realization dawns on me. Oh My God I Am A Lesbian. And not one of those hip stylish ones who write avant-garde movie scripts and get their pictures taken in nightclubs either. I'm some sad old thing sitting at the bar while my little femme fatale girlfriend cheats on me with anything, male or female, that happens to be around. In other words, I get treated the way I've treated certain men in my life, which as a thought is worse than thinking about car accidents. So I say to Lara, would she like some popcorn, my treat. She's so short I want to put my hand on her shoulder, but I don't. I put it instead into my pocket to dig out the money. My friend comes out of the men's room and we go inside the theater. Then there's the thing about who sits where, which I can't stand either; it's more of that kind of thing that makes me pull at my hair when I'm sober. We could sit with my friend between us, but I don't like the looks of that—like he's got two girls, one on either side, nudge, nudge, lucky dog, heh heh. But then again if I sit on the outside of Lara, it will look like I'm some sort of third wheel, some kind of duenna, or some horrible thing like that. I'm standing in the aisle, thinking about what it would be like to be someplace else, sitting in my kitchen for instance, or watching my insane and sorrowful upstairs neighbor Katasha write down lists of her enemies, when here comes the thought, to my rescue, like Superman. Just sit, Gloria, it doesn't matter where, because No One Is Looking At You. Hard to believe, and yet it's an ontological starting point I must adhere to, at times, even just to get out of my apartment.

Anyway, I forget about all that noise as soon as the movie starts. Let me tell you about this movie. It was amazing, and it made me cry at the end, not the kind of crying where they trick you into it with violet-colored lights and a certain kind of music that attaches itself directly to your tear ducts and pulls at them like an invisible, milking jellyfish, so you feel a little ashamed of yourself for being so easily run through the maze to get your money's worth; but the kind of crying where you've just gotten a sense of the fact that there is life, and people go through it, and they die, some of them kill each other, but a man who knew nothing, not even how to talk to people, was somehow able to learn to make things grow out of the earth. Something like that.

The movie put me in a wrestling hold of excitement. Whenever I see something like that every single tendon in my arms and legs seems to buzz a little, and I feel like twitching and jumping. What this is, really, is the desire to do something like that, make that picture, paint that painting, walk that walk, talk that talk. I want to do something like that, something good. What I do when I feel like that, usually, is kill that energy as soon as possible. I go have a drink, or I eat an entire Philadelphia cheesecake, which will make it impossible to think about anything but my intestines for the next three hours. But now I've got to go for coffee, coffee of all things, and I'm walking fast, turning around every now and then to the couple behind me, saying, "Incredible. It was incredible. Fuck." My friend agrees with me. "Incredible," he echoes, but when we get to the coffee shop it turns out he's got reservations, he thinks the filmmaker could have gone further with the atrocities depicted in the war scene.

"What," I say, "the depicted atrocities weren't enough for you? You can't stand it when anyone does anything well, is what your problem is."

"I'm not saying he didn't make a good movie," my friend says. "I'm just saying that when push came to shove, he sold out." When my friend says "sold out" he bangs his fist down on the table and the coffee sloshes over his cup, running thinly over the Formica and down the ridged metal edge of the table, dropping off in little beads. He doesn't notice. Lara sops it up with a napkin. Meanwhile I'm saying, "Yeah, sold out? Sold out to who? Is this man going to become rich off this film? No, I think not. Who did he sell out to then? Who?" I raise my hands in question and knock over a bowl of sugar. I make a plow out of my hand and wipe the sugar to the floor. There are principles here, and I mean every word I'm saying. We keep going. The waitress asks us to lower our voices. Cigarette butts pile up in the ashtray. I compare the narrowness of his righteous unbending rigid thinking to that of Mussolini. He compares all my old boyfriends to Hitler. I draw an analogy between the alchemy of the movie and something about Madame Curie. Which brings up radiation, which brings up Hiroshima, and the ashtray clatters to the floor spilling gray dust and cigarettes everywhere. We work quickly to get it all up before the waitress sees it, and we continue through the Kennedy assassination, the Vietnam War, various pop stars compared to the blues singers they ripped off their music from. And finally, finally my rudeness dawns on me like a wet gray November morning. I pull in my gesturing hands, which are leaping about like struggling swordfish on a tight line. I narrow the big opening my mouth makes in my face and look at Lara, who has been sitting quietly through the whole discussion, looking pleasantly first at one of us, then at the other.

"Well," I say, "what about you, what do you think?" Lara takes a moment to answer. She takes so many seconds to answer that I am about to throw another question at her, because I just can't wait, I'm jumping out of my seat; but before I can, Lara says, "well." She says, "well," and slowly, slowly, clears her throat.

"The thing about the scene you were talking about," she says and gives a little apologetic smile, "is it was about the First World War, not the Second."

The First World War. Not the Second. It's like hitting a wall of air. If this movie is about the First World War and not the Second, everything we've been saying is either completely beside the point or ludicrously wrong. For a moment there is actually no sound at all at our table.

"Did you know that the whole time?" I ask.

"Well," she says, "yes, pretty much."

"Why didn't you stop us?"

She looks absolutely frank and undisturbed as she says, "What you were saying was interesting."

I just sit there, my arguments and brilliant parallels drifting down around me like invisible balloons with the air let out. Those people from the Midwest. Oh, they're clever. Watch the snowflakes fall, observe the sky change from blue to black to blue again, and think and think and think before they speak.

You can't trust them, you just can't. But what if she hadn't been there, what if we had gone on all night calling something that was obviously blue red—eighteen different shades of red.

"Listen," I say to my friend, "I'm not kidding, marry this woman."

The Garden

by Devika Mehra

When Pia walks into his flat in Bombay, she thinks it's a joke. She looks up at Adil, the man she has agreed to marry, waiting for him to ask the rightful occupant of this miniature box to step out of his hiding place.

"So, what do you think?" he asks, mistaking her smile for approval.

Her instinct is to pick up her bags, say No thanks—this was supposed to be romantic—and return home to Delhi. But Adil looks so proud.

"I like the windows," she says.

"Really?"

She unzips her bag and takes out a fresh T-shirt. He offers her a hanger. Pia wonders if she should move to her girlfriend's house, which, in any case, is where her father thinks she's spending the weekend.

It isn't just the room's tiny size or squalor. It's the impermanence of the furnishings, essentials thrown together with no design. The largest object is a metal cot clothed with mismatched linen and shriveled pillows. A curry-stained stove rests on a counter along the wall, its umbilical cord connected to a gas cylinder. No telephone, no air conditioner. The only features are the waist-to-ceiling windows on two of the four walls. Half open, they draw in the saltiness of the Arabian Sea, the smell of fish and damp gutters.

Pia asks for the key to the toilet, more to compose herself in private than out of physical necessity. She moves down the hallway, unlocks the door, and squats over a simple hole in the ground. The stink of human waste hangs in the air. Her thigh muscles twitch; she steadies herself. Pia can't help but think of Adil's room. Had he noticed her hesitant step that could neither go forward nor turn back? Crossing the threshold meant giving up a way of living, all those high standards she had been schooled in since childhood. Good breeding, her father called it.

Yet the ugliness of his place has already begun to seduce her. Its illegitimacy is a sort of comfort, like the time she crept into the servant quarters at the back of her house and lay curled up for hours on a thin, soiled mattress.

Pia met Adil six months ago, when he was in Delhi modeling for a condom advertisement and she was studying journalism. He pressed his fingertips against her many books, marveled aloud at the knowledge encoded in her brain. Before he knew her, Adil confessed, he'd done cocaine, freeloaded on women, posed nude for money—now his ass was hanging in black and white in some rich faggot's dining room.

Then, during a hiking trip to Ladakh, she agreed to marry Adil. A week later, she informed her family.

"What does he do for a living?" her father asked.

"Adil's an actor. And he isn't rich or anything."

"Oh," her father said, too self-conscious to take on the role of a

Hindi-movie parent. "Well, it's up to you. At twenty-three, you're mature enough to know who you want to spend your life with."

Some part of her was disappointed by his tempered reaction.

Now, Pia wonders if she is being foolish. There is a loud thud on the toilet door. "*Arre*, hurry up, or I'll *su-su* in your Kelvinator." The knob wriggles like a netted fish.

The neighbor, Mackrand, she guesses. Adil has told her about him.

"Stop playing with yourself, *bhainchod*, save something for your rich girlfriend."

Pia pulls up her panties. She can hear Adil's voice in the hall, then the neighbor's. "So, who's in there? Some slut?"

Pia stands with her hand curled around the knob. She doesn't want Adil to witness her embarrassment. She collects herself, and, a moment later, steps out. A stocky man with a towel around his bare shoulders faces her.

Mackrand smiles, his round cheeks making dimples, then he turns and glances up as Adil approaches. "*Aaay*, give me an intro to her, *yaar.*"

Pia avoids Adil's eyes and wipes her hands on her jeans. "I'd better go back." She motions to his room.

"Man, she's much taller than her photo. She looks like a cross between Kareena Kapoor and Preity Zinta. Fair and innocent. Sexy, too."

Pia shuts the door. The baby blue Kelvinator stands in the corner like a spectator; fruit flies hover around its sticky frame. Adil has unpacked, folded her clothes away in his closet. He comes in as the kettle on the stove steams.

"Tea?" He turns off the heat.

"Why didn't you say something to him?" She already knows: It's because Mack has set him up with some big-shot director.

Adil looks at his feet, a sulky droop to his lips. "Mack's like a brother to me. What could I do?"

"Anything. You could have said anything." Pia realizes this could become an excuse to move to her friend Maya's house. "You just stood there like a chicken," she says.

"Look, I'm sorry. It won't happen again."

She allows Adil to put his arms around her and rock her gently. His spontaneous affection surprises her, like a sudden rain, and she soaks in it. By comparison, her parents' kisses are dry, careless brushes against her cheek.

Adil goes to the counter, picks up a tall steel glass of tea, and holds it out to her. It is cupped in his palms like an offering.

"Sit," he says and pulls a chair toward her.

She takes a seat. The tube light makes her feel like they're in an examination hall. "I need to call home."

"I'll take you downstairs. We can go to the beach after that. But tell me what you want for dinner, I can cook some fish."

"I'm not hungry."

"Eat something, no?" Adil selects a coconut from a stack. He slices the crown off with a butcher knife and empties the liquid in a glass. She sips slowly and watches him. He is beautiful—tall, with narrow hips. His lean body is almost hairless; tight muscles define his shoulders and legs. His face is oval, widest at the cheekbones, tapering down to a square jaw. He has dark eyes and a protruding, wet mouth, like a fruit.

Adil carves the milky flesh from the shell in bite-size pieces and feeds it to her with his fingers.

"Shush," says Adil when they reach the landing where the landlord lives. "Uncle doesn't allow women to stay overnight." Pia smiles and puts a finger on her lips. Invisibility is new to her. She takes exaggerated steps, hums the *Pink Panther* tune in her head. When they reach the ground floor, Adil introduces her to a third paying guest: an up-and-coming veejay who calls herself Fleur.

"Adil talks about you all the time. Everything is always Pia-says-this and Pia-does-that." Fleur speaks in a birdlike voice. She wears pink hipsters that show off her pierced belly button.

"I've heard about you as well," Pia says, though she hasn't. Adil rarely talks about his female friends.

"Really, like what?" Fleur turns to Adil and ruffles his hair. Her gunmetal eye shadow accentuates her light eyes.

"Only your finer qualities, don't worry," he says. "Pia needs to call Delhi. She'll pay for it."

"All yours," says Fleur.

Pia dials the number on the ancient phone. She watches Fleur, the way she jokes with Adil. Her body sways into his—one bump for every sentence. Adil and Fleur talk about the film industry: no work these days, bullshit money. *Arre*, did you see that new Venus flick? Big hoo-ha and now it's flopped. Producer gave Twinkle the role 'cause she's Dimples's daughter. Big name, influence and all, so what do you expect? And who the fuck lip-synched for her, just horrible, *yaar*.

On the phone, Pia's father picks up. "Where are you?" he says. "Your cell phone is out of range."

"At Maya's house." Pia cups the receiver to block the noise.

"Uncle's been looking for you," Fleur says. "He wants rent."

"I'll deal with it," Adil says quickly as Mack walks into the room. "Janeman," he whispers into Pia's ear, and presses a hand to his heart.

She tries to concentrate on her father's voice. "Our filly runs on Sunday in Bombay. Hope you're going to be there."

"Adil, you're on for the screen test Saturday," Mack says. "Better show up."

Fleur cocks her head to one side and sticks her finger at Adil. "You're the man! Isn't he, Mack?"

Mack scrapes his ear with a hairpin. "The *chutiya's* not a man, he's Superman."

"Is your friend Adil joining us?" Her father will be coming to Bombay the day after tomorrow for the annual derby. He'll stay at the Oberoi Hotel, two hours from Adil's flat in Lokhanwalla.

"Yes," she says. "We'll both come."

Adil laughs. "Fleur, you have the MTV act nailed."

"Yo!" Fleur jumps in the air. Her breasts jiggle and then settle in her tank top.

"I'll send a car for you," her father says. "You know that Adil needs to be properly dressed. What's that racket in the background?"

"The television. I'll call you later." Pia puts down the receiver and turns to Adil. "My father is sending the car to pick us up on Sunday."

"A Porsche or a striped Jaguar?" Fleur says, sucking the tip of her thumb. Adil tries to hide a smile.

"Neither, actually." Next to Fleur, Pia feels dowdy in her tailored pantsuit. "Adil, we should leave. I want to get to the beach before dark."

"Don't mind her. She's not potty-trained," Mack says, pinning Fleur's arms behind her. "Stop by when you come home."

Home? The word rattles in her head.

Chowpatti is nothing like a beach. The sand is filthy. Jagged seashells poke out like warnings. The only people in the water are squatters shitting or washing their laundry against salt-bitten rocks. Adil and Pia sit on plastic bags, shelling roasted peanuts, inventing ways to describe the sea.

"The waves roll toward us," Pia says, "like huge fists. Your turn."

"Erm . . . the waves roll toward us like a forming thought."

"Nice." She thinks of how they'd watched the blue waters of Pong Yong Lake in Ladakh turn a mysterious emerald at noon. Adil had asked her to recline on the shore to pose for his camera, but the photographs mostly showed her long fingers interlacing across her face. Now, she turns toward Adil and surprises herself by kissing him.

"There's Kareena Kapoor," an impish beggar boy screams. *"Aay-haay,* Kareena is giving Akshay Kumar a *chummi."* A group of potbellied boys form a circle around them, tittering like thin-legged chicks. Adil lifts his arm and chases after them.

"Let's go." He looks impatient.

They walk against the wind. Lame ponies pulling carriages trot at their heels, the drivers begging them to take rides. On the slope above, overlooking the sea, the homes are mini fortresses surrounded by barbed wire and guards. They remind Pia of her own house.

"When I get famous," Adil says, "we can move into one of those."

"And in the meanwhile?" she says. Adil likes to talk about his future.

"You can redecorate."

"I can't live like this. In these sort of conditions, I mean."

He doesn't reply at first, just looks out at the horizon. "Okay, I'll join Daud's gang as a hit man and buy you an eight-bedroom apartment. Happy?"

She grins. "Only if all the rooms are sea-facing."

"How about if I build you a houseboat? Great view even when you take a shit."

"How about if I, say, get famous first?"

"Pia, you ever taken the ferry? Come on."

She and Adil squeeze into a rickety wooden boat, squashed among mothers and children in synthetic clothes, half-asleep cows, sweaty workmen, and motorcycles. Adil looks at her and laughs. "What?" Pia yells over the drone of the engine.

"Remember when I met you at that pool party?" he says. "I was dripping wet, and you stood there, this graceful woman I hardly knew, listening to my crazy ideas."

"You're lying." Pia strokes a sleepy cow on its neck.

At night, Adil drags the mattress to the floor so they can lie side by side. The table fan doesn't keep the mosquitoes away—they're like a net around her. Adil faces her, the blanket bunched around his heels. His skin is tanned and glossy, except for the birthmark on the rise of his hipbone. The mosquitoes don't touch him. Familiarity, maybe.

Pia keeps her cotton nightdress on. Sleeping naked, she has been taught, is inappropriate. Having sex isn't appropriate either. Sex is the mysterious blackout in Hindi movies, the missing frames after rainswept song-and-dance sequences, the lovers' clothes wet with longing.

But lying here with Adil, she feels comfortable enough without Wonderbras or blow-dried hair. As a kind of game, he shows her how to tear open condoms with one's teeth. Pia pokes her thumb into the condom's sticky mouth, laughs, shakes her head, and watches Adil demonstrate different sexual positions. "For posterity," he says. He rolls on his back and pulls her on top of him. Pia giggles. She bounces up and down. She can feel him beneath her, sense his desire, but of course it is only make-believe. Pia knows how to control herself. "It's not right," she says. "I feel dirty." She is a decent girl, a virgin, the type men want to marry.

Pia returns Adil's overtures timidly at first: stroking his chest. When it feels safe, her tongue traces a slow line to the bottom of his stomach, pausing where the dangerous dark hair emerges. "But what will you think of me?" she says when Adil asks for more.

"I'll think you're a whore, so what? I'll say it right now, you'll be a whore, a slut, a cheap *rundi* . . ."

"Stop it," she says.

"Your father's not watching," he tells her, placing his hand between her legs. "No one cares over here."

The morning sun floods the room like a searchlight. The sound of the sea, the water's tug-of-war with land, is unfamiliar. Heat sinks into her. Adil has left without waking her. She lies between the clutter of clothes and bedding and last night's dirty dishes. The shadow of a palm tree flickers across her body like a reptile. If a man, say Mack, should come in and drag her by the hair to the toilet, rape her, and throw her into the opaque sea, no one would know.

The streets below are narrow and wounded, teeming with beggars and stray dogs eating litter. Shacks sprout behind hoardings painted with busty starlets clinging to bare-chested, mustached heroes. Lokhanwalla smells like a ghetto. But the advertisements still accumulate like obstinate desires, attached to street lamps and dilapidated houses. It's the neighborhood of strugglers: kids who were conditioned to be engineers and doctors, but flocked to Bombay determined to reinvent themselves into Shah Rukh Khan, or disco kings like Govinda. Adil's no different. His father was clubbed to death in a workers' strike when Adil was thirteen. But he doesn't like to talk about the past. "That part of me," he has told her, "is dead."

Pia pictures her own father in his black satin pajamas and embroidered slippers. He laughs over her mother's latest antics—her foolish fear of cats, her failing memory. He and Pia are the intelligent ones: a team. Then she thinks of Adil. When he meets her father, Adil wants to ask ridiculous questions about his beginnings, his struggles, his business strategies, the road to riches. She tries to remember what Adil knows about thoroughbred racing. Nothing.

The mattress she slept on feels hollow. Even so, she wants to lie here forever, to vanish into the dirt and clutter all around her—lose herself. She looks out the window and sees a *hijra* lurking on the neighboring terrace. The hermaphrodite walks with one hand on her torso, swaying her thick hips. Her hair hangs in thin spikes over her brightly painted, manly face as she hides beneath the clothesline and chews her betel leaves. If the *hijra* gets caught in a decent home, she will be beaten. She spots Pia staring and spits juice at her. The shiny red saliva spatters against the window. The *hijra* lifts her sari, threatening to display her double sexuality, then disappears behind the drying clothes.

A moment later, Adil comes in, holding paper plates. He wears tight Levi's and rubber Bata slippers. He puts the food down and throws himself on her, kissing her palms. Her skin feels damp under his lips. "You're still here," he says.

"Where did you expect me to be?" says Pia. "On the moon?"

"Yes, on the moon, but you're still here." He wraps one arm around her neck, nibbles the tip of her nose.

How easily she surrenders to his affection, sinking into his lap, cradled, whispering nonsense—baby talk. She can't help herself, and it scares her. Pia strikes out at him. He ducks her blows, eyes half-closed, amused, still holding her firmly and planting kisses in between the violent gestures.

Adil pushes her to the ground and pulls down his jeans. She removes his penis from his underwear and squeezes, feeling its pulse as her thumb reaches its smooth tip. She inhales his smell, the curious essence. "Fuck," Pia says in a throaty voice she doesn't recognize. He tries to free his dick from her hand, but she will not let go. She watches him wince as he pries open her fingers, stubborn tentacles, one by one.

Adil lies between her legs and encircles her wrists, placing her arms on either side of her head. He hesitates as he looks down at her.

"Don't think," she says, and pulls him inside her.

Her body yields to Adil's weight, the shock of his immersion. She feels him rise and fall inside her. Behind him there are half-open windows and unknown streets, and beyond that acres of deep sea. Nothing seems impossible. She feels the suck and swell of water, tastes its salt on her tongue as she bites his skin.

"Ouch," he says.

The plain sound of Adil's voice makes her wholly aware of lying here pierced and naked. Adil's face comes closer. It seems twisted, as if in pain. He is so close his black pupils smear into a single gaping eye. "You look creepy," she whispers.

He stops, still inside her.

"What?"

"Talk to me. I need to hear something. Tell me what makes you sad or happy. Just tell me things."

"You already know about me, you mad woman." Adil places his hands under her hips and lifts her toward him. "So, I'm creepy?"

"I didn't mean it like that. Just your eyes. Can we go on?"

Adil raises himself on his arms and begins to move quickly. She hardly recognizes him as he punches into her.

In the afternoon, Adil takes Pia to watch a platform skit at Prithvi Theatre. He stands behind her, his arms fitted comfortably around her waist, and she leans back against his body. After the performance, they sit in the café. Fleur smokes a joint and talks to Adil. "I gave a blow job, the works, and the *chutiya* still said no. That's what a loser I am."

"I think you're a great veejay," Adil says, and squeezes Fleur's hand. "Right, Pia?"

Pia tries to compose a clever reply, something that will make her belong. "You can do better. Fuck him."

Fleur sneers and stubs out her cigarette. "Yeah, right. What the hell would you know? Adil, want to watch a play tomorrow? It's free. She waves two tickets at him.

"Can't. I have my screen test." He practices a fight move: a left jab. "Just watch, Natraj is going to launch me. I feel it in here." He thumps his heart.

"Do the test first, then—" Pia begins.

"Wowie!" Fleur says, cutting her off. "My Aby-baby's going to be a superstar."

"When I get famous," Adil tells her, "I'll make you queen of veejays."

Fleur claps her hands, and then hugs Adil. "I love you, you fucker, you know that?" She wipes her eyes dry with her fist.

Unsure of what to do, Pia looks away.

On Saturday evening, Pia goes with Adil to Film City. Mack waits for them outside Natraj Studios. "You're late," says Mack. He spits his sum and opens the door for her. "Welcome to our funtastic abode."

The rumbling sound from the industrial generators makes the sweltering space seem alive, as though they were inside some huge ravenous beast. Thick black tubes snake around the walls. Stage lights stud the ceiling. A shapely, baby-faced actress bedecked in a shimmering sarong reads a Bollywood magazine. Beside her, a pudgy man wearing a lime green suit sits surrounded by his sidekicks. Adil and Mack join the circle. Spot boys weave through, serving glasses of tea.

Pia listens to Adil talk to the man. "It would be a great honor, Natrajji, if you could give me a small chance to work under you." His voice is sweet and hopeful.

"What about her?" Natraj points his tiny cell phone toward Pia. "Would she like a small chance, too?" He sputters into laughter.

"Oh no, sir. Pia is my fiancée." Adil gives her a little push. She steps forward.

"Nice choice," Natraj says.

Pia has the urge to slap his baboon face—inform him exactly who and what her father is. For Adil's sake, she stays silent.

Natraj shifts his weight. "Okay, the story is boy loves girl, parents create a big *hungama*, couple elopes, then some *bukwas*, let's see, few songs, dances, and a happy ending." He pats the actress on her bum. "Shilpa, go do a sequence with our hero. Let's get some action."

Shilpa stretches her arms languidly. The magazine on her lap slips to the floor. KAREENA DUMPED! the cover reads. "Where's Tiny?" she says.

A midget carrying a makeup kit follows the actress into her dressing room.

Adil removes his watch, gives it to Pia, and steps onto a junglelike set. A backdrop of snowy mountains and trees flickers on the wall. The dance tutor hops in a circle, demonstrating the steps. Adil faces the camera and stares ahead at some distant spot that is secret and urgent. For a brief moment, Pia sees him detached from the ordinary, like a painting, exquisitely framed and held up to the light. When Adil stumbles over a word, she feels responsible. When he delivers a line with ease, it's as if he has spoken only to her.

A technician asks Pia to move. "Your shadow's in the way," he says, and makes her shift to a corner. She sits on an abandoned prop and glances around. Mack walks up beside her. Pia is grateful; she pinches his arm and grins.

The set thunders, the roof pours rain. A disco beat unfurls from the speakers. Fog machines cloud the stage, and Shilpa emerges from the smoke like a miracle. She closes her eyes, rotates her hips. Tiny jumps onto the director's chair, unbuttons his trousers, and mimics her movements. The crowd of extras hoots and shrieks.

Maybe he *will* be a star, Pia thinks, watching Adil's lips slide over Shilpa's quivering, wet navel. And what will I be?

Adil slithers up Shilpa's body and lip-synchs to a love song.

The next day, her breakfast is placed on a turquoise dish embellished with white daisies. Adil has his eggs on a paper plate. He eats fast, doesn't daydream or shift his food around. The fork's trajectory is a straight route: into his mouth and out again to stab the eggs. Adil finishes, then lies down, his head propped by his elbow. They've had sex again, and now he gazes at her, as though nothing she can do will disappoint him.

"What?" Pia says. "I can't eat if you stare."

"Okay, I won't." He picks up her left foot and kneads the sole with his thumbs. "You eat like a bird."

There is a knock at the door, then a man yells, "Adil, are you there, *beta?*"

"Oh, shit," Adil whispers. "One minute, Uncle." He pulls on his shorts. Be quiet, he signals to her, and goes out to the corridor.

The landlord's voice is only slightly muffled by the closed door. "Last month's is overdue, Mister. I'm not a charity, you know."

"I'll pay by tomorrow latest, Uncle. I've even asked for those passes for you and Aunty to watch the shooting at Sun and Sand Hotel."

"I heard a girl's voice last night," the landlord says. "You know the rules. No hanky-panky in my house."

"There's no one here, Uncle, by god," he says. "Just my sister from Delhi."

A door slams in the hallway. "Adil, shweety," Mack teases. "Why are you standing here in your *phunky* knickers? *Yaar*, put on a tie, there's a producer-looking guy asking for you. I told him to come upstairs."

Pia hears sharp, measured footsteps. Instantly, she recognizes them. Her heart clenches.

"Is Pia here?" asks a familiar voice.

"Mr. Burman, sir," Adil says. "Yes, but let me tell her you're here. She's resting."

Pia feels a sickness inside her as if she is falling from a great height. It can't possibly be him, she thinks.

"Sleeping till noon. What is she, ill?" says Uncle.

"May I go in?" says her father.

Adil opens the door and her father faces her. Pia tries to sit up, but her body doesn't respond and she lies stretched on the mattress, shirt inside out, no makeup, her hair disheveled. For a moment, her father looks uncertain, as though he wants Pia to be someone else, not his daughter, sprawled on the floor. She expects him to back out in horror. But he stays.

"I thought I'd stop on my way from the airport and pick you up myself," he says, averting his eyes almost casually and looking out the windows. "Your friend Maya said you asked for the car to be sent here."

"Yes, I came in the morning," Pia says in a choking murmur, and then sits up, holding the sheet tightly around her chest. She can smell his lime cologne. Its fragrance floats around Adil's room and turns it back into the tiny box she walked into when she arrived.

Her father straightens his silk tie as if to set everything in order: the damp heat, his half-naked daughter, Adil in his underwear, the gutter stench, and flies that litter the shoulders of his jacket.

Pia searches for something to say. Why did you come? she wants to ask. You have no right to be here, this is your fault. Instead, she reaches for her jeans and puts them on under the sheet. She tucks in her shirt and stands up. "What time is our race?"

"Four P.M." Her father glances at his watch, then places his hands in his pockets. "I want to get there early. Are you still interested in going?"

"Yes, I am." She wishes he would growl or scream, slap her, drag her out of here, do what he needs to do. But he will never be tempted into forgetting who he is.

A small, balding man with owl-eyed spectacles now stands in the doorway. "So, this is your real sister?" he says, examining Pia as if she is a rotting fruit he'd cut open.

"Yes, Uncle," Adil says softly.

Pia looks at her father as he processes things. She tries to remain calm, but all she wants is to hide her face.

"I'm not listening to any more 'Uncle, please,'" the landlord tells Adil. "If you don't have rent, I'm throwing you out—sister and all."

"Uncle, give me till tomorrow."

Her father snaps open his briefcase with a solid click. "How much is it?" He takes out ten thousand rupees stapled together with a bank sticker. "Will this do?"

The money lies on the counter like a weapon. Uncle stares at it, his fingers pocketed deep in his trousers.

"It won't be fair to accept this, sir," says Adil.

"Well, this is hardly the time to be concerned about being fair. Just take it."

Adil takes a step forward and picks it up. "Sir, I'll definitely pay you back this evening." He wipes the bundle against his shorts. He takes a look at her father and then hands the money to his landlord.

Uncle counts the cash quickly. "It's good," he sniffs and slips out the room.

Adil closes the door. His eyes look shifty. "Pia, if you want to leave with your father now, it's fine."

"No, I'll wait for you," she says, because it seems the right thing to say. Pia slips on a sweater over her shirt and buttons it.

Her father studies his watch. "I'll go ahead then. Why don't you follow when you're properly dressed?"

"Mr. Burman, sir, I'm really sorry about all this. I'll return the loan."

"Forget about it. Just wear a suit or you can't enter the members' enclosure."

Her father picks up his briefcase. Wait, she wants to say. Pia tries to hold together something inside her: maybe a hope, an unmanageable emotion that topples under its own weight.

Kabhi Kabhi plays on the radio in Mack's room. Pia waits in the corridor for Adil to lock up. Mack's door is ajar. He lies on the floor, staring at the ceiling, arms and legs spread wide. His large, watery eyes flick to the side. "Hey, Queenie," Mack whispers. Pia looks away and hurries downstairs.

She and Adil climb into a yellow and black rickshaw. "Mahalaxmi Racecourse *chalo phatafat,*" he tells the driver. The open flaps allow the dust rising off the road to strike their faces—no tinted windows to buff out the glaring sun. A beggar boy chases after the rickshaw, his bare feet slapping against the hot tarmac.

Pia wonders where she would be now if she had never met Adil. Gossiping with family at Sunday brunch? Playing golf with her father? Home, she thinks.

Adil places her hand on his thigh and rubs it. "You're not angry, are you? I'll pay your father back, even if I have to turn into a horse myself and run the races."

She tries not to smile. "Stop acting silly."

"You're so sexy it makes me silly."

She pushes him away. "You saw what just happened. I mean, my father caught me undressed. Do you have any idea what that means?"

"It means you love me and no one can change that. Not even him."

"I've been humiliated in front of everyone. My father must think I'm a . . . I don't know what. And all you can do is play the fool."

"I told you I'd pay him back. I promise, okay?" He lifts both her legs and swings them over his knees. "You have the sweetest toes."

"You probably use the same lines to *pataou* all your girlfriends," Pia says, putting her legs back down. Despite his softness, she realizes Adil is tougher than she is. He knows how to move on.

Their rickshaw halts abruptly at a major intersection. Coca-Cola billboards tower over the fuming traffic like new gods. A cart stops alongside them. It has shutters on three sides and a barred peephole. School children sit silently in the dark. They stare out onto the street, their tiny fingers poking through the mesh wiring.

"Look at that," Pia says. "Like chickens being sent to a slaughterhouse."

He glances at the children. "They look happy."

As happy as we look, she thinks.

The driver cranks up a hit tune. He shakes his head and hums along.

"You liked *Zadugar?*" Adil asks him.

"*Wah!* What a *phlim,*" the man says. "Aamir Khan has double role, eleven songs, and tip-top dancing, but fighting was so-so. No *dum* in villain."

"Pia, let's go see it tonight," Adil says.

"Don't you understand? For god's sake, he caught us. He *knows.*"

"So?"

"What if it were your father? How would you feel?"

"My old man is dead." Adil stares at the moving white stripe on the road and starts singing along with the driver.

When they reach the racecourse, Pia joins her father in the owners' paddock, and they watch his filly, Secret Treasure, trot by. The diamond shapes on her father's midnight blue tie match his gray flannel suit. Pia stands near him; her shoulder touches his arm. She is foolishly satisfied with her father's appearance. He is tall, like Adil, but his features have a harder, authoritative look.

Secret Treasure waits to be mounted. She strikes a practiced pose: left leg forward, ears pricked, head held high, sun hitting her smack on her shiny coat. "Get a good jump, lie third or fourth," her father instructs the young jockey. "Make your run in the straight, and don't try any tricks."

Pia smiles at his advice. Always practical. Do what you know and get home free.

Adil waits for them at the gate to the paddock. "You missed the fourth race," her father says. "Mystique won by four lengths. I had a big one on her."

"That's great, Mr. Burman." Adil shakes his hand. "Sir, who do you think will win the main event?"

"The bookies are pretty hot on my filly. Two-to-one favorite." He looks at the race book. "The colt Indictment could cause a few hiccups, but I'd say the field's fairly clear." Her father takes out his wallet. "Place your bet at the first enclosure—they give better odds. And here, put twenty thousand rupees on Win for me."

Adil takes the money and heads toward the bookmaker's ring where the serious punters in their old jeans and Terylene shirts stand.

"Pia, you look exhausted," her father says. "I hope you haven't caught something. You have to be careful of your health."

"I'm fine."

"You don't look fine to me." He turns up the collars of Pia's shirt, removes a stray thread stuck in her hair. "What you need is a warm bath, a nice clean bed, and some rest. No more vagabond nonsense. Now let's go to our box and order you a drink."

"What about Adil? They won't allow him in the members' enclosure without us."

She and her father stand in awkward silence. Pia stares at a pair of men walking past her. Kabir Oswal: twenty-four, single, chauvinist, heir to Oswal Steel. Jeh Mehta: twenty-seven, married, unfaithful, source of income uncertain. They blend together into a single stroke of crisp suits, monogrammed shirts, and veneered faces. Pia imagines Fleur in her pink hipsters and pierced belly button among this jeweled crowd. She envies her.

When Adil returns, her father leads the way to the long, white balconies on the second floor that perch over the track. "I borrowed four thousand rupees from Mack. I've put it all on your horse, number four," Adil tells her. "Damn thing better win."

Her father stops to greet friends before they sit down. "Pia, you sit in the middle," he says, placing her between Adil and himself.

The Topiwallas, an old Zoroastrian family, have the box in front of them. It is designated by a brass nameplate. They own the chestnut colt Indictment. The large family sits as though enthroned there by nature.

"Good luck," her father says to old Mrs. Topiwalla. "May the best horse win."

"May the best horse win," she repeats, flashing a smile. She wears the same canary yellow crepe-de-chine dress every time her horse runs. "I can't say exactly how my Indictment knows, but he always does his level best when I wear this lucky outfit," Pia has heard her say.

"You've met my daughter, Pia, haven't you?"

"Of course. And what a lovely girl she's become." Mrs. Topiwalla waves a finger toward Adil. "And this is your . . ." Her eyes scan the skinny knot of Adil's tie, the absence of cuff links on his sleeve, a coffee stain at the kneecap of his khaki pants, his bulky white socks. The valuation, Pia thinks.

"Oh, he's a friend who lives here in Bombay," her father says.

Mrs. Topiwalla pulls out a scented tissue from a tin and dabs her neck. "Well, good luck all."

Pia looks up at the suspended monitor and watches the horses move into the gates. Adil leans over and speaks to her father about the race. She shifts her right leg and nudges Adil's elbow from her thigh. He is talking too much. Nervous chatter. Her father sits back in his chair, his left foot tapping the floor, and listens. Pia tries to visualize what her father must think. How dramatic Adil is. How he speaks with his hands, his features vibrant, his voice too loud.

A shrill bell rings. Her father adjusts his binoculars and leans forward. The gates open. *Under starter's orders . . . they're off,* says the commentator. A storm of pounding hooves moves past the boxes, and the jockeys' colors flash kaleidoscopically in the sunlight. The horses bunch together, galloping along the mile-and-a-half track. Mrs. Topiwalla shuts her eyes. She keeps them closed during the race, says it's too much pressure. *As the field hits the straight, it's the pacemaker, Baywatch . . . followed by Arabian Rose . . . hotly pursued by Aerogramme, and Indictment close behind on the rails.* The hurried tempo of the commentator's voice quickens the heartbeat. *But the favorite . . . found a gap . . .*

Adil stands up and yells, "Secret Treasure—move your butt!"

The Topiwallas glare at him. "For god's sake," Pia hisses.

"Sorry, sorry." He places a finger on his lips and sits down.

*In the home stretch, it's Indictment, followed by Secret Treasure . . .
quickly making ground . . .*

The crowds in the first enclosure press themselves against the railings of the track and yell out the favorite's name.

Her father shouts, "Come on, Secret Treasure!"

Pia follows his lead and stands up. Mrs. Topiwalla mutters a cryptic prayer. She wonders if old Mrs. Topiwalla has ever played puppet with her thumb stuck up a condom. *It's Indictment and Secret Treasure, running neck . . .* Pia wants to ask her, "Does your lover blush when you brush those huge teeth?" *Secret Treasure is pushing . . . she's giving it all she's got . . .*

"You can do it, baby!" Adil yells, throwing out his arm. Voices crescendo as the horses gallop past the boxes; dust from their hooves rises like a funeral fire. *It's Secret Treasure and Indictment, still Secret Treasure and Indictment.* Pia wants to ask her, "Have you cleaned a window stained with a *hijra's* red spit?" Mrs. Topiwalla sticks her fingers into her ears. Tell me, old woman, have you ever tasted the sea? *Yes, oh yes . . . the hot favorite . . .* Pia watches Secret Treasure stick her head forward, just a nose ahead of Indictment as she races past the finishing post.

Her father slaps his hand against his knee. "We did it!"

Adil lets out a whoop and kisses Pia, then embraces her father. "It's quite all right, thank you," her father says. He smoothes his hair, excuses himself, and hurries down to lead his filly into the paddock. Photographers surround him. Acquaintances try to catch his eye. The crowds do a little jig, and throw rose petals on her father and his horse. "*Wah! Wah!* Burman sahib! Well done, Secret Treasure."

"Let's cash the booty," Adil says. He leads Pia downstairs to the bookmaker's ring. The bookies sit on high stools. Desperate punters clamor around their knees as though they were selling nonstop fares to heaven. Adil gives the man his slips.

The bookie glances down and hands them back. "Sorry, no good."

"What do you mean? My horse—number four won." Adil points to the chalked results on the long blackboard behind him.

"Mister, your number four hasn't even seen the track yet. Your bets are on the next race." The man sighs. "Odds are fifty to one. What are you? A fortune teller?"

Adil looks confused. He opens his mouth, then shuts it again.

"I can't believe this," Pia says. All the confusion she felt in his room is balled into a mean fist. "I've put up with your friends' snide remarks, watched you flirt with every woman in sight. I was ready to give up everything to be with you. And you can't place a simple bet. You can't even pay your own rent. How the hell do you expect me to marry you?"

Adil's eyes are empty.

She is going too far, but she wants to go even farther—get Adil to do what she can't—make him shake her by the shoulders and say, This won't work, I'm leaving.

"That was all Mack's money," he mumbles.

"What about my father?" she says, working herself up. "What's he going to think?"

"What about me?" says Adil. "How do you think I feel?" He tosses the slips in the air. "You people think you know it all, don't you? Money, horses, fucking suits and ties, but what about love? You know shit about that. Shit."

"Stop shouting. This isn't some stage set," she says, and turns to leave.

Pia joins her father behind the track at the stables. The filly stands sweating; a white residue stains her bay coat where the saddle was.

"You should write a little essay on the race for college," he says.

"Yes, Papa."

Flies buzz around the horse's head. Her eyes are dilated, and she breathes heavily. Pia puts her arms around Secret Treasure and buries her face in the animal's neck.

"I'm going home," Adil says when he catches up with her after the prize ceremony. "What's your plan?"

"My father and I are having tea at the hospitality tent." She shifts the enormous silver trophy to her other arm. "I'm staying with him at the hotel tonight."

Adil's arms hang at his sides. "I'll call you."

Pia nods and watches him walk away. She thinks Adil might turn around, but he doesn't, and then he vanishes into the crowd. Left alone in the paddock, she listens to the amplified voice of the commentator declare the day's winners and losers.

Her father reads a novel: *The Other Side of Midnight*. He pushes his gold-rimmed glasses firmly against his nose. She'd like to speak to him about Adil, tell him how she feels so she can make sense of things.

Pia fiddles with the knobs on the console between the twin beds that control the piped-in hotel music.

"Turn down that noise, please," her father says.

Pia switches it off. "So, what did you think of Adil?" she says before he can resume his reading.

"Decent chap," he says, without looking up at her.

"Then you like him?"

"It's not a question of like or dislike. A man is known by his profession, his deeds, and a woman is judged by . . . by the dignity she keeps. At least that's how I've tried to bring you up. What I saw this morning, well, you could hardly call that place a garden."

"Adil loves me, doesn't that mean anything?"

He looks at her curiously, as if the notion of love is something she has invented. "Darling, if you think you can live happily ever after in a filthy box, then go ahead. The decision is yours." Her father reaches to turn off the light. "Good night," he says, his words harmonized with the click.

Pia turns to her side and hugs the pillow. The linen has a scratchy texture, as if no one has ever slept on it. If this were a movie, she'd climb out the window, desperate to join her banished lover, who'd wait below singing some melancholy song. They'd dance like Laila and Majnu under the moonlight, make love in discreetly edited footage, and drink from silver cups of poison.

The hotel operator has put the line on DND. Pia wonders if Adil has tried calling. She misses rubbing her toe against his leg; she misses the weight of Adil's body behind hers, his hand cupped resolutely around her breast.

The air conditioning deadens the sound of traffic on Marine Drive, the main road that wraps around the shoreline. Adil says the city was once a group of small islands, but greedy developers pumped out the sea and dumped earth in its place until the land ate up the water. An unearthly green light from a neighboring skyscraper blinks at her. The windows are still wet from the evening rain.

Pia goes to the bathroom, sits on the toilet seat, and checks the messages with the operator. Nothing from Adil.

She looks at herself in the mirror and pulls a face. "How lovely I have become," she says, mimicking Mrs. Topiwalla's British accent. The fat hotel towels look tempting. She runs a bath. Do what you know and get home free, she sings to a made-up tune, as the water splashes into the tub.

Her cell phone rings in the silent, dark bedroom. Pia runs to get it. She looks at the flashing number. It's Adil.

"Why is your line on Do Not Disturb?"

"My father's sleeping," she says, walking back to the bathroom.

"I was going to mail this letter I wrote, but Mack says I should read it to you. It's not elegant or anything. It's about me, how I feel, okay? So no sarcasm."

"Just read it."

"Okay, here goes: *It has stopped raining and the sun from behind the clouds is making everything in my room look yellow. I can hear crickets outside, and I want to tell you about this small village in Assam, where I lived with my family.*"

I don't want to know, Pia thinks. It's too late.

"*It rained ten months in the year, and there was always this diffused light, which makes me remember all this in black and white. There was never any electricity, and our home was lit by kerosene lamps. They have a thoughtful flame that made everything look graceful, and during my bath, I'd love to watch the water shimmer down my skin.*"

Sentimental, but she knows what he means. Soft towels lie at her feet.

"In the evening, the drives on my father's scooter felt like victory laps. I was nine years old and I rode in front with him, holding the handles. The roads were hilly and winding, lit dimly by the scooter's headlights. We could hear the hum of grasshoppers and crickets and fireflies, it was as if God (if there is one) had lined them up like an orchestra along the road to sing for us, and the darkness ahead made it seem like we could go on forever."

Pia digs her nails into her fingers, and curses him silently. Just when she has made up her mind, he talks about forever, about miracles.

Adil pauses. "There's more, but you'd call it silly. I'll read it anyway. *I wonder what put me in this time capsule? Maybe the crickets outside my window. But now they are gone and there are too many mosquitoes.* That's all I want to say. Tell your father I'm sorry."

She can hear Mack's voice in the background. "*Yaar,* let me say hi to Queenie. Is she coming with us for the film?"

"I have to go," says Adil. He hangs up before she can say a word.

The hot water gathers in the shallow tub and the rising steam blurs the mirror she is looking into. "I am a lovely, lovely girl," Pia says to herself. She engraves her full name on the smoky mirror. Lovely fool, she thinks, watching her eyes emerge through the clear lines. She imagines herself with Adil, Fleur, and Mack with all his crazy talk, telling her to stop by. How successful Adil and his friends are, living alone, independent, and Pia is furious at herself for who she is.

She enters the bedroom, the numbing, air-conditioned darkness. Her father's eyes are shut. He makes no sound. She walks to the windows and pushes the shutters open. A strong wind hits her face, whips through the thin fabric of her nightgown. Leaning over the sill, she watches the waves roll in, full of hope and vigor, only to break against the rocks and wash away again, taking bits of the shore as they retreat toward some invisible future. Tireless motions. If it were possible, she would set the sea free, release it from the pull of gravity, the dutiful opening and closing.

She turns around. Her father still sleeps. Stripped of consciousness, he looks faded. She sits beside him, nudges his shoulder. His head droops off the side of the pillow into his chest; a strand of spit worms out from the corner of his half-open mouth. For a second, she thinks she has somehow killed him. Her fingers tighten into an unbreakable grip, determined to wake him; and she shakes his body so hard that her whole world seems to shake with him.

The City of Brotherly Love

by Karen Herman

They are all fire ants. I can wave a blowtorch, set them alight, and listen for the crackle of tiny bodies. It ignites into a feathery curl of dark smoke. I asked my brother, I said, "Who did you see down by the river?"

He said, "Colonel Sanders."

I said, "No!"

He said, "Yes! I saw Colonel Sanders sitting in a car by the river and he had a blowtorch."

Along the Schuylkill River, where canals were built and streams rerouted and dammed, is the City of Brotherly Love. There is a bell with a crack in it and an eternal figure of a woman sewing a flag.

In the City of Brotherly Love, my brother loves to catch things. Under the Spring Garden Street Bridge, he caught a twenty-one-pound cream-colored carp. At the Market Street Bridge, he snagged a ten-inch bull-head.

Along the Schuylkill River, which means "Ganshowahanna" or "falling water" in the language of the Lenni Lenape, The Men Among Men, is a mental asylum that will shut down and flow with the river. Some rooms will contain live streams and the basement corridor will be filled with rushing water. The upper floors will have the wind and the rain and migrating birds. But for now, the psychiatric ward has nurses, doctors, and patients. They are all interchangeable. Like pieces in a strange puzzle a child could arrange, the nurses placate the patients, the doctors placate the nurses, the patients are out of their heads on all sorts of medication or else supine, fish on a slab, restrained by leather straps.

It is this kind of efficiency and one out-of-tune piano, a community room with a television, a candy and soda machine, and books like *How German Is It* and *Black Pow-Wow* that define this particular psychiatric ward. My brother has been a member of this psychiatric ward ever since the LSD he took at twelve years of age backfired on him at eighteen years of age. He said he could see all the planets and stars crashing down on Walnut Street. He said he could talk to Betsy Ross. He said he cracked the Liberty Bell with a crowbar. He could walk on the moon.

He could hear God whisper in his ear.

One day, my brother left the psychiatric ward. He simply walked out of the door and kept going. He crossed Roosevelt Boulevard like The Men Among Men and went south. He walked from the Schuylkill River to the Susquehanna River, America's sixteenth largest river, then he trudged by the Potomac in Washington, D.C. He continued like an Indian, a pioneer, sleeping in the great pine forests of the past, scrambling over farmers' barbed-wire fences in Virginia and makeshift stone and shale walls from the Civil War days. By the time he got to the bottom of Florida, there was no place left to go except Cuba, so he turned back. But first he stole a Camaro. Then the police gave him free accommodation in jail. Somebody kicked him in the crotch. Somebody hit him over the head. He sat in a corner on the cold cement floor and wept because he could still see the moon exploding on the sidewalk and nobody would listen, nobody wanted to see. It's hard to see sometimes.

When my brother wasn't having an acid flashback, he returned to his greatest joy, fishing. He had subscriptions to *Fly Rod & Reel*, *Field & Stream*, *American Angler*, *The Fish Sniffer*, and *Boating World*. He had a tackle box to keep all his hooks and flies. His whole world was chaos, except when you opened his tackle box. Before he left home, I used to sneak into his bedroom just to have a look around and to fiddle inside the box. There were three tiers of lures and flies, plastic beads with painted eyes wearing tiny grass skirts. There were lead weights, metal hooks, and neatly wound rolls of line.

He talked a lot about his fishing adventures, but he rarely took me. He talked about the cold, clear streams and creeks that fed the Schuylkill River and overflowed when it rained too hard. He talked about pike and pickerel, trout and bass, like they were beautiful flowers in bloom. He could talk about fish the way he could talk about drugs, the way he could talk about his paranoia rising behind him, and the fish swimming below him, and he'd cast in his line to wait while the moon rose between his shoulders.

Once, behind the Philadelphia Museum of Art, he caught the same carp twice. Its lip hanging off a little to the right, like a poorly hung painting, he said, "Hey, brother. I know you."

When my ancestors still lived along the River Thames, or in some dark Welsh village by the sea, people were running to the City of Brotherly Love. They bundled up their heartbeats and dreams and fled into the rapids and torrents of life. Like the wind, it blew their heads adrift, floating above the rich green and black earth. Then they would sit down on a strange rock. Between black maple and white ash, they watched the moon rise for the first time as free people and realized what The Men Among Men have known forever: Beyond ourselves are long fields sloping down, filled with the forgotten seeds of sunflowers. The light shifts, creeping across the face of the mountain. Night and stars hold hands. We do this and we do that.

We go down to the river, to cast in a handful of stones.

Borderlines

by Calla Devlin

Neighbors called us brats, unruly, yelling monsters who picked fights with their children, littered their lawns, and screamed at night when we should have been asleep. We heard, "Where is your mother?" daily, a question that became as boring as bedtime prayers. Adrienne, my oldest sister with the filthy mouth, always yelled back, "She's dying, so why don't you shut the fuck up?"

Adrienne was beautiful, her strawberry-blonde hair and yellow sundresses disguising her poisonous tongue. A cream puff with tacks inside. When we walked down the street, a tidy row of deceptively sweet-looking girls, I trailed behind like an afterthought. I wanted to be a mixture of my sisters, gathering fragments and putting them together to create a mix-matched whole. Unapologetic, like Adrienne. Gentle, like Marie. Irreverent, like Vanessa. I walked with a swift gait.

Adrienne took after our mother, inheriting her pale hair and round face. She rode shotgun. Vanessa, Marie, and I crammed in the back, our legs sweaty against the vinyl seat. I could taste the heat in the car. Adrienne said that we should drive along the ocean because just looking at the water would make us cool down. Vanessa squeezed in the middle, impatient and restless. Marie curled up behind Adrienne. I sat behind my mother and rested my head against the window, watching her hair whip around her face in the rearview mirror.

San Diego was a strange mix of border town and resort. We drove through the neighborhoods and, by age nine, I could identify the rich from the poor with ease. Vanessa insisted on asking the name of each neighborhood, even though we made this trip often. The rundown houses with cracked stucco blurred into larger, freshly painted versions of themselves. Some streets were tree-lined; others were dusty and filled with potholes. My mother offered sighs instead of answers. Adrienne told Vanessa to stop asking the same fucking question over and over again. Vanessa closed her eyes.

I loved the car, the simple act of being in motion. Marie would climb over the emergency brake and turn on the radio. Adrienne would take requests for stations, and sometimes we would sing along to Neil Diamond or Carly Simon. I pretended that we were taking a road trip. A vacation to the Grand Canyon or Lake Michigan or Mount Rushmore. I sang Neil Diamond loudly. "I love your voice, Amy," my mother said. Adrienne agreed. "You have a goddamn angel voice."

The highway curved against the ocean, the shore so close that the salt water stung our eyes. My mother told us that if we looked hard enough, we could see dolphins in the water. Marie and I stared for what felt like hours, dying to see the arched gray backs emerge for a brief moment before disappearing into the surf. Vanessa said that she was more interested in the debris floating in the waves: logs, seaweed, a broken surfboard. She wanted to see sharks and teeth.

We pulled up to wait in line for the border crossing. The heat caught up with us and filled the car, flooding it with a mixture of sweat and exhaust. Adrienne turned up the radio until guards glared at us. She was fourteen and defiant, confident, having just outgrown her training bra. My mother looked at the guard and then at Adrienne, who smiled. My mother smiled back and turned down the radio. Being blonde made the crossing effortless. The guards waved us right through. We were halfway there.

My mother said that Tijuana looked like a city that had been bombed. In the streets filled with pedestrians, our pace slowed, breaking the breeze. We passed refrigerator boxes that housed families. Children younger than I, younger than Marie, who was seven, ran after the car begging. "Be grateful," my mother said. Marie leaned against the window, needy, the youngest. "When are we going to eat?" she asked. She wanted a bottle of Coke and maybe a pastry. My mother answered, "When we're out of Tijuana."

My father told me that my mother first exhibited symptoms when she was nineteen. They were students at UCLA. She studied nursing and he studied architecture. My mother had a tumor. A small, ugly bump on the back of her neck, ruining the perfect line of vertebrae. My father hated touching it, his fingers and palm skipping over the growth as his hand traveled down her spine. He said it was the only ugly thing about her. She explained that it was cancer and had it removed. When she was thirty-six and I was nine, she told my father that she was dying of leukemia. During that time, cancer possessed us; we were its hostages. We occupied a world of illness. Our once-sunny rooms darkened with closed curtains and the kitchen sink overflowed with dirty dishes. We were ungrateful. We didn't appreciate the present or the past. We wanted more, and each unmet need germinated into a nagging resentment, multiplying like infected cells.

Laetrile is cyanide. Its origins seemed harmless: apricot pits. It should be nutritional, like a vitamin or dietary supplement. In the 1970s, thousands of people diagnosed with cancer—mostly leukemia—went to Mexico for laetrile treatment, staying in the clinics for days or weeks or months. It was illegal in the United States. At first, we visited the clinic weekly, staying a night or two at a time.

Our blue Datsun station wagon approached the school, collecting Marie and me. Then we swept by the junior high to pick up seventh-grade Vanessa, surly with her braces, her blue eyes flashing from another day of adolescent drama that both intrigued and intimidated me. Vanessa was twelve and filled with the awkward anger and self-consciousness of her age. Outspoken and popular, she was surrounded by friends, other girls filled with energy but already learning to conceal enthusiasm with nonchalance. They all wore miniskirts. Vanessa climbed into the car, smoothing her coral-colored skirt over her thighs.

We drove across town, past strip malls and grocery stores, and then pulled up to the expansive lawn of the high school. Adrienne was waiting, sitting on the curb. A boy was with her, smoking. This must have been Ben, the boy who Adrienne talked about with Vanessa. Marie and I were too young to understand the longing for a boy's tongue in our mouths. Vanessa pretended she understood passion, but it was out of her reach. Adrienne said that Vanessa would have to wait until high school to fully appreciate desire.

We drove. We sped through neighborhoods until they became familiar. We learned to say "*por favor*" and "*gracias*" and "*dónde está el baño?*" We liked the children at the Mexican clinic because they were as loud as we were. They didn't appear full of fear. They didn't pity us for having a dying mother. Their parents didn't banish us from their slumber parties because we uttered phrases like "shit-faced rat-fucker." Later I realized how easy it is to simplify people when you don't share a common language. When you can't ask questions and hear answers. Like my mother.

When summer came, we went to the clinic three or four times a week. It was there that my mother found a community among the dying. She began to work in the clinic—treatment one afternoon and nursing the next. Almost every day, we would leave our San Diego home to visit the Mexican hospital. I remember driving down the coast, crossing the border, and following the sea south. We always sped through Tijuana, slowing down as we approached Ensenada. There, we would eat lunch in the clinic's courtyard, looking out at the ocean as though on holiday.

I didn't want to believe my mother was dying. She didn't feel well enough to ride her bike; she stopped going to the grocery store; she never cooked; she stopped visiting with friends; she threw out her makeup. One afternoon, we were alone in the house and I wanted to go to the park. I whined and begged and threw pillows across the room. I told her that I hated her cancer and I hated her and I insisted that she get better. My mother was the only person who could be quieter than I. She stood and absorbed my tantrum. Minutes passed before she knelt down and pulled me close to her. "Wait for me, Amy," she said. "Wait for me to get better."

A nine-year-old unacquainted with burying a cat or stumbling across a dead bird couldn't grasp the complexities of cancer. My mother was ill, but I applied the laws of the common cold to leukemia. Her illness was elusive. My parents were strained with each other, always tired and preoccupied with something larger than our family. Now, I realize that it was the grief of living each day as though it could be the last.

The clinic became as familiar as school. The white stucco buildings of the hospital had curved arches that opened up to a courtyard where we played kickball and hopscotch. The sun filled the garden in the middle of the building, multiplying my freckles until I appeared almost tan.

My mother picked up Spanish, becoming almost fluent. My sisters and I befriended dying children. Cancer became our way of life. I remember the warmth of the afternoon sun as we drove home, which was more comfortable than driving to the clinic. We left late in the afternoon, past the peak of heat. The air was breezy, a relief. But I wished that we were driving toward the clinic, rather than away. I grew comfortable with the climate of illness. At home, I was constantly questioned: "How is your mother?" At the clinic, everyone knew how my mother was doing. There, the nurses asked how I was doing.

Vanessa kissed her first boy at the clinic. He was older than Adrienne, seventeen. He was dying. Most of the American children were dying except for us. Michael was from Seattle; his parents had packed up their car and headed south in search of a cure. A temporary remedy to his illness. He was doing well. Laetrile was offering a remission, my mother said. *Remission.* Could my mother get a remission? Could a doctor prescribe it to her like he had for Michael? Could our visits to Mexico come to an end? Could we return to our father?

Marie broke her ankle playing soccer with some of the sick children. It was an easy game. Low impact. Nothing to tire them out. I watched as they played in slow motion, their legs moving cautiously. Marie was the fastest, but she tried to slow down, only to speed up again, forgetting that she shouldn't show off her natural athletic abilities to a group of sick children. But, at the age of seven, she understood disadvantage. She slowed down and resisted the opportunity to score over and over again. She was the polite one.

I read Nancy Drew and sat in the sun. I waited to go swimming; wearing my floral printed bathing suit. The bougainvillea was my only shade, small shadows in the shape of open petals and thick leaves. I concentrated on my book, on the clues of the broken locket. I didn't look up when Marie screamed. "Amy, get off your fucking ass and go get Mom," Adrienne hollered. I looked up to find Adrienne hugging Marie. Vanessa was inspecting Marie's leg, which looked twisted and disgusting. Marie was quiet except for her initial scream. I rose and ran into the clinic and yelled for my mother. I ran up two flights of stairs, passing rooms with beds full of cancer. "Mama! Mama!" I ran faster, forgetting my plans to swim in the ocean. I found her on a bed. Her pink lips now gray. The color gone from her cheeks. Her hair messy and her smock hanging open, revealing sweat pants and a T-shirt. "Marie's hurt. You have to come." Another nurse, a woman named Lupe, came up to me. My mother spoke to her in Spanish. I caught *"m'ija,"* and that's it. All of the other words were foreign to me. I kept telling her that Marie needed her. That Adrienne was getting pissed off. That we needed her help. Lupe took my hand and let me lead her to the courtyard. Marie was crying now. Lupe scooped her up and took her inside. Adrienne said that it was the perfect motherfucking place to break a leg. There were half a dozen doctors on duty.

My mother stayed in her clinic bed for the next two days, slow to recover from her treatment. Lupe assumed my mother's responsibilities, feeding us, telling us in broken English to brush our teeth. At night, I left my bed to sit by my mother's side. She slept soundly, not rousing when I spoke to her. I whispered her name and borrowed Adrienne's profanity. I demanded that she take care of us. I wanted her to wake up and take us home, to notice that we were there. She slept through the night.

Marie got a cast, and we spent the next few weeks covering it with Magic Markers. We were instructed to restrict our play with the other children to board games. Monopoly in Spanish. The clinic became boring. The sun grew too hot. We never made it to the ocean to swim. I outgrew Nancy Drew.

"I'm not going," Adrienne said. "Go without me." She stood next to my father. "I'm not getting into that fucking car." My mother didn't resist. My father never resisted.

Vanessa graduated to the front seat. Marie reached to turn on the radio, but Vanessa kept the volume low. The open windows let in the sound of the freeway, drowning out the music. I caught random bits of songs, incomplete melodies that couldn't hold my attention. Vanessa spoke in an envious voice, almost yelling, making sure we could hear her in the back seat. Marie curled up against the window. Vanessa talked about Adrienne's plans for the day: a car wash benefiting the high school baseball team. Ben played second base. I closed my eyes and imagined Adrienne telling Vanessa to shut the fuck up.

Once we were settled at the clinic, my mother disappeared. The landscape looked the same regardless of the season. A year of Mexican weather was like one long day. Always sunny with some cool spells and periods of unbearable heat. Marie had taken to talking with God. She found a pocket book of saints. Lucy was her favorite, a waif of a woman who carried her gouged-out eyes on a plate. Marie started walking with her eyes closed, bumping into walls and closed doors, knocking over medical supplies. She learned the floor plans by heart.

Vanessa pitched a fit. She was in high school now. Our family split in half like a sliced avocado. Slowly, we were repossessing our father. First Adrienne, and now Vanessa. I waited for my turn. Vanessa wanted to play the piano. Her teacher called her a natural, her fingers instinctive. She needed instruction and practice; she came to the instrument late and had to catch up. Her hands worked the keys, and soon her exercises became songs. Beethoven's sonatas and Chopin's nocturnes. My father bought the old church piano from our new church, Our Lady of Immaculate Conception—Marie's choice. The parish was small, not many children. My father brought it home in a borrowed truck, and four men carried it into the family room. Vanessa never went back to Mexico.

Once Vanessa was a freshman, Adrienne guided her through high school. Adrienne bought Vanessa her first erotic book. Initially, it was tame—Judy Blume's *Forever*. Then *Flowers in the Attic*, with those seductive brother-sister incest scenes. Within a year, she graduated to *Penthouse*. Adrienne thought Vanessa would be shocked by sexuality and was thrilled by her hunger for pornography. Vanessa kept her stash in the piano bench, *Our Bodies, Ourselves* and *Hustler* hidden beneath sheet music. After Adrienne, I was the only one who knew of Vanessa's reading material. Adrienne said that she would personally kick my ass if I told anyone. Adrienne could always keep a secret.

As my mother's health declined, we left the house less and less. Our trips to the hospital became infrequent, and we never traveled on a Sunday. That day was off limits—reserved for rest and play. For everyone except me.

Marie attended first communion classes after mass. She only wore pastels because she believed God preferred pale colors. Adrienne told Marie that God was a smoking pile of horseshit, and maybe she should wear the color red once in a fucking while. Marie stuck to baby blue and pink. She drew pictures of saints on her T-shirts. Bloody-eyed Lucy. Flame-licked Joan. Horrible portraits drawn with an amateurish but sincere hand. My father was faithful and escorted Marie Sunday after Sunday, leaving my mother in bed, leaving me to watch her. Adrienne was off with Ben at some sports game. Vanessa was wedded to her piano and porn.

I asked my father if I could leave, not caring where I went: church, music lesson, or baseball game. "Someone has to take care of your mother, sugar," he said. My father praised me for being the perfect nurse, mistaking my silence for compassion. I stayed with my mother, reading books as she slept.

Our visits to Mexico decreased. My mother slept all of the time, losing weight and fading away. She called me her little nurse. I stayed indoors, freckles fading from lack of sun. I caught up on my reading. Vanessa said that we were becoming a real family again.

I don't remember my father interacting much with my mother during that last year of her illness. I became the conduit between them. He would come to me to ask if she needed anything. They rarely spoke and never touched. I parked myself on the floor and worked on homework or read or

47

stared off into space. Sometimes I slept on the floor. My father came home with a puppy, a border collie. "He'll keep you company while your mother's sleeping." Panting. Smiling. Ready for a nap. My father said that he liked having another male in the house, even if it was just a dog. He named the black and white puppy Smiling Jim. He said the dog was mine.

I rarely walked him, keeping him in the room with me. He slept with his head in my lap, rolling over so I could pet his belly. Leaving me in the dark house with my mother, my father and sisters would be gone all day. My mother asked for water, tea, soup, or medicine. I told her to get it herself.

In the summer, my mother wanted to go back to the clinic. It was Sunday. My sisters were scattered about attending recitals and baseball games and church. Our air conditioner broke down, and the house felt hot and musty despite windows left open for days. My mother carried a terrible odor: sweat and urine. Even the dog seemed to dislike being in the room with her.

Marie inspired me and I tried to pray, but my insincere words embarrassed me. I begged for her to die. Disappointed, I looked away when she opened her eyes after a long nap. I hated the sound of her voice, soft and helpless. The rhythm of her breath—the perfect beat of inhaling and exhaling—suffocated me. I yearned to smother her with her own pillow.

Maybe we would die on the road. The car would skid off the highway, stumble over the roadside railing, and trip into the ocean. Water would seep through the cracked windows. I would finally have a chance to swim.

She made me leave Smiling Jim at home. We crept down the freeway in the car, neighborhoods both familiar and foreign. Now I rode shotgun and controlled the radio. We didn't talk. We just sat there, my mother's hands on the steering wheel and mine in my lap. We waited in a long line at the border. Guards standing next to low buildings wide enough to house semitrucks. The guards smoked, and I wanted to bum a cigarette. I wanted cancer. I pulled out a quarter from my pocket and flipped it in the air. Heads: My mother would die. Tails: I would.

"What are you trying to decide?" she asked. Her first words in the car. I turned up the radio. Now eleven, I was old enough to be rude.

I loved the clinic. I remembered it as a time when we were orphans. Vanessa kissed boys. Adrienne turned heads. Marie played sports. No one told us to start or stop or shut up. But this last time was different. The pink bougainvillea didn't impress me with its contrast against the white stucco walls. The courtyard was empty. The dying children simply dying, and no longer children. Death had lost its charm.

I sat and waited, but my mother was quick. She returned in ten minutes holding a brown paper bag. Once we were in the car, she pulled out four folded dresses, all made of the same crisp white cotton, like sheets. Each was embroidered with different colored thread. One had birds. Another roses. She handed them to me. "Lupe made these for you and your sisters." I ran my hand over the cool fabric. "Let's go walk on the beach."

I looked at her disbelievingly. She could barely get out of bed and now she wanted to take a walk. "Do you feel well enough?" I asked her.

"I feel fine."

We left the clinic grounds and drove down the coast ten miles or so. She was chatty, saying that Lupe was well and how good it was to be back in Mexico. I closed my eyes and felt the wind, breathing in the smell of salt water. The ocean felt so different in Mexico, only a few dozen miles away from home. We pulled over to the side of the road and walked down to the shore. The breeze cut the heat's intensity and I yanked off my shoes, anxious for the water to cover my feet.

"You always wanted to swim when we came here," she said. "You should go in."

I shook my head. "I don't have my suit." I knew that it would be useless to bring it.

"Let's just walk then."

I walked slowly, trying to keep an easy pace, wondering when we would have to go back and drive home. Her illness always took over, cutting everything short. But she walked quickly, and I quickened my stride to keep up with her. "You don't look very sick today," I told her. "You never take walks."

She stopped and turned to me. "I feel good today. It's nice to be out of the house." We walked for twenty minutes without saying anything else. I pretended she wasn't there and wished Smiling Jim walked next to me. When she was gone, I would ask my father to take the dog and me to the beach. Maybe Mission Bay, where we could swim.

In my memory, that day feels both compressed and drawn out. I don't remember coming home. I don't remember climbing in and out of the car. I couldn't tell you what was on the radio. The only thing I remember is my mother telling me to not breathe a word about our walk. She wanted my father to think that we had spent our time at the clinic. "He would worry too much, Amy," she said.

My father waited for us. He sat on the couch, with all of the windows and doors open. Smiling Jim barked and wagged his tail. He wiggled his butt and ran to me.

"How was the clinic?" my father asked.

"It was fine," my mother said. "I think this last treatment helped." She took the brown paper bag and pulled out the dresses. "Look what Lupe made for the girls."

He looked at me. "Did you have fun? It looks like you got some sun." I could feel the warmth of my cheeks. I looked at my mother.

"She sunbathed in the courtyard, didn't you, Amy?"

I nodded and petted Smiling Jim. My father told me to take the dog for a walk and to pick up any shit with a plastic bag. I grabbed the leash and left the house.

My mother told my father that she had to go out. She wanted me to go with her and leave Smiling Jim at home. It took her an hour to get dressed, and she emerged wearing lipstick and a pink dress. I hadn't thought of her as pretty in years.

"You look nice," my father told her. She nodded and told me to get in the car.

I wondered if we were going back to the beach and stuffed my bathing suit in my backpack. We drove for twenty minutes, away from the border, leaving San Diego and heading toward the northern part of the county. Brush replaced grass as we followed the ocean. When we finally pulled into a parking lot, I was surprised to see a movie theater instead of the ocean or a doctor's office. "Come on," she said. "Let's see *Star Wars*."

The theater was cool and dark. I ate popcorn and drank an enormous Coke as my mother sipped a small cup of 7-Up. We sat in the middle of the crowded theater and watched the movie. I realized that I hadn't seen one in three years. Struggling to focus on the plot, I thought more about what we were doing in the theater. Commonplace activities were foreign at this point.

I watched her more than the movie. She sat, engrossed, and watched the spaceships fly across the screen. She lifted her cup to her face and drank from the straw, swallowing slowly. All of her movements were delicate. I munched on my popcorn and wondered how long it would take her to die. I wanted to join my sisters and my father and Smiling Jim.

We drove back, silent, with the radio turned up loud. At one point, she reached for the knob and turned down the volume. "Things are going to be different from now on, Amy." She reached for my hand and gently squeezed it.

I sat quietly and looked at our hands in my lap. My fingers were longer than hers. Soon, I would be taller, all of my limbs longer than my mother's.

"I'm leaving," she said. If the radio had been on, I wouldn't have heard her. Her voice was thin and wavering. "I wanted to tell you first. Your father knows, of course, but I wanted to tell you first."

"Where are you going?"

"I'm going to a hospice. Do you know what that is?"

"It's a kind of hospital, right? Is it in Mexico?"

"No." She shook her head and squeezed my hand before taking hers away. Her fingers circled the steering wheel. Her wedding ring glinted in the sunlight. "It is a hospital where people go to die."

When I looked at her, she had her eyes on the road. She grabbed my hand swiftly and tucked it under hers. "It will be like the clinic, right?" I stared hard at her. "I'm coming with you?"

She focused on driving and didn't look at me. The car was filled with a hushed silence. I could hear her breathing. "No, sweetie, I have to go alone."

"But I'm the one who takes care of you," I insisted.

"Amy," her tone grew stronger, "you've taken care of me for too long. You're beginning to hate me for it."

I was crying openly now. "No," I barked. "You have to take me with you." I looked her straight in the face as Adrienne had done.

"No, Amy, you can't come with me. Only your father is allowed to visit." She met my eyes briefly before returning hers to the road. "I want you to remember me like I am right now." Her hand remained on mine.

Smiling Jim rushed to meet me, wiggling his butt before rolling over for me to scratch his belly. I leaned my face into his neck, hugging him. He jumped up and barked; he was ready for his walk. It would have to wait.

"How was your afternoon?" my father asked.

"Fine." She looked at me. She had reapplied her lipstick in the car, a pale pink shade that matched her dress. I was still crying. Smiling Jim barked at me, tail wagging. My mother reached out for me and I leaned into her. She kissed the top of my head. My sisters came in, tan and smiling, returning from a baseball game. Vanessa asked what was wrong.

"Girls, why don't you sit down?" my father said.

We all claimed a seat on the sectional couch. I sat next to my mother, huddling close. Smiling Jim lay at my feet. My father was the one to talk. "Your mother is getting sicker," he said. He kept his eyes on her, his eyebrow raised as though he were asking a question. "She needs to go live at a hospice."

"I won't be coming home, girls." She paused and I could her the sharp sound of her taking a breath. She was struggling. "It's really important to me that you don't come to the hospice, but I'll call you as much as I can." I couldn't stop crying. First I looked at Vanessa, then Adrienne, and finally Marie. We crowded in close to each other, trying to eliminate the distance that had grown between us.

My father packed up her things in boxes. I folded the clothes and put them in a suitcase in tidy piles. I don't remember her act of leaving. I remember the phone calls that followed. She told me she loved me. She thanked me for taking care of her. She asked about school and if I was making friends. She wanted to make sure my sisters were looking after me. The space between her calls grew longer and longer until they finally stopped. Then we gathered again in the living room and my father told us she was gone.

Without her, my father retreated even deeper inside of himself. He established a routine that included family dinners every night, when we crowded into the kitchen and cooked together. He directed us with few words, but with a soft touch. We attended church, where the parishioners called us pretty and polite. My father sat next to Marie, and Vanessa and Adrienne passed notes throughout the service. After seeing The Thorn Birds on television, Vanessa decided she was sweet on the priest. She returned from communion with a smile on her face, licking the wine off her lips. I sat on the other side of my father at the end of the pew, missing my mother.

The end of the summer approached and we started to think of back-to-school clothes. Adrienne prepared for her last year of high school; Vanessa her second. Marie was the last in grammar school, starting fifth grade. Gradually, I spent less time alone in my room and allowed my sisters to initiate me into their world of boys and sports. I had imagined that they were somewhat the same as before our mother got sicker. Taller versions of themselves. But they weren't.

Vanessa smoked cigarettes and had more than one boyfriend. I only met the one she went to school with, but she received many phone calls in the evenings. After dinner and piano practice, she'd retreat to her room. Our only link to her was the long phone cord trapped under her door. She'd come out flushed and full of stories. We'd pile on Adrienne's bed and listen to Vanessa compare each boy with the others. Adrienne approved, but it seemed to me Vanessa was running away from something. Otherwise, she'd pick her favorite. When I said so, Vanessa winced and Adrienne reminded me Vanessa's favorite had been the sick boy at the clinic.

When our older sisters asked Marie and me what kind of boys we liked, Marie swore she'd never marry. After that, we all called her the nun. Our routine began to include evenings of the four of us in Adrienne's room. Our father worked in his study, and we spent time talking about everything but our mother.

I followed them to football, softball, and soccer games. I allowed Adrienne to find a boy for me. I held his hand and kissed him, hoping that my manufactured affection would grow into sincerity. All the while, my mother remained with me, a quieter presence than even my father, a phantom limb.

The Trash
Collector's Song

by Anna Sophie Loewenberg

I t was when she first met Song Qin, when her face was still swollen from his kisses, that the paint box exploded. They were making out, so she turned the lights off and balanced a candle on top of her compact traveler's paint set. She woke to Song Qin shaking her, his face coated in a mask of black ashes, the box in flames. Song threw the burning box out her window. They lit cigarettes and spent the rest of the night giggling from shock, and because their faces looked so funny.

Next morning, when she looked down into the courtyard for the charred pile, everything was white. First snow had come. The ground was coated in pale frosting, a blanket over their secret night of mischief. She ran down and rescued the disfigured paint box like it was a dried flower.

She wanted to remember her first year in Beijing, when they were like a paint box on fire.

It is a bright, cold day in April when she moves her things into Landlord Zhang's place. She mops the linoleum floors until the smell of boiled cabbage and old rag mats vanishes. She scrubs the greasy kitchen walls and the laundry room windows until everything looks shiny and the endless Beijing sky beams through clean glass. Her own place. Still, the gritty street always finds its way back to her windowsill. Song helps her tear two grease-stained propaganda posters of the Great Helmsman, Chairman Mao, from her kitchen wall. Instead, they put up her favorite album cover: Dead Kennedys, *Bedtime for Democracy*. She folds all of her trash bags and stuffs them under the kitchen sink. When everything is in place, they sleep naked under the furry American flag quilt that Sarah Ann gave her. Sarah Ann was an expat from Minnesota. "I bought that quilt in Las Vegas, my honeymoon with Larry. Those were real wild times, the 1970s," Sarah Ann had said, before divorcing her fat Texan husband and leaving China. There isn't much else in the apartment, but when Song is lying next to her, the place feels full.

She always wakes up before Song, in the early hours, and lies very still, without opening her eyes. She is listening for the rise and fall of Song's breath. She could be anywhere: Japan, Norway, California. But the melody of the morning trash collector always carries her back to Beijing.

"Shou fei pin! Shou fei pin!"

Beijing trash collectors belt their morning arias high enough to reach top-floor apartments like hers, only to swing Mandarin tones down low into basement factories and boiler rooms. They make sure everyone hears their song: "Collecting extra stuff, collecting your garbage!"

She's moved so many times that she hardly has anything to throw away anymore. It's never easy finding a place in Beijing. This time she had called her best friend, Rabbit. Rabbit copied the ad in her dainty Chinese characters so they could tape it to telephone poles around the university district:

```
Mandarin-speaking Jewish girl with cute green
glasses looking for apartment in the city.
Can pay first and last months' rent. Is re-
spectful and quiet, but likes to have Chinese
musicians and artists over, including her
boyfriend, who smokes pot, is a high school
dropout, has bleached hair and tattoos, and is
a totally great guy.
```

"But Fei Fei," Rabbit protested as she traced the characters. "Don't you know what happened above the Third Ring Road? They tore everything down last week, even Global Disco and Angel Bar." So she trashed the poster in favor of urban development.

Her next plan was that Rabbit could hold a loudspeaker and she could stand on an overpass, above the exodus of moving vehicles on Peace Boulevard. Her ad would read:

```
Nice, young American girl, university-
educated, looking for an apartment! May have
Chinese friends frequent the apartment without
notice or neighborhood committee approval.
Will pay first and last months' rent in full!
```

The only hitch in the loudspeaker plan was the bad state of her lungs. Beijing is so far from the California coast where she grew up. Still, on humid nights, she dreams of seagulls and vast open spaces, but her lungs have long since purged every last grain of that salty sea air. They are now packed, like preserved duck eggs, with coal dust, construction dust, and Mongolian sandstorm dust. So she finally decided to hang her advertisement from a red kite and fly it above the city. The kite would start at Hou Hai, the Back Lake. She would walk the kite south through an old maze of alleyways and across Tiananmen Square, and on to the Jianguomen Financial District. On the banner, she would write:

Nice, American-educated girl has been living like a no-good hunzi. She has moved apartments so many times that she keeps her clothes in a suitcase. She has lived in an all-male dormitory, but that was just until her final exams at the Beijing Language and Culture University were completed. She left early after being tormented by drunk Korean men from the dorm who pounded on her door at night, screaming at her. She hid under her bed and was afraid to go to the bathroom. She was offered a job at a magazine with "housing included," but once she started the job, "housing included" meant moving in with her editor. She lived with her boyfriend in a one-bedroom with running water, but no hot water, stove, or telephone. That was a fine place until autumn came. They had spent the summer watching a pair of sparrows build a papier-mâché nest on the balcony. Then, it was five o'clock one morning when the Beijing Housing Authority came banging on their door:

"Who is in the bedroom?" She could hear the policeman questioning her lover in the hallway.

"Open the bedroom door." The policeman was wearing a green uniform.

"You in the living room. She stays here." Song joined the rest of the guys in his band who where sleeping on a pile of raunchy DVDs.

"Whea ah you from?" The policeman closed the bedroom door. She felt dizzy and sat in a chair. If she didn't speak Chinese, if she played dumb and only spoke English, he would leave her alone.

"Passport. Show me passport," he said. She glanced at a trash bag on the floor. It was filled with the weed Song had bought on their last trip to Southern China and stuffed, like a pillow, between her chair and the bed.

"Your *huzhao*, your passport," the policeman raised his voice at her. She reached for her suitcase and pulled out a dark blue passport.

"American," he said, grinning. Then the policeman touched her.

"You name?" he asked, flipping pages. The policeman took his free hand and brushed it over her chest, across the front of her pink nightshirt.

"What is going on in there?" Her lover knocked at the door.

The policeman walked into the living room and left her there, her face burning pink as her nightshirt. He collected resident's permits from the boys.

"She has to be out in twenty-four hours, or she'll be taken to the station." The policeman rifled through a stack of pornos. "I'm confiscating these," said the policeman before he left.

Maybe the neighbors had complained. Maybe it was that time when Song got stoned and threw a six-foot Styrofoam lion off the balcony. That was during a summer rainstorm, and they wanted to see if the lion would fly, but it just crashed into the downstairs neighbor's roof instead.

As the policeman's footsteps faded from the stairwell, she grabbed a trash bag and began to stuff it with clothes. The apartment started to shake until a fracture appeared in the bedroom. As the apartment grew smaller, the crack became a giant fissure. It was growing between her running shoes and his slippers, her passport and his identity card, her breasts and his pornos. But where would she go? As she packed her things, the fissure became bottomless. It looked just like that construction site near the Back Lake where their favorite noodle shop had been. The restaurant was a bright spot at the end of a decrepit alleyway. Song grew up around the corner, and he had brought her there in summer to eat cornbread noodles and garlic tofu paste. Then, one afternoon, Song took her for noodles, but they found that the shop had been reduced to a rubble pit.

"Stop right there, Fei Fei," Rabbit said. "*Bie leile!* Don't tire yourself out!" She grabbed the advertisement. "There are way too many words to fit in the sky, even above Tiananmen." Rabbit's pale face was still fragrant from the Dabao cream she had used the night before. By this time, Rabbit looked like a displaced nymph who should've been sleeping, but was made to labor in the midday sun.

"Besides," said Rabbit, "even if you could have fit that entire ad on a kite, you'd be targeting the businessmen who eat their lunch in the Financial District, and they are always looking into their cell phones and never into the sky." So she dropped the kite idea.

Rabbit's real name is Jiang Mei. Jiang is for the Long River country where she was born, in Central China. But now that she is an artist living in China's capital, home of the Forbidden City, the Communist Party, and long-haired musicians, everybody calls her "Rabbit."

Since Rabbit isn't from Beijing, she knows how to get important things like fake identity papers, hash from Xinjiang, and illegal apartments. So Rabbit paged Comrade Li, and Comrade Li paged Landlord Zhang, because Landlord Zhang had an extra apartment awarded by his work unit that he wanted to rent to a foreigner.

"Foreigner? No problem," said Landlord Zhang. "Broken window? We'll fix it before winter," said Landlord Zhang. "And a king-size bed is included," said Landlord Zhang.

Now Landlord Zhang and his family sleep one floor below her bed of farmer's cotton and wooden slats. That's where she waits for Song at night.

The first night Song comes for her, he invites the stench of stale beer and he's not alone. Fang Pi, the guitarist in Song's new band, trails in with a beer in his hand. Fang's flaunting a freshly shaved Mohawk and an ugly, drunken grin. *"Zamen che ba,"* Fang spits words like peanut shells. *"Che ba, che ba!* Let's get outta here."

"Fei Fei," Song mumbles a drunken apology. He is wearing her Dickies and her Vans skating kicks, like some suburban kid from Los Angeles. But he's not that. He's from the backside of the Forbidden City. Cars can't drive to where he's from, the alleys are too narrow. Bai Huar

Hutong is the Alley of One Hundred Flowers, where the willow trees are so old they extend long, knotted fingers, making canopies over cobblestone. Where, from above, the call of homing pigeons echoes across blue skies and off of ancient gray walls with red gates. His family sleeps beyond one of those mysterious red gates in a single room, with all of their fish and talking birds and turtles. They cook in the courtyard and shit in public toilet stalls in the alley around the corner. But that is where they've always lived, and his mother likes it there. Already the looming *chai* character darkens their neighborhood, "condemned" by forward-thinking city planners. The family will move soon, and Song's mother wants to know where she'll buy stuffed eggplant and hand-pulled noodles when the city relocates them to a high-rise.

After lunch with Song's parents, they often took meandering walks around the Back Lake. His slender hands cupping hers, he would tell stories about Sun Zhongshan's wife, who lived in the courtyard on the right, and ghostly ashes of death spewing from the crematorium chimney in the courtyard on the left. "We used to sneak in there after school." Song told the same stories, and she always wanted to hear them again. She loved his lips and the lull of his voice, she wanted to live there.

But Fang is taking Song with him to a karaoke bar tonight. "Sex Pistols!" Fang proclaims as they head for the door. The guys will stay up all night smoking Turkish hash. "This place is so boring—*wuliao*," says Fang, his T-shirt clinging to seventeen-year-old shoulders, a bony new framework called manhood. Fang takes Song away and leaves her alone.

By morning, she is sure that the trash collector's song is for her.

"*Shou fei pin, shou fei pin!*" he calls to her.

She carries her burnt paint box and rushes downstairs as he approaches. Pedaling in slow motion on plastic sandals, he is dragging a bamboo trailer stacked with TV antennas and bedposts. She hands over the charred box. He'll like it. The acrylics inside are from America.

"Can't use that junk!" The trash collector turns his coal-stained face in disgust and pedals away.

"*Ni mabi!*" she screams at Song when he shows up the next night. He spills beer on her fuzzy slippers.

"We're just drinking, that's all," Song says. Tonight, his smile is for his friend Fang. She stares at the ground because she can't bear to look at his lips anymore.

"You had better go." He grabs Fang and they barrel out the door, knocking over winter cabbages on their way down the stairwell.

"*Cao ni ma, Fei Fei!* Fuck your mother, Fei Fei!"

Fang's curses cut through midnight silence and right into the hollow of her chest as they drive away. His curses cut deeper than the roar of Song's World War II sidecar motorcycle as it turns the corner of her building. Fang says her name wrong, nothing like Song. When Song says "Fei Fei," his deep voice hangs on each tone. He says it like a careful question.

She calls the only person who has a phone and will be awake at this hour, Rabbit.

"Fei Fei!" Rabbit's breathy voice warms her. At 2 A.M., Rabbit is standing in a basement hallway phone booth in blue long johns and yellow slippers. She has been busy painting her nails green on a cot in the windowless room she shares with three other girls from the countryside. At night, they talk about the foreign men they will meet and marry in Beijing.

"Song Qin is just a *xiao hai'r*—just a kid," Rabbit says. They talk until she wallpapers her apartment with the familiar cadences of Rabbit's voice. "My friend is holding a DV salon at Blue Jay next week. Wanna go?" Rabbit continues. They should be living together, but Song wouldn't have liked that because Rabbit is "country trash." He laughs at her bumpkin accent, but Rabbit is the only girl in Beijing who shaves her head. Rabbit is expert at flipping Chinese authorities the finger. She doesn't have a city resident's permit, and she doesn't need one to cruise the clubs. In the summer, she wears cutoff Levi's and platform boots.

Slam! The downstairs door. A Korean neighbor was murdered in that courtyard two weeks ago. Must be the wind. Maybe the police. She pulls at her furry American flag quilt. Probably just some greasy business-man leaving that all-night massage parlor on the first floor.

She picks up a paperback that a Canadian expat once gave her. She is fighting hot tears, but they fall on the cover anyway: *1984*, by George Orwell. The kind of book her father reads. She turns to the first page:

> *It was a bright cold day in April, and the clocks were striking thir-teen. Winston Smith, his chin nuzzled into his breast in an effort to escape the vile wind, slipped quickly through the glass doors of Victory Mansions, though not quickly enough to prevent a swirl of gritty dust from entering along with him.*
>
> *The hallway smelt of boiled cabbage and old rag mats. At one end of it a colored poster. . . . It was one of those pictures which are so contrived that the eyes follow you about when you move. BIG BROTHER IS WATCHING YOU, the caption beneath it ran.*

So this is what the rest of the world thinks about China. Communist China. She laughs. She never imagined she would be reading such an old book, about such a faraway place, and that it would feel so close now.

Around her building, the local grannies wear red armbands and watch her coming and going from the courtyard. They are the neighbor-hood committee, flaunting toothless smiles when she walks by. She wants them to love her like they love their grandchildren, but when she turns her back, they tell her landlord about the "hoodlums and artists" who visit her apartment.

All of those years she was in school, and she never learned much until she got to China. Then she found Beijing, the city that draws the world's wanderers and escape artists and lets them free-fall from the other side of earth. North Korean, South African, Nepalese, Canadian, American.

By night, she cracked sunflower seeds and spat on the kitchen floor. For breakfast, she ate sweet-and-hot crayfish. She stayed close to Rabbit, Song, even Fang, as they ducked below Big Brother's contrived eyes. She lived in nightclubs, cheering on Chinese rockers, started up local magazines. She went to school and fell in love. But where was she supposed to go when she decided to stay?

When morning comes, it's not the trash collector who wakes her up, but Landlord Zhang. He's standing over her bed, jarring her from dream to upright. His thin skin exposes blue veins. When his bloodshot snake eyes scan the bedroom, hers follow, relieved that Song and his friends aren't sprawled across the floor, lost in drunken snoring.

"The police are raiding the building tomorrow night. You have to be out by noon," Landlord Zhang says. He didn't even have a chance to fix that cracked window yet.

She pages Song, and he comes for her. They put all of her belongings into trash bags. They'll move her stuff to the Alley of One Hundred Flowers until she finds another place. Song scours the room to see if they've gotten everything.

"Where's the paint box?" Song asks. Sleep is still crusted around his slender eyes. Her bags are nearly full, but still, she has enough room for that paint box, spared from the trash collector's pile.

What Happened

by Janis Harper

I shouldn't have gotten into that car accepted the ride but how else was I to get home after midnight mass on Christmas Eve in Sydney soon after I had arrived in Australia to live for the second time but this time escaping from somewhere else deliberate not just stopping in Sydney while on the road

And so feeling depressed empty what was I to do now and midnight mass was nice I guess all the people squeezing together in the cathedral downtown and I didn't know any of them though later I found out that a future roommate was there and if I knew him then if I knew anyone then I could have asked for a ride home because as it turned out the trains had stopped running and the buses too because it was late on Christmas Eve and people are usually together with their loved ones and if they're out at midnight mass they all came together and will go home that way

So it was only me all alone like how I arrived in Sydney from Canada the week or so before with about a hundred bucks and a couple of friends I could stay with so I didn't have money for cab fare home or I didn't want to spend the little money I had on cab fare and I didn't know until later that the house wasn't that far away from downtown and I could have walked or I should have taken a cab because it wouldn't have cost very much at all

But instead I ask the group of friendly easygoing Aussie blokes where they're headed and they say isn't that something this guy lives a block away from you so of course come with us

And they were all pumped up and jostling each other joking but in that laid-back kinda macho way some Aussies have and I thought I knew who they were the kind of people simple down-to-earth traditional values talking about sheilas teasing each other about women but so what not harming anyone they know what's right know whose shout it is at the pub real gentlemen true-blue fair dinkum never'd hurt a sheila opens doors for them knows the rules good people really good regular folk

The first revelation was these guys were just at a bar a disco drinking partying all evening I didn't know anybody went out drinking on Christmas Eve I thought it was a quiet cozy family night reflective or at the very least a last-minute shopping frenzy who the hell went to clubs on Christmas Eve these guys

And I was feeling trusting having just attended church which is something I don't do often at all but feeling trusting because of the feeling of all those people all squeezed together in the cathedral at midnight all there to celebrate something of the spirit something lasting something they hardly understand but can feel somehow when they all come together like that

And I was feeling a little desperate well a lot after having run down to underground stations through empty echoing cement corridors trying to catch whatever last train there was so I thought of asking someone on the street someone who had just been to mass one of the mass of people there

When I asked the group of friendly young men who made it easy because they spoke to me first I assumed they had attended mass we were just down the street from the cathedral but when I told them I had they elbowed each other hey she's just been to church hey

Their car was the last one in the underground parking lot and walking to their car with them I felt just a bit nervous for the first time and was relieved when I saw another person in the lot

Now comes the part I am embarrassed about the part that I brush over sometimes alter when I tell the very few people I have told the part that makes it maybe partly my fault my poor judgment but I was just trusting people and why is that so wrong and I've always been right my instincts intuition assessments of situations have never misled me and I've lived an exciting anything but sheltered existence so far and so far I have never felt fear

What Happened

There are four of them they are young about twenty maybe younger I am
only a couple of years older two of them get in the front and one gets in
the back tells me to slide in I hesitate come on in so I do cheerfully of
course I create my own reality I am not afraid of anything and the fourth
guy the hugely muscled one gets in after me and I am squeezed in between two men in the back seat

There it is I don't like to admit it feel a little embarrassed but I am in the
middle I am between these two guys I didn't insist against it I didn't say no
I'd like the front seat please or at least a window seat I am polite I let myself be seated and here I am squeezed in between two men in the back seat

But it was a night for people close together like in the cathedral nothing
wrong with strangers packed in together on Christmas Eve and it was a
small car and they are nice enough to give me a ride home

then the comments start
hey she's not wearing a bra

the driving in the wrong direction
just taking the scenic route

the touches
they're nice I like the pointy kind

the plans

I am not naïve not innocent left a broken home at fifteen traveled
through Southeast Asia worked as a musician in Penang worked as a se-

cret agent for Australia's Central Intelligence Bureau in Sydney as an ac-
counting clerk in Vancouver knew lots about life knew men well had serious and not so serious but always intense relationships this all by the
time I was nineteen and of legal drinking age

the plans

what they were going to do

to me

Well the truth is I needed a ride to where I was staying and I shouldn't
have gotten into that car

Shouldn't have never say shouldn't have I never say
shouldn't have implies regret shouldn't have regret
shouldn't have

gotten into that car

that is unless on some level I wanted this experience

At some point I realized that these guys hated me they actually hated me
or what I meant in their world she's a smart one I bet your boyfriend is a
wimpy bloke with glasses a professor or something right so at that point
even my seemingly lightly tossed off but really carefully measured re-
sponses even my ability to know how to talk to different people in their
own language even my wits failed me turned against me nothing I could
do or say nothing I tried on was right

What Happened

That was when I started getting scared I guess though I still couldn't believe it and when I did when I finally realized there was nothing I could
do this time this was for real these guys are for real then I got scared and
almost threw up I'm going to throw up I tell them no you're not just relax
sit back and relax

just relax

Since then I know not to trust anyone any man who says those words to
me other than maybe doctors

Once when the car was stopped at a red light I got the attention of a
woman in the car in the next lane I mouthed help help me looking
frightened desperate hoping she'd know this was no joke

The muscle guy looked at me funny did he notice or not maybe he
did he was pretty quiet hadn't said much if anything so far so I thought
I would appeal to his sense of goodness compassion humanity very
basic humanity I whispered to him unlock the door and let me out
now do it now come on and he just looked at me funny dumb smile
slight shake of the head no he is not my ally and soon after he spoke his
first word   yes
    you want to fuck her don't you
    yes

And the woman in the car beside us just looked at me with a little frown
and I wondered why I came back to Sydney

We started driving by dark bushy areas parks and I started pleading just
let me out feeling reduced to my very basic self all the layers of experience

social skills intellectual verbal abilities dissolved and at the bottom the core was a person needing to survive

But even still I was aware that perhaps this pleading frightened person no longer smart and witty would perhaps touch them convince them this wasn't right even still I could remove myself from the situation be objective even in the grip of fear don't do this please don't do this
but we always fuck the girls we give rides to

But I was different was I so different I don't go drinking on Christmas Eve I don't wear heavy makeup tight clothes I don't want it did the others if there were others and it's because I'm different isn't it it's because I am not of their world it's because they hate me

I don't know where we are
we drive down a deserted lane by an empty lot
there are no houses in sight no people
and the lane stops dead end
and the car stops
the guy next to me the slim good-looking one
the one who's been doing most of the talking
all of the touching
stops talking quiet everyone is quiet

I scan the area if I got out and ran which way would I go how fast could I run could I escape one way the lane stops and there is the empty lot a field and something industrial-looking and the other way is the road where we came from but it's so far away my god where could I run to I could not escape there is no escape no

What Happened

My words come out in small breaths

okay but
      just you

               no one else

The slim one and the driver get out together go away from the car talk argue I hear but she says she'll fuck me she wants to

And suddenly there is a different possibility a chance a hope

Something in me switches on I do some fast talking to the short guy in the front seat who's now looking pissed off I say when I got in I memorized the license plate I know the license number I can give it to the cops I can describe each one of you I even know your name

He's nodding his head is he an ally I've found my ally I do some more talking I use the word rape I talk about attempted rape sexual assault how even he is implicated even if he doesn't do anything finally he says as if I've offended him
      we don't rape girls

The two guys return the slim one is red-faced angry silent they get in the car the short guy says to the driver quietly she knows your license number she says she'll tell the cops

The ride back to where I'm staying is very short we were right in the neighborhood

Before the driver lets me out he says no hard feelings right I say nothing
he repeats it louder slower aggressive
> *no hard feelings*
> > *right*

right

On Christmas morning I tell my friend I'm staying with what happened
I try to tell him but nothing I can say can come close I keep saying the
word helpless I felt utterly helpless there was nothing I could do and he
nods his head as if he understands but I think how could he because I can't
describe it it is too much there is too much mixed in with the fear now
there is fear now I will never get into a stranger's car now I will never feel
invincible strong and he asks me if I'm going to tell the police what happened but I can't how can I and besides nothing really happened they

didn't do anything

to me

London Routemaster

by Amy Prior

Sick as I am
confused in the head
I mean I have
endured this April so far
visiting friends
—William Carlos Williams

An ambulance travels high speed down Commercial Street, making a cab driver pull in so sharply to make way that he almost swerves into the front of an Indian restaurant. It is 7:18 P.M., a rainy Thursday night in April, and her breath makes strange patterns on the glass of the windowpane as she views this scene from inside the cozy domestic warmth of her flat. She pauses briefly before hitting the SEND key. Sadie is emailing Richard Hell, a musician from New York whose CDs were first played for her by a boy she used to like, a boy from school who was chess champion, who was so cool he hardly spoke, the one who was the first she knew to be online. (Later, she heard he moved to Tokyo, did sites for Pepsi.) She is asking Richard for an interview for her zine, one she photocopies for free when no one is looking at the offices of the corporate trade magazine publisher where she is temporarily answering telephones. She wants to meet him for some drinks, maybe more, now that she sees on his website he is visiting London on tour. She thinks he might be up for it. She hears another siren, goes to the window, sees two fire engines and another two ambulances racing down the street. There's some kind of accident, she thinks, some kind of drama.

Richard Hell is staring at the keys of his laptop in room 176 of the Great Eastern Hotel. He is wondering what to write next. Maybe he should use emoticons, or is that too flirty? Her picture was good, sweet eyes like his first girlfriend, Julie, in high school, and she knew stuff about his films the others didn't. Once, he met one of his online girls in a bar in Virginia who said she wanted to interview him for her dissertation on "The Female Gaze and Rock 'n' Roll." He thought otherwise, but she really did just talk about her college courses, then asked him about the seventies, about the Blank Generation and what it was like living through all that, and he paused and thought, then said, *Well it never really disappeared.* He stares at his screen. It stares back. He lies on the bed, looks up. The ceiling is white, like the whole room: Cream towels sit alongside lily walls, white-with-a-hint-of-pink bedspread, and beige-white coffeemaker and cups.

At that moment, his girlfriend, Ramona, who has already been away from the Great Eastern far too long a time just to be picking up some coffee, is emailing in a Web café. Her fingers dance across the keys with lightness, but also with speed, like the way her voice became when she spoke to a guy she met at a record company party last week, the one she is emailing now, a music video maker ten years younger than she is, who is still at that brief and almost imperceptible early-twenties stage when pretty boy is on the cusp of chiselled man, who sat out with her on the roof of 93 Feet East and rolled cigarettes while her boyfriend was interviewed downstairs by a feature writer from *Rock Classic* magazine. She remembers him touching her hair, brushing it behind her ear when the wind picked up, has revisited this thought several times.

The electric pulse of physical attraction she is experiencing now as she formulates this thought again moves from her fingertip to the keyboard and then—as she hits the SEND key—it is translated into more regulated electric impulses that are transported along a route miles and miles from her—first to the service provider in Holborn, then branching out along tightly entwined cables of tiny diameter. At that moment, the Web café is playing host to numerous other electric connections between lovers—substitute, future, and potential—networks of intimacy-at-a-distance communications from this tiny corner of East London; connecting people right across the city, so they are almost touching.

Though the place is mainly still, quiet, there is an oppressive background hum of keyboard movements, occasionally punctuated by short beeps of electronic detraction, or confirmation. A hundred, maybe more, bodies together in this strip-lit space, a flickering host for flickering screens and eyes, some tight and sleepless, but coffee-sustained for hours through the night, some darting from screen to Webcam and back again, as if they were frightened animals caught up somewhere against their will, occasionally some furtive communication between them—signaling a hot photo of some body, a flirtatious email.

Jane, a.k.a. gothteen66, whose long-sleeved top hides a crisscross history, posts intense messages to reno99 in an unspecified city location on the Suicide.net notice board. Later, they will meet, and it will transpire that reno99 is, in fact, in between tenancy agreements, so that the next day, she will move in with gothteen66, who lives alone even though she is only seventeen years old, on account of being recently rehoused in a council flat to escape a stepfather who used to blacken her eyes. Reno99 takes the sofabed in the living room, and gothteen66 loves to have her around; most nights, they sit close on the sofa watching soaps and quiz shows until after one, but after a few months, gothteen66 starts to get annoyed at the way reno99 leaves her clothes lying around the kitchen, rarely buys bread or Coke or other foods, and spurns contributions to the gas bill. The end comes soon after the time when gothteen66 comes home early from her retail job in a supermarket to find reno99 on the Internet when she is supposed to be at work (the nature of which is unclear), specifically in chat rooms, and it becomes clear that reno99's attentions are now focused on other suicide girls and boys, and she moves out soon afterward, having acquired a copy of raya101's house keys. Later, gothteen66 will end up in casualty, suffering from hypothermia, having trailed the streets of London in bitter winter sleet trying to find her love that never happened, and this will continue to be the pattern for a number of years, until someone kind and wise and much older than her intervenes. But this is before all that, before all these difficult things, when gothteen66 is just a pale, etched sliver of an unknowing girl, who is calmly sitting here typing in a strip-lit room with strangers.

And in a corner directly opposite her, unhampered by the close attentions of other users and close to the gentlemen's toilet facilities, is Jesus Magdelanio, part-time English language student and waiter, who has purchased the attention of Sabrina (offline, Shirley of Hackney) on sexychicks.com, and is in lengthy and urgent discussion (where spelling and grammar have become quite irrelevant) regarding his current pleasure requirements. Shirley is glancing up at the clock as she is typing, calculating when she should wake her baby for a feed. Her job is a secret from her boyfriend, though unfortunately for her, it is not one that will be kept much longer.

In the other corner of the Web café sits Melissa, currently studying communications at the graduate level, who is mailing Charlie about flier design for an arts project, but it is not *actually* about flier design, though neither of them is aware of the fact at this moment; it is only something that will become clear in retrospect, after months of emailing and dates that are not classed as dates but meetings, ones that start with lingering glances at inappropriate moments over lemon and ginger tea, end being meetings of souls, so the fliers never get done, but they do end up living in a studio just off Hackney Road, quite happily, for a short while.

Outside now, Ramona rushes back to the Great Eastern, her passage across the highway blocked by lanes of traffic slowing to a stop, and now an ambulance turning into the junction, then another waits behind, some kind of talk of a situation eastward, she hears, but it is fleeting because she speeds by, making up time, her coffee under her arm, her eyes on the Great Eastern Hotel sign up ahead, her mind on her boyfriend's face, the way he will look when she walks through the door and smiles brightly. *I had to walk three blocks for this*, she will say breathlessly (though not suspiciously so), handing him the package, waiting for a reaction, *and it's not even Colombian.*

The pretty boy, the recipient of all Ramona's misspent attention, whose online name is teenstar, whose real name is Lloyd, is at that moment, looking with his pretty eyes at the blog of someone he's never met. He feels like an intimate friend of this girl, though it's a relationship without the commitments of the real. He likes this, what's good is that he can check her out at a distance. He already knows Amber likes the same films as he does, so that is a start, but he is worried about her obsession with Cindy Sherman, the way she snacks on pork scratchings for breakfast. He will have to take that one further, but not now. He is tired still from the club last night. He sits, a slight figure, clothes hanging off his thin frame, a loose arrangement of fleece materials, longish hair dangling down shapelessly like when he was a kid. The kind of androgynous look that's so fashionable at the moment, he gets attention from style magazine photographers when he goes out, which he simultaneously courts and spurns. He sucks on a cigarette slowly, flicks the ash on a textbook beside the monitor. He has just finished art school, works part-time in a video shop, and later, looking back on these years, he will view them as the slow ones, the ones when most of his key career choices were made without much deliberate thought or action.

At this moment, from her houseshare in Heneage Street, Amber is updating her blog. Someone is calling her to watch *EastEnders* on TV in the other room, and there is dinner waiting. *Okay, Okay.* Amber has been typing her entries and emails for so many hours that the joints in her fingers ache and her eyes are glazed over, straining to see the words on the screen. When she goes to eat, finally, one part of her is in the real world, one part is still in the virtual. She will watch *EastEnders,* forking some tuna salad into her mouth every so often, but her mind will be on her inbox, imagining electronic replies. She has an addictive personality—this is something a therapist will tell her later—and there are no boundaries to its nature. The TV will hum like constant background chatter, but over the top, there'll be something else, the whir of helicopter blades circling up above the roof. She will hear them, and for a moment be distracted from the screen, then look outside. There is a kind of glow in the sky, a kind of dazzling, like there are searchlights or something.

Online at this moment, and reading the blog a few streets away from Amber, is Sadie, who, due to lack of an immediate response from Richard Hell, has begun to check up on people she has never met to see how they are doing. On an entry that interests her, she stops reading, briefly touches the glass of the screen, lacing her fingertips around its rounded corners, tracing a circular path that loops text and image and colored advertisement. Then they move to a stuffed toy animal, a sloth, on top of her monitor, a present from her first boyfriend, who is helping the less fortunate make local communities in India, has been for two years now. *You could have worked here,* she always said. She'd just moved to London from the south coast, didn't know too many people. For a while they mailed, him snatching turns on an old Mac in an iron-roofed backstreet—but long-distance never works. She picks up the animal, smells it. She can still sense his scent, like a mixture of smoke and joss sticks and cheap cider. She used to dream about him traipsing dusty tracks, that intense frown he always wore starting to etch lines on his forehead. Now she has begun to have a recurring nightmare. Always the same scenario: The whole world had been blown up two years ago, right to smithereens, and everyone was just floating around on parts like they hadn't even realized what had happened yet.

There's been some kind of accident, some kind of problem, that much is clear. In the next street, traffic has slowed almost to a stop, and helicopters fly overhead to record the situation for the TV news. Things are not good: An aerial photo shows problems on routes within much of the London Orbital. A light map of traffic flow shows some continuous currents westward, allowing for road works, but eastward there is disruption in the charge of cars, interruptions in the chain of vehicle lights at certain points, and one black, insulated spot where their conduction has completely malfunctioned. And it is here Sadie stands now, finally aroused from her virtual world into the real one by the sirens nearby. The fire engines got there too late, too much traffic with people coming home from work, and the flames are touching everything. *Some kind of problem with the electrics,* they said, *some kind of short circuit, two wires meeting when they weren't supposed to.*

Onlookers gather at the fringes—a teenager walking home past curfew hour; a man in a wig and stilettos going to a club where he would speak to no one, where he would sit sipping rum and Coke in the corner all night on a high stool, legs crossed awkwardly to hide regrowth; a Bengali kid, fifteen, weaving his way in and out of the cars to get closer to the spectacle, his pupils dilated so the vision appears lighter and more dazzling than the real thing, like it is a kind of apparition.

An elderly couple standing next to Sadie are so shaken up they hold on to each other tightly, and after a while, Sadie walks them home to their flat, part of a block similar to the one that's been ruined. Standing in the kitchen, searching for glasses, Sadie hears the couple's voices, calm again in the other room, something about blackjack and poker, and briefly remembers her grandparents, the way they played patience for hours—outdoors in summer. There was nothing they liked more. She sees them on the patio, with sun hats and iced tea, the way one's eyes would take quick glances at the other's hand, then read the other's face to second-guess the next move. She pours bourbon into a tumbler, hears ice cubes fracture, little hairline cracks that grow, then slowly melt away.

Country Songs
about the City

by Sara Jaffe

I went to go see a boy I know play country songs at a bar on Polk Street. The bar is located on the lower part of Polk Street's upward climb, the sketchy midsection between the Tenderloin and the tonier environs of Nob Hill. Up until the early seventies, Polk Street was the hub of gay life in San Francisco. Now that the Castro has supplanted it, with rainbow flags flying from every telephone pole, Polk Street lacks a unified identity. Indistinctness assails tradition and foils real estate, and so people scramble to define this blurry region. Nobody can agree on what to call it: the Tendernob? The Nobberloin? City maps equivocally refer to it as Polk Gulch.

This bar was a new bar, but it used to be an old bar. What I hear from a friend who used to have a painting studio up the street is that it used to be a watering hole for aging drag queens; I hear from someone who went in there once that it was too big and always felt empty. Now, the new owners have left up the painted sign on the building's façade bearing the bar's old name, whether out of laziness or in some small tribute to its history, I do not know. Now, as I show my ID and walk through the door, I notice that this bar is too big, but it feels crowded. The bar itself is a round island in the middle of the room, with service at any point around its circumference. The light is dim, but it catches on certain surfaces—the polished wooden countertops, the patrons' hair, their shiny shoes. The room rings around the island bar in a larger oval, and I recognize the people I know arced into the shadowy areas along the walls' outer curves.

When it is time for our friend to start playing, we shuffle through the crowd to the back room where the music takes place. We pack into the room's narrow confines, jumbling chairs up close to unsteady little tables with candles lit on them in bell-shaped glass jars. Our friend sits on a high stool, black Western shirt with white piping tucked into tight blue jeans. He rests his feet on the lowest crossbeam of the stool, so that his knees come up to form a ledge on which to rest his banjo, which he holds at a forty-five-degree angle, the neck projecting up to the low ceiling, as if he is securing the body of the instrument against his belly as the neck tries to flee, as if the banjo must be held at just this precise, precarious angle, or the strings will snap and the tricky mechanism will split and crack open, revealing only a splintery mess of thin wood, and none of its secrets about how it brings forth song.

Our friend greets us, thanks us for coming. He takes a long gulp of beer and gives a quick shake of his head. He takes a deep breath, says, "Here goes," and starts to play. His right hand opens and closes as it scratches across strings, as if the sound is coming from unleashing something inside his palm and not the actual strumming motion. He jerks his leg slightly up and down, in rhythm to the music. He just recently moved here from Iowa, and that is the place he sings about. He uses the language of the country songs he heard, we assume, growing up, that we city dwellers have come to know in the last few years and imagine we heard when we were young. He sings, *The ground is dry, the corn is growing high, the sky is so blue and so wide, my love left me, where's my shotgun, how do I find my way home, I am too blind with whiskey and tears to tell.* Everyone's favorite song is one about how the rain falls hard on the roof of a shed, and the sky is as black as the coal from a train. We like its internal rhymes and the intensity that builds up with the speed of it. Tonight we would rather see the words galloping to get out of his mouth like he has no choice but to sing them than watch him wring forth meandering, heartfelt ballads. The faster songs remind me of my own experience of his home state, rushing past on the interstate, blacktop and cornfields and bluest sky rushing together into a postcard blur.

We are not all of us in this room city kids born and bred, or reluctant children of the suburbs, but I wonder if I am the only one who wishes I could hear country songs about the city. Can these kinds of songs exist, or do our survival tactics for city living preclude them? Must we only always face the city cement and its few scattered trees with resolve, trusting surfaces and resisting the urge to find something rawer and truer lying beneath?

Our friend is still tapping his foot and singing about the loneliness and freedom of wide open plains, but I am right here, wondering what would happen if we wrote our own songs as we make our way through the paths and mazes of the city streets. As our friend describes the Number 9 train, whose far-off whistle gets louder as it thunders past, I think about the 9 San Bruno bus, its orange and white, bulky body lumbering past me several times a week, though it is not a bus I have ever taken. As he sings about old dirt country roads that bear the marks of all who've passed in their deeply rutted, dried-out tire tracks, I start to imagine a new song, about Polk Street, how it runs uphill like a scar, sewing up disparate neighborhood parts, skin and bones and surfaces and stories getting mixed up in the stitching. A song about the heat created by the friction of these incongruous parts patchworking up against each other, creating the energy of a bigger city, where such undertones of chaos are commonplace. A celebration song, about washed-up drag queens and fresh-faced young boys just out from the Midwest, lured to Polk Street for danger, for sex, for relief. A ghost-town song that asks what happens when the new seeps in through the tired foundations of the old, like an anesthetic to history.

I wish I could hear country songs about the city, but I wonder: Could buildings still stand if we infused their concrete structures with dreamier constructions? Would we be drowned out by the cacophony of city sounds, or would the car horns and streetside rants become our accompaniment? Would we be censored for singing past artifice? Would we trip over each other on the sidewalk and stumble over our own feet if we only walked around looking up, looking down, glancing in wonder around us with songs on our lips and our hearts in our pockets, rattling around like change?

Summer of Mopeds

by Courtney Eldridge

S ay there's this woman whose accountant makes her cry. Say there's this woman who wakes, showers, goes to her accountant's office, and he says, What's that look on your face? And then the woman starts to cry, or she leaves his office and then she cries. Or, say the woman wakes, showers, gets dressed, goes to therapy, and then goes to her accountant's office. Then her accountant says, What's that look on your face? And the woman says, What is what look on my face . . . ? Then they fight and the woman leaves her accountant's office, shaking with anger, and she almost starts to cry, waiting for the elevator.

Or, say she wakes, showers, gets dressed, goes to therapy, and then walks to the subway. She catches the subway, walks to her accountant's office, and then passes his building. The woman walks right past her accountant's office, distracted, and then realizes that she's missed her accountant's building. She turns around, walks back, and grimaces, entering her accountant's building. Then she gets in the elevator and pushes the wrong button, but doesn't realize her mistake until she steps out into the penthouse suite, looks up, and thinks, *Where am I . . . ? Whoops—wrong floor.*

She turns around and gets back in the elevator and pushes the right button, waits for the doors to close, then pushes the DOOR CLOSE button, waits, and then pushes DOOR CLOSE again, sighs, and says to herself, What the fuck? She pushes the button a few times in rapid succession, as if to teach the button a lesson, and the doors close. Then the elevator stops at her floor and she swears, getting off the elevator, and walks down the hall.

She enters her accountant's office and sits down in the chair in front of his desk, and then he says, What's that look on your face? She takes offense and says, What is what look on my face . . . ? They fight about Social Security, and then she leaves, shaking with anger, and she almost starts crying but doesn't, because she doesn't want to give her accountant the satisfaction and because there are too many people on the elevator for her to cry freely.

She thinks of possible insults to keep from crying, as if she could do it all over again and insult him first, but can't in either case, then returns home and calls her friend who recommended this accountant. He is *such* a character, her friend had said. And then her friend said that this accountant was cheap and charming and he had a voice like Barry White. What's his name? she asked, and her friend said, Klaus. Klaus Winchester. And she said, A CPA named Klaus who's cheap and sounds like Barry White? And her friend said, You'll love him. So she calls this friend and tells her friend that, Barry White or not, if the man ever speaks to her like that again, she'll go off.

———————

Or, say she wakes, showers, drinks a cup of coffee, and checks her date book. Then she dreads her appointments, thinks of canceling, thinks her new accountant is mean and he scares her, thinks, Yes, he does, but not as much as the IRS, then nods, grabs her keys, and goes to therapy. At therapy, then, she talks about a suit; she thinks to mention a red-and-white, horizontal-striped, one-piece bathing suit she wore as a girl. She says, I loved that suit. Then she talks some more about swimming and high school girls she knew and kids she looked down on, growing up, then feels badly, and then she cries, dries her eyes, thanks her therapist for her time, leaves, and walks to the subway.

At the subway, then, she waits and steps forward and looks for rats, then down the tunnel, sees nothing but a single blue track light, and then quickly steps back. She puts the image of herself being shoved in front of an oncoming train out of her mind, crossing her arms and leaning against a metal beam, and listens to other commuters complain. Fuckinaye, says one guy, and she rolls her eyes, wishing the other commuters would just shut up.

She clenches her jaw, hearing the announcement that the R train is having electrical difficulties and passengers should ... etc., etc., and thinks, Thanks for fucking telling me, like you couldn't, etc., etc. Then she leaves in a huff and runs down the stairs to catch another subway and almost trips, headfirst. She catches her breath and steps on the subway, sits, and smiles, feeling pleased. Then she realizes she's headed in the wrong direction and gets off and catches the subway headed in the right direction.

She gets off the subway and walks up the stairs to Canal Street, then smells something rank and covers her nose. She crosses the street and walks in the right direction, and then walks past her accountant's office, wondering whatever happened to that suit ...? She looks up, notices the numbers on a building, and turns around, swearing at herself again, etc., and walks two blocks back to her accountant's building. She grimaces, entering the front door, gets on the elevator and pushes the wrong button, and ends up at the penthouse, with fresh calla lilies and a receptionist wearing an ivory silk blouse, and she thinks, Where am I ...? Etc.

She gets back on the elevator, sighs, checks her watch, pushes DOOR CLOSE, etc., then waits as more people get on the elevator. The elevator stops several more times and several more people get on the elevator, and someone steps on her and she shouts, Watch it! Then she gets pushed by more people getting into the elevator and keeps her mouth shut this time, and then grimaces again, recalling the thousands of fingerprints she saw on the glass doors when she entered the building. And again she's disgusted by the idea of thousands of dirty hands touching the glass in the middle of flu season and couldn't they pay someone to clean the front doors once in a while . . . ? She steps aside once more as the doors open and she waits as more people try to get on the elevator and she wants to tell them it's too full! No more fucking people, all right?

She takes a deep breath and scolds herself for having thought, while being pushed and stepped on, that because every other person on the elevator is Chinese, they don't mind being sardined together. Then she feels ashamed of herself for having such thoughts and tells herself to calm down, considering she wouldn't be here if she'd pushed the right button in the first place. Push the right floor next time and this won't happen, will it? No, she tells herself, and then tells herself, Okay, then.

And then she says, Excuse me, excuse me, please, Jesus, etc., gets off the elevator, and rings the buzzer outside her accountant's office. She enters his office, sits, waits in the waiting room, and then walks into her accountant's office. She sits down and then her accountant says, What's that look on your face? And she says, What is what look . . . ? Etc. They disagree about Social Security and then they fight, and she leaves shaking, and almost cries but doesn't, because, etc., etc., and then she tries to think of an insult that would reduce the man to tears, but can't. She returns home and calls her friend and says, Who the hell does he think he is? And then she becomes angry with her friend as well.

Or, she wakes and rolls over, closes her eyes, and dreads the day ahead. She gets up, showers, dresses, pours a cup of coffee, then looks at her date book and thinks about her accountant, etc., etc., then nods, grabs her keys, walks to therapy, and waits in the waiting room. She leafs through *Newsweek* and *Food & Wine* and thinks, God, I want to go home. I just want to go home and go back to bed and I want this all to be over.... Her therapist walks into the waiting room and smiles at her and she smiles back at her therapist and returns the magazines to the coffee table. She follows her therapist down the hall, into her therapist's office, and then she sits in her favorite chair, the one farthest from the window.

Her therapist sits and smiles and says, How are you? How was your week? And she says, Fine, fine, and then she smiles, and her therapist says, Good, good, and nods and waits. She looks at her hands, thinks, ignores the thought, and then she mentions a swimsuit she wore as a girl: a red-and-white, horizontal-striped, one-piece bathing suit. I loved that suit, she says. I loved that suit so much I slept in it all summer long, she says. Then she talks some more about the striped suit and swimming and high school girls and her brothers shouting, Two for flinching! Two for flinching! Then her therapist nods and asks a question, and then she nods and tries to answer her question without crying but only cries harder. Then she stops crying, dries her eyes and blows her nose, thanks her therapist, and closes her therapist's office door behind her. She checks the mirror in her therapist's bathroom, wipes the mascara off her cheeks, and leaves.

She walks to the subway and waits and frowns, watching a guy check out some teenage girl standing nearby, wearing stretch jeans and white patent platform boots, as the guy's friend hawks and spits onto the tracks, and then she steps forward and checks the tunnel again. She listens to other commuters complain, Fuckinaye, and, What the hell is taking so long? I haven't got all damn day, and then she hears the announcement that the R train is, etc., etc. In a huff, then, she walks back upstairs, then downstairs, then she almost trips, grabs the rail and gasps, and steadies herself, etc. She catches the subway in the nick of time and sits down, only to realize she's heading in the wrong direction, and thinks, Oh, goddamnit ... etc., then smacks her forehead with the palm of her hand.

She gets off the subway headed in the wrong direction, then she gets on the subway headed in the right direction, and then she gets off again and walks up the stairs to Canal. She smells something and checks the street signs, etc., and walks in the right direction, etc. Then she walks right past her accountant's office, distracted by thoughts of that bathing suit and whether or not her mother threw it away after she got her brother in trouble or if she threw it away or . . . ? She stops, notices the numbers on the building in front of her, swears at herself again, and then turns around and walks to her accountant's building and grimaces, etc.

She gets on the elevator and pushes the wrong button and ends up in the peach penthouse with the beautiful Asian receptionist, who reminds her of an ex-boyfriend. Then she gets back on the elevator and gets pushed and shoved and checks the elevator's weight capacity and thinks racist thoughts about Asians as more people cram onto the elevator, etc. Then she yells, Watch it! at an old lady and scolds herself for yelling and for getting shoved in the first place. Then she excuses herself, snaps, Jesus, gets off, and makes it to her accountant's office, only five minutes late.

She enters and waits in Klaus's waiting room, overhearing him talk to another client, as the two men enter the waiting room from his office. Then she tries not to stare at the man with whom her accountant is surprisingly cheerful, not at all like he is with her. Then, watching the two men on the sly, she wonders why her accountant doesn't seem to like her when he likes her friend and even her friend's two coworkers, neither of whom she particularly likes. Then she tries not to take it personally and decides that it doesn't matter because she disliked her accountant first, anyway.

Then the black man—or rather, the very handsome black man—the very handsome black man, wearing a tailored pin-striped suit and purple dress shirt and a dark gray silk tie with a handkerchief, says good-bye to her, and she realizes she's been staring at him the whole time. She says, Good-bye, after he's already turned and opened the door, and then she worries that the delay in her response has made her seem unfriendly and she frowns again. Then her accountant invites her into his office and tells her to sit, and she does, not caring for his tone.

Then he says, What's that look on your face? and she says, What is what look on my face . . . ? Etc. Then she removes a letter from her purse and asks her accountant to take a look at the letter and he does and then they fight about Social Security. Then she leaves, shaking, etc., and almost starts to cry but doesn't because, or because, etc., etc. She returns home, thinking of something mean she could say about his face or his person or his ugly tie, as if she could, but can't, and can't think of anything particularly mean, either, etc.

Angry, she calls her friend and says, I don't give a fuck who he sounds like. Barry White or not, I think he's a total fucking asshole. And if he ever, *ever* speaks to me like that again, I'll go *off*. Her friend starts to speak, and she interrupts and says, I should call him boy, see how he likes that. Hey, *boy*, finish my taxes yet . . . ? Then her friend says, You just have to get his sense of humor, and then she becomes that much angrier with her accountant and her friend and she hangs up the phone.

Or, she wakes, rolls over, and wants to hide, knowing that it's going to be a long day, sighs, and finally gets up. She showers, dresses, pours a cup of coffee, dreads her appointments, and wonders why in the world she scheduled these two appointments on the same day. Crazy.

Then she remembers that her accountant gave her no choice and left her a nasty message on her answering machine. And she remembers how she had tried to break the ice with her accountant the first and only time they met, by confessing her fear of being audited, and instead of showing any compassion, he treated her like an idiot. And then she remembers that afterward, when she mentioned her fear of this new accountant to the friend who recommended him, her friend said, Oh, you just have to get his sense of humor, that's all, and she really didn't care for the insinuation that she didn't get the man's sense of humor, either. She assures herself she has a very good sense of humor, nods, grabs her keys, and heads out the door.

She walks to therapy, buzzes, waits, dreads, and thinks, I just want to go home and go back to bed, etc. Her therapist walks into the waiting room and she smiles at her therapist and follows her down the hall and sits in her favorite chair and then scans the room, checking the time and the Kleenex box and the candy basket and whether or not there are flowers on the metal stand in the corner, near the window. But no, no flowers today. . . . Then her therapist sits in the chair across from her, etc., smiles and wipes her nose with a pink Kleenex, and says, How are you? Then she says, Fine, fine, and her therapist says, Good, good, etc., and waits. Then she looks at her hands and says, Well, to tell you the truth, I was dreading coming here today, and her therapist nods again and asks why.

She thinks for a moment, ignores the thought, and then she mentions a swimsuit she wore as a girl, a red-and-white, horizontal-striped, one-piece bathing suit. A Speedo—it was a Speedo, she says. I loved to swim so much that I slept in my bathing suit all summer long. Then she smiles and says, So I was riding my bike home from the pool this one day. I was walking my bike up the hill, and this friend of my dad's drove by and he stopped and offered me a ride home.

Then she talks some more about the man and the summer of mopeds and her brothers and how her brothers teased her, making her stand by the television for hours sometimes, during severe thunderstorms when television stations used to broadcast the emergency message, Please Stand By, because if she didn't stand by the TV, the storm would never end and it would be all her fault for being so damn lazy, so get your butt over there, they said. And then if she refused, they'd tackle her and play typewriter or, simply, tappers, as they called it, and her therapist leans her head to the side, curious, and asks, Tappers? And she says, One of my brothers, whoever got me first, would pin me down on my back by straddling my chest and digging his kneecaps into my shoulders and then tapping my chest as hard as he could with his fingertips until I screamed, and then *bang!* He'd slap me upside the head like he was hitting return on a manual typewriter. . . . Then she starts to laugh, then she starts to cry, etc., blows her nose and dries her eyes and leaves, etc.

She walks to the subway, waits, sighs, steps forward, looks, loses patience, etc. She rolls her eyes as a guy wearing a navy cotton sun visor turned upside down and backward on his forehead says, Fuckinaye, while his friend checks out some hottie with a spit curl on her forehead and red lips lined in black liner. Then she hears the announcement that passengers should etc., etc., and she walks back upstairs and catches a subway headed in the wrong direction, etc. She gets off and on and off the subway, then walks to the street and smells something rank, etc. Then she walks past her accountant's building, distracted, thinking of her brother calling her a lying bitch and how they never really got along after that and feels bad and wishes she could talk to him, really talk, but still, the suit. No idea what happened to that suit.... She looks up, frowns, turns around, and walks back to her accountant's building, swearing at herself, etc. She gets on the elevator, pushes the wrong button, and ends up at the penthouse, with the beautiful Asian secretary looking at her as if she's obviously in the wrong place, and she nods in agreement.

She gets back on the elevator and smiles at the receptionist and then steps away from the open doors, worrying that her face is still puffy from crying, then pushes the right button and waits and gets shoved and stepped on and yells at an old woman and snaps, Jesus, etc. She gets off the elevator and walks into her accountant's office and sees her accountant talking to a very handsome man whose shirt is more like lavender, and she whistles to herself. Her accountant laughs at something the man has said and says to her, Be with you in a moment, and she smiles and says, Fine, no rush, then she wonders why her accountant isn't as nice to her as he is to this man or her friend or etc., etc., and the handsome man says goodbye to her and she etc., etc. Then she follows her accountant into his office, and he says, Sit, in a brusque tone, and she tries to smile.

Yes, she smiles, although she's very nervous about what her accountant has to say about how much money she owes the government. And she wants to protest, simply because her accountant told her last time that she probably owes several thousand dollars this year. If you're lucky, he said. If I'm lucky? she asked. Then he sent her away late on a Friday afternoon, he waved her off, after telling her that she'd find a way to pay. Then she asked how she was going to pay her taxes if she had no money? And then he shrugged and threw her file on top of a pile of manila files, waist-high and haphazardly stacked in a corner of the room, behind his cluttered desk.

Just to top it off, her accountant turned around, looked at her, frowned, and then told her she should be grateful and to get out and have a nice weekend. There are more important things in life, he said. And she wanted to say something barbed in response, but she felt too sick to her stomach. Though she did manage to protest, asking him if he was certain she was going to owe this year? Then he said, We'll see what we see, and she asked him what he meant by we'll see what we see. Then he said, Just go. Go on, git. And she thought he might smile, speaking to her in that tone of voice, but he didn't, and she couldn't respond except to do as she was told.

Then she smiles, anyway, sitting down, still scolding herself for not having said good-bye to the very handsome man in time, because she wants Klaus to like her even if she didn't like him first. Then he says, What's that look on your face? And he says this not in a good-humored way but rather insultingly, she thinks, like there's an ugly expression on her face, and she says, What is what look on my face? And who are *you* to talk about looks, anyway . . . ?

She begins to shake, realizing what she has just said, feels the blood rise to her face, then her accountant stares at her for a moment, considering her comment, and then she looks down and removes a letter from her purse. He says, What's that? Then she shows him the letter and then they disagree about whether or not she should call the Social Security Administration. Then they fight about his payment and she leaves his office, shaking and thinking of saying something insulting about his freckled mulatto face or his ugly tie or his filthy windowless office and its fake wood paneling and piles of shit everywhere, that little shithole in the middle of fucking Chinatown . . . etc., etc. She can't think of anything, becomes angry again, and returns home.

She then calls her friend and tells her friend what Klaus said to her and she says, Who the hell does he think he is? And she interrupts her friend and says, Well, you know what? I don't care. I don't care who he thinks he is. And then her friend suggests he was just trying to be funny. You just have to get his sense of humor, her friend says, and then she becomes that much angrier with her accountant and her friend and she says, Yeah, well, you know what? I *don't*, okay? I don't get his sense of humor. Guess that means I just don't have a sense of humor. Then she gets in a fight with her friend and hangs up the phone and thinks, Some friend.

Or, she wakes, rolls over, dreads the day ahead, gets up, showers, and drinks her coffee while looking at her date book. She bites her nails and stares off, wondering why her accountant sent her friend her friend's tax forms and her friend's coworkers their tax forms, but her accountant won't send her tax forms. Why? Not even after she called and left a message sweetly requesting he send them to her, because that day was really not going to be a good day for her to make the trip to his office right after therapy. Her accountant simply ignored her request. Or rather, Klaus called back and left a message telling her to stop by and pick up her tax forms, no matter how inconvenient the trip might be. He said that her busy schedule really wasn't his concern; he was her accountant, not her secretary. Then, chewing the skin of her ring finger, she worries if her request made him feel subservient for any reason. She was just asking if he could mail her forms to her, that was all, but no time to fret about that now, seeing as it's April 14. She'll just have to go, like it or not.

Well, then, no, she doesn't like it, and she thinks he's mean and etc., etc., nods and leaves, etc. She walks to therapy, buzzes her therapist's office, enters and waits, etc., and then her therapist enters and smiles and she follows her therapist to her office. She sits and scans the room and her therapist sits and smiles and throws her pink Kleenex in the wastebasket beside her chair and says, How are you? Etc. And she says, Fine, fine, etc., and her therapist says, Good, good, etc. Then she looks at her hands and says, Well, to tell you the truth, I was dreading coming here today, and her therapist nods and asks why. She looks away and shrugs and mentions a red-and-white striped suit. It was a Speedo, she says, a racing suit. But my dad said it made me look like a tan candy cane, she says, and smiles.

Then she says, The best part was when we used to get out of the pool during Adult Swim and lie down on the hot cement for five minutes. And by the end of the summer, the front of my suit was shredded from snagging on the cement. It was a rag, but I was so proud, I still wouldn't take it off.... So I was riding my bike home from the pool, and there was this hill. I was pushing my bike up the hill, and this friend of my dad's drove by and stopped to offer me a ride. Well, he wasn't a friend, really, he was just someone who worked with my dad. Then she talks some more about the man and her brothers and her family and about being the only girl and the youngest, etc. Then her therapist asks a question, and then she tries to answer the question, but she can't, and then she tries not to cry but only cries harder. She dries her eyes and blows her nose, fishes two individually wrapped green Life Savers from the candy basket and leaves, etc.

She walks to the subway and waits, etc., etc., and gets annoyed with the fat guy with the baggy jeans to his knees checking out the hottie's ass, and she thinks, Oh, as if, and then his friend, the guy with the upside-down and backward Nike sun visor steps forward and snorts and hawks and cocks his chin and spits on the tracks. Disgusting. She winces, rolls her eyes, checks the track again, then hears the announcement and thinks, Thanks for fucking telling me, etc. She runs upstairs, then downstairs, then almost trips and breaks her neck and jumps on the wrong train just in the nick of time, etc. She realizes her mistake, swears at herself, gets off the wrong subway, etc., etc., and walks up the stairs to the street, etc. Then she walks right past her accountant's office building, distracted, just can't remember what she did with that suit. She remembers her brother saying, Hey, Ugly, where you been? And she remembers telling him to fuck off, and his tackling her, and her crying because it hurt so badly, and she started crying, telling him to get off, he was hurting her, and he said, Oh, you gonna cry, baby? Let's see you cry, then, cry! And then she started screaming at him to get off and her mother ran in and yelled at her brother, telling him to get off, but then . . . ? She stops, turns around, walks back, and enters her accountant's building, grimacing, etc.

She gets on the elevator and pushes the wrong button and ends up at the penthouse with the crystal vases on the reception desk and the beautiful secretary with the high-collared silk blouse and her hair pulled in a bun, looking like some tourist ad, she looks so perfect, sitting there, she thinks, and steps away, etc., etc.

The elevator stops again and again and more and more people get on, and then someone steps on her foot, someone very heavy, and before she has a chance to look, she yells, Ouch! Watch it! Would you watch where you're stepping next time! Then she looks down to find a very old lady with a little boy who looks like he must be the woman's grandson. Then the little boy hides from her gaze, as if she's a mean woman for yelling at his grandmother, and she wants to convince him that she's really a very nice woman, but he won't look at her, so she looks away, too. Then she feels guilty, because it is her fault, really, that she got stepped on in the first place, etc., as more people get on the elevator and etc., etc.

She excuses herself, snaps, Jesus, and gets off the elevator and buzzes her accountant's office, enters, and waits while her accountant talks to a very handsome man, and she notices he's so well dressed she can't imagine what he's doing here. Then she thinks that she would have sex with this man. And then she wonders why Klaus is so nice to this man and her friend, etc., and then chooses not to think about why her accountant doesn't like her. And, instead, she wonders if this man would have sex with her, too, and feels much better. Then the handsome man says good-bye and then she says good-bye as he closes the door, then frowns, having missed the opportunity to make eye contact before he closed the door and swears at herself again, etc.

She enters her accountant's office and he says, Sit, and repeats himself. Sit . . . Sit . . . Then she thinks that apparently Klaus is big on the sit and git, and she almost smiles and then remembers her last visit and his response when she said she was afraid she might be audited. I'm a little nervous, she said the first time she sat in his office. And since he didn't ask, she added, I'm afraid I'm going to be audited. Really, he asked or said, furrowing his brow, looking over the receipts she had Scotch-taped to blank sheets of Xerox paper, causing her to worry that she hadn't taped them correctly or maybe he thought it was a bogus expenditure or something, what?

She peered to see what receipt he was frowning at and she said, Yes. I just have this feeling. Then she sat back and said, I guess everyone probably worries about being audited, right? He stopped, looked up at her, and said, No, not really. Then, still looking at her, he took off his wire-rimmed glasses and put them on his desk and said, Don't flatter yourself. And she said, I didn't mean to flatter myself—, and he said, Don't interrupt me, please, and she said, I'm sorry, I—, and he interrupted her and said, Listen. You don't make enough money to be worth their time, and she said, I know, but a friend of mine— And then he waved his hand and said, I'm not here to discuss your friends. Save it for your shrink, and she balked, and then he told her to have a nice weekend, now git.

I said, Sit, he repeats, and then she sits and keeps smiling, remembering the shrink comment and the message he left on her machine last week, the secretary comment he made, as well as his having told her to get out and enjoy her weekend the first time they met, after he basically dropped a bomb on her personal finances and then he behaved as if she were overreacting, etc., etc. Then she hears her accountant say, What's that look on your face? And she answers, What is what look, and who are you . . . ? Etc., etc. She gets in a fight with her accountant over Social Security, and she tells him that she's going to call, and he calls her a fool and tells her to do as she pleases, then, and she says, yes, that's exactly what she plans on doing, thank you. She signs her returns and then she leaves, shaking and thinking of something scathing she could say to make him want to cry, too, as if she could do it all over again, but can't, etc., etc.

Then she calls and tells her friend what her accountant said and she threatens to call him boy, see how he likes that, and again her friend says, You just have to get his sense of humor. Then she says, That's fine, but, you see, I don't, okay? I *don't* get his sense of humor. I think he's a fucking asshole. And if he ever, ever speaks to me like that again, I'll go off. Her friend insists that the man was just trying to be funny, and then she becomes that much angrier with her accountant and her friend, and she asks her friend why she's defending him, and her friend says she's not defending him, she just thinks he was teasing her, and she says, How would you know? You weren't there, were you? Then she fights with her friend, hangs up, and tells herself never to listen to that friend again. The woman obviously doesn't know what the hell she's talking about.

Or, she wakes, rolls over and sighs, gets up, showers, drinks a cup of coffee, dreads her appointments, thinks, then thinks, etc., etc., then grabs her keys and heads out the door. She walks, buzzes her therapist's office, waits, etc., etc., smiles and follows her therapist to her office, down the hall. She sits in her favorite high-back chair, locates her therapist's Starbucks grande latte cup, etc., and her therapist smiles and says, How are you? and she says, Fine, fine, and her therapist says, Good, good, and nods, etc.

   Then she looks at her hands and says, Well, to tell you the truth, I was dreading coming here today, and her therapist nods again and asks why. And she thinks, Because I've talked about this before and it doesn't change anything, not a damn thing, so this is basically an incredible waste of time, that's why. I think my being here is a waste of time and your being here is a waste of time and I don't really believe talking changes anything. I think people are the same, and it's the same fucked-up world and nothing's improving, anyway, and it's just so self-obsessed. Person after person after person who thinks they're the center of the fucking world? The whole cliché: I talk and you listen and the whole, *Oh, poor me, poor me,* blah blah blah, it makes me sick, it really does. Turns my stomach. . . . Then she sighs and looks away and shrugs and thinks to mention a striped Speedo racing suit that her dad said made her look like a tan candy cane.

   She says, When I was a kid, I went to the pool every day. Every single day of the summer. I loved to swim so much I even slept in my bathing suit. I showered and took baths in my bathing suit. I wouldn't take my suit off. I couldn't be talked out of my swimsuit. . . .

I was always the last out at night, and so I was riding my bike home from the pool, wearing nothing but my swimsuit, with my towel wrapped around my neck. She says, And there was this hill. It was great going down, on your way to the pool, but on the way home, back up the hill, it was a bitch. So I got off, and I was walking my bike up the hill, and this friend of my dad's drove by. He wasn't really a friend, he was this guy who worked on one of my dad's crews and came over sometimes, with some of the other guys. But, anyway, he stopped and offered me a ride.

Then she crosses her legs and says, I didn't really like him, but it was getting late, so I said all right. And her therapist says, Why didn't you like him? And she says, Because . . . because he always complimented me. He used to compliment me, she shrugs. And her therapist says, You didn't like him because he complimented you? And she says, No, I didn't like him because he complimented me and I liked being complimented so much. Nobody ever said stuff like that in my family. That's not the way we talk in my family, don't you look pretty or whatever. I mean, just the opposite. You mean one thing, you say another. If you want to say, You look pretty in that dress, then you say, *Hey, fat ass* . . . And my brothers— she nods. We'd be in the car and a sign would say, CATTLE CROSSING, and my brothers would make me get out and walk back and forth in front of the car, and then she laughs and looks at her hands.

So I said yes and he got out and put my bike in the back, and I climbed in the front seat. He asked if I wanted to go for a drive and I said, No, I should probably get home. Then he said, Well, that's too bad, be- cause he was thinking maybe I'd want to drive his truck and he asked if I'd ever driven before, and I said no. He said, Well, I was going to let you try, but if you don't want to . . . and I was like, shit, I want to drive, so I said, Oh, ... He smiled and said we'd have to find a back road so no one would see me driving, and I started to get really excited. He stopped the truck and he said I'd have to sit on his lap and steer, and he'd do the gas. And he said, What's wrong? And I just shrugged. . . .

Then she says, There was this one time, sometime the year before, and I was sitting on the kitchen counter at home. We weren't supposed to sit on the counter, but I was. I was sitting on the counter, and then I jumped off—I kicked out my legs and pushed off the counter, but I didn't look below. I didn't see the cupboard door was open beneath me, and I landed with my legs spread on the cupboard door. Right on my crotch. I thought that was the worst pain I'd ever felt. I couldn't even scream, it hurt so bad.

Then her therapist talks and asks her a question, then she tries to answer, but she can't form the words, she's trying so hard not to cry that she can't speak, and then she starts to cry. She sobs, answers the question, blows her nose, and dries her eyes. She stands and thanks her therapist for her time because she doesn't know what else to say for herself, closes the door behind her, heads to the bathroom, etc., and leaves.

She walks to the subway and waits, etc. She catches the wrong subway and gets off, etc. She walks up the stairs to Canal Street and walks right past her accountant's office, etc. Then she grimaces, entering his building, and pushes the wrong button on the elevator and ends up at the penthouse, etc. And then she steps out, looks up, sees the gorgeous woman sitting behind the lilies, and wonders how much the woman gets paid to sit there and look beautiful or do whatever it is she does and what the nature of this company is, anyway, and thinks about an ex-boyfriend who had an Asian fetish, which is probably why it didn't work between them—well, that and several other reasons—and wonders what her ex-boyfriend is up to. Then the receptionist catches her looking at her and she smiles and looks away and pushes the DOOR CLOSE button again, then more and more people get on the elevator, then she snaps and pushes her way out of the elevator.

She walks down the hall and enters her accountant's office, sees her accountant and another man talking, thinks the man very handsome, wonders why her accountant doesn't like her, etc., and then thinks about having sex with the man and then feels much better. Then the handsome man catches her eye and she stares at her feet and wonders why she's never had sex or been in a relationship with a black man before and answers her own question, Well, probably because you're a racist. She frowns, stares at her feet again, feels her toe throb, and wishes the old woman would have been more careful where she was stepping.

Then the very handsome man says good-bye, but she hears the man too late to realize he was paying her any attention, and she says good-bye to the man a few seconds too late and she looks very rude, she knows, thinking, Oh, swell, racist and rude to boot. But why can't you at least smile when a handsome man smiles at you? What's the matter with you, are you *retarded?* Then her accountant asks her into his office and tells her to sit, he says, Sit, which reminds her of her last visit, when he told her to git, which reminds her of his response to her fear of being audited and the secretary comment after that, etc., etc. Then her accountant asks about the look on her face, and she says, What is what look and who are you to talk . . . ? Etc. They fight and she leaves, shaking with anger, etc., etc.

She calls her friend and tells her friend what her accountant said and swears, If he ever, ever speaks to me like that again, I'll go off. Then her friend starts to speak, and she interrupts and says, I should call him boy, see how he likes that. Hey, *boy* . . . Finished my taxes yet, *boy?* Her friend laughs and says, You just have to get his sense of humor, and then she becomes that much angrier with her accountant and her friend. Well, that's fine, but I don't. I don't get his sense of humor. Besides which, I'm paying him to do my taxes, not some fucking standup routine, all right? Her friend laughs as if she's making a big deal out of nothing and she says, Look. You know what's funny? What's funny is that I don't remember seeing you in the room. And then her friend starts to say something and she interrupts her friend and says, You weren't there, were you? No, she answers her own question. No, you weren't there, so how do you know? She hangs up the phone and thinks, Some friend. She doesn't like her accountant, and she doesn't like her friend, and she wonders why people can't just leave her alone. Then her phone rings and she thinks, Whoever you are, go away. Please. Just go away.

Or, she wakes, dreads, etc., showers and dreads, etc., pours coffee and thinks, etc., grabs her keys and walks to therapy and waits and smiles and follows her therapist down the hall, etc., etc. Her therapist sits and smiles and says, How are you? Etc. Then she looks at her hands and says, Well, to tell you the truth, I was dreading coming here today, and her therapist nods and asks why, and she sighs. She looks away and shrugs and then she mentions a red-and-white, horizontal-striped Speedo racing suit and her dad saying it made her look like a tan candy cane. And then she smiles, thinking of her dad and any number of things he'd say over and over, never tiring of his own jokes. And how he used to say, You look like a giant candy cane in that suit, or, Christmas in July, huh . . . ? Etc., etc., and she nods, rolling her eyes.

Then she says, I loved to swim. My parents would get us all season passes when we were kids. So instead of getting your hand stamped for the day, you just walked through the front doors and yelled, Season! And I thought I was so cool, you know. I thought I was so much better than the country kids who came in once or twice a year, swimming in cut-off jeans and doggy-paddling in the shallow end. Afraid to get their faces in the water because they didn't know how to swim. I really looked down on them, plugging their noses with their fingers if they wanted to dunk their head beneath the water. . . . That wasn't very nice. It was just the one time of year that I got to feel rich, you know?

She stops and looks at her hands and says, So my suit. One summer, when I was about eleven, I had this bathing suit—I loved to swim so much I slept in my bathing suit. She smiles and nods and says, Yes. Just so I wouldn't waste time, I even showered and took baths in my bathing suit. My mom used to beg me to take it off, but I wouldn't take my suit off. I couldn't be talked out of my swimsuit. . . . Anyhow. So I was riding my bike home from the pool, wearing just my swimsuit. I had my towel wrapped around my neck, whatever. And there was this hill. It was great going down, on your way to the pool, but on the way home, back up the hill, it was a bitch. All the kids had to get off and walk their bikes up the hill. . . . So I was walking my bike up the hill, and this friend of my dad's drove by. Then he stopped and offered me a ride home. Well, he wasn't a friend, really. He was this guy who worked on one of my dad's crews, and he'd come around with the others, whenever we had parties. . . .

It was really hot that day, the end of August, and I didn't really like him, but I said all right. And her therapist says, Why didn't you like him? And she says, Because he always complimented me, that's why. He used to compliment me and I loved it. Part of me, at least. He'd say, You have such pretty hair. I always remembered that, too, and I'd show off my hair. This one time, he was over for a barbecue or something, and he said, Your hair always looks so pretty, the way it blows in the wind. . . . It sounds so corny, I know, but nobody ever said stuff like that in my family. My brothers—my brothers teased me mercilessly, that was affection in our family. We'd be in the car, and a sign would say CATTLE CROSSING or DIP IN THE ROAD, and they'd make me lie down in the road, and she starts to laugh but begins to sob. I liked him saying how pretty I was and it confused me. So then I'd ignore him or I'd be openly snotty, just because I knew I could, and she shrugs.

So it was getting late and he said, Come on, I'll put your bike in the back. I didn't say yes right away, I had to think about it. The hill or the guy? And finally, I said all right, and then he got out and put my bike in the back, and I climbed in the front seat. Then he did something. I remember thinking it was weird, but I didn't ask when he U-turned. It was no big deal, but I didn't know where he was going. So I said, Where are we going? And he said, I thought we'd take a drive, and I said, I don't want to take a drive. And he said, Oh, well. I was going to let you drive, but if you don't want to . . . I didn't know what to do, because I wanted to drive the car, so I said, Oh, all right. Like I was huffy, you know.

He started making small talk, asking about the pool and my friends and was I ready to go back to school. And we had just gotten out of town when he said, You never take that suit off, do you? And I said no, and he said, Then you must be really dirty underneath, and I said, No, I soaped up in my suit, I was clean. And then I told him how, by the end of the summer, when I took the suit off, you could see stripes, from where the fabric had worn and the sun would shine through the white stripes, and he said, Really? You mean your skin is striped? And I said yes.

She tucks one foot beneath her legs and clears her throat and says, He smiled and then he said we'd have to find a back road so no one would see us driving, and I started to get really excited. I saw myself cruising down the dirt road. . . . He drove over to the fairgrounds and took this turn, then he stopped the truck and he said I'd have to sit on his lap and steer, and he'd do the gas. I said I wanted to do it alone, but he said my legs would never reach, so I agreed. He turned off the engine, and I moved over and sat on his lap, and then he asked if he could see the stripes. He said he wanted to see this striped skin of mine. I said no, I showed him my tan lines at my shoulders, but I told him I couldn't show him the stripes without pulling down my suit. And he said, It's just me. No one was going to see. And then I didn't want to drive anymore. I got off his lap and I just wanted to go home at that point, and I told him. And he said, What's wrong? And I just shrugged.

I said, Nothing. I want to go home now. And he said, Why are you being such a crybaby all of a sudden? I give you a lift, I offer to teach you to drive, and you act like a spoiled brat. There was nothing more shameful in our family than being called a spoiled brat, so I didn't know what to say. I felt really ashamed, and I must've looked pouty, because he said, Stick that lip out any farther and a little birdie's going to come along and shit on it, or whatever that saying is. I hate that saying. Then I felt angry, you know, and he poked me in the ribs, and I said, Don't. Then he poked me again, and he started laughing, and I said, Don't do that, and I told him to leave me alone. He poked me in the ribs again and then he squeezed my knees, and I slapped his hand away. I told him to stop it and he did it again, and I started to hit him and he caught my hand and clenched it in his palm.

He moved the seat back and pulled me back over on his lap, and I could feel his erection beneath my butt, my thigh, right here, but I honestly didn't know what it was. I kept moving around thinking there was something in his pocket. . . .

My brothers, the oldest two, Tim and Jaime, they once tried to get me out of my suit by pinning me down and then my dad walked in and he pulled them off so fast. Oh, the veins in my dad's neck were bulging— it was scary. Then he told them if they ever did that again, he'd beat their asses so hard. . . . Jaime almost started crying and he said, We were just teasing, Dad. . . . And they really were teasing, they'd never have taken my suit off. They just wanted to hear me scream. So I thought—I kept thinking he was teasing or he just wanted a reaction, too. At worst, I kept thinking he'd get tired of my screaming, like my brothers always did, or he'd stop when he saw my stripes. But he didn't.

Then she says, There was this time, sometime the year before that. During the school year, I guess. I was sitting on the kitchen counter at home. She smiles and her therapist smiles and her therapist nods and she nods and she says, But I was sitting there, on the counter, and then I jumped off—I kicked out my legs and pushed off the counter, but I didn't look. I didn't look below. I didn't see the cupboard door was open beneath me, and I landed with my legs spread on the cupboard door. Right on my crotch. I thought that was the worst pain I'd ever felt, landing on the cupboard door, but it hurt worse than that. . . . She says, Have you . . . Says, Have you ever taken a cotton sheet in both hands and torn it . . . ? Her therapist stares, says nothing. It was like that sound, but inside, she says.

Then her therapist says, When did you know? And she says, When did I know what? And her therapist says, What was happening? And she says, The whole time, in a way. I felt it in my stomach from the time he pulled me on his lap, this sort of queasy churning. But I don't—because even when he pinned me down on the seat and he was pulling off my bathing suit, I kept thinking, Please don't rip my bathing suit. Please don't rip my suit . . . I didn't—I, no. I'm sure I knew what he was doing, I knew what it was called, but I don't remember it being discussed, or, you know—no. No, she says, and nods her head. She says, He had Wet Ones in the glove compartment. I remember he had all these fast-food ketchup packets, and those little salts and peppers, too. The ones they throw in your bag at fast-food places. And napkins, he had a ton of napkins in the glove compartment. And so then he cleaned me up. . . . I remember getting out, or him opening my door after he took my bike out of the back, but I don't remember driving home. And then her therapist says, Did you tell anyone? No, she says, and her therapist asks why not. And she says, Because I decided there was nothing to tell.

She shifts in the chair, tucks both feet beneath her butt, and she says, I locked myself in the upstairs bathroom. The window was open and I heard some girls drive by on mopeds. It was the summer of mopeds; everyone had them, all the cool girls. She smiles, remembering. Then she says, I heard a couple girls drive by outside, I heard their voices for a moment, yelling at each other, and then I remembered something I'd heard one of the girls say on the bus. One of the coolest high school girls. Missy Thorstad. We took the same bus together, and one time, in the back of the bus, she said it smells like fish when you have sex. We didn't have much fish, Mrs. Paul's or an outing to Red Lobster once a year, that was about it, so I didn't really understand. But then, lying on the bathroom floor, I realized I didn't smell any fish, and I thought, Thank god. I got all excited, and I sat up and got off the floor, and I started smelling my arms, just to be sure. I smelled the top of my arms, then underneath, my shoulders, and then my hands. She says, All my fingers, my knuckles . . . I kept sniffing and sniffing, making sure there was no fishy smell anywhere, and then I leaned over—to smell between my legs, my crotch, and I almost puked. He'd missed some blood.

She says, I keep trying to figure out what it was, what he enjoyed. What did he enjoy? She says, Was it my size? Because I was so small or was it my . . . She says. She says. She says— When . . . ? What moment did he get hard? Or was it . . . She can't say the word. She stops, thinks, Say the word. Say it. Terror. Say terror. Say, Because I was terrified? Can't— She says, Was it . . . Again. Says, Was it . . . Starts to cry. Can see the word, but can't say it. She can't say the fucking word. Again. Says, Was it because I was so terrified? Is that what I did wrong? She starts to sob. I just want to know, she says. Was that what he enjoyed? What got him off? And which moment was it, then? she says. When he pulled at my swimsuit straps? Or was it when I slapped his hand? What if I hadn't slapped his hand then, or the next moment? Or what if I'd laughed when he kissed me instead of shoving him away? What if I'd kissed him back, would he have left me alone? Because there has to be a moment, there's always one moment when you can turn back, but I missed it. I can't figure out when it was.

She takes a breath, uncrosses her legs, frowns. Says, If I could figure out what it was and which moment, I think I would be all right. Was it any one thing I did or was it all of it? Says, If I hadn't screamed, you think? Says, What should I have done? Says, I know there's something. There must be something. Maybe if I'd kept swimming. Or if I'd left earlier with my friends. Or if I'd said no. If I wasn't so lazy. Or if I'd kept riding straight instead of turning left at the hill. And her therapist says, You think that would have changed anything? She says, Yes. Yes, I do. If I hadn't been there when he drove by, it never would have happened. And my entire life would've . . . Would have what? Would have been completely different, she says. Everything would have been so different. So you think it's your fault, then? She starts to answer then begins to cry again and says nothing or says yes or . . .

She cries, dries her eyes, blows her nose, thanks her therapist, and shuts the door behind her. She wipes the mascara off her cheeks, leaves, and walks to the subway. She waits on the platform, etc., etc., then gets on the wrong subway, etc., etc., then she turns around and gets on the right subway, and gets off again, etc., etc. She walks to the street, sighs, etc., etc., checks the street sign, etc., etc. She walks to her accountant's office, then walks right past her accountant's building, etc., etc., etc., distracted, etc., etc., and afterward, after she took a bath and put on a pair of sweatpants and made her way to the TV room and her eldest brother, Timothy, said, Hey, Ugly. Where you been? And she said, Fuck off. Her brothers stopped and stared at her before Tim tackled her, and later she told her mother Tim tore her suit and she cried and cried and her mother told her to calm down, calm down. No use crying over spilled milk, and then Tim got in trouble and wouldn't speak to her for weeks and called her a lying little bitch. But after that, what became of the suit . . . ? Then she stops and frowns, turns around and walks in and pushes the wrong button, etc., etc., etc.

She enters her accountant's office and sits down, etc., and he says, What is that look on your face? And she says, What is what look on my face, and who are you to talk about looks, anyway? And she feels the blood rush to her cheeks as he stares at her.

Then she removes a letter that Social Security has sent her and asks him what he thinks of the paperwork. He says he thinks she should ignore it and forget about Social Security, even though it says she must call their offices immediately because there is a problem with her Social Security number that could complicate her return, etc., etc., etc. Ignore it, he says, handing the letter back. She protests and says it might be important and he says, All right, all right. Let me see that again, and she hands the letter to him, and he looks at the paperwork and then he says, No. Don't call them. Waste of time, and she says, I just want to know what the problem is. Why would they—and he says, Doesn't matter. It's a waste of time, throw it away, and she says, I'll call them, just in case. And he says, No. What did I just say? She says, I heard you, but I want to make sure they have my correct Social Security Number on file. And he says, You're acting like a fool. He says, Don't be an idiot, all right? And she says, I'm not. That's why I'm going to call. Then he says, If you aren't going to listen to me, what are you paying me for? And she says, My taxes, I think. Are they done? And he shakes his head, in disgust. Then her accountant hands her two stuffed envelopes from a stack of forms on his cluttered desk, removes her tax forms from their envelopes, and tells her where to sign, handing her a Bic pen. Here and here, he says, and then he removes his glasses and rubs his eyes.

She looks at the forms and then he opens his eyes and says, Are you done signing? And she says, No, I was just looking them over. I'll sign later, when I get home. And he says, No. Sign them now, and she says, I said I'll sign them when I get home, and he says, No, there's no use not signing them now, and she says, No, I'll sign them—, then she feels the blood rising to her cheeks again and her hands shaking, so she signs her tax forms. There, she says. Then she hands him back his pen and he gathers her forms and puts them back in their respective envelopes, and then he says, Why am I doing this? They aren't my taxes. You can do this! And she says, I didn't ask you to, and he says, You didn't ask me to? She says nothing, stares at her hands, and then he says, And here's your bill, and he jots down a number on a piece of paper and hands the paper to her, and she says, Oh. And he says, Oh, what? What oh?

And then she says, Oh, nothing. Nothing, and she searches for her wallet in her purse, then finds her checkbook first, and he says, Didn't you bring cash? And she says, No, why? And he says, The rule is, pay when you pick up, and she says, I will pay—I have my checkbook and plastic. And he says, I don't take plastic and I don't take checks from first-time clients. Can you bill me, then? she asks. And he says, Didn't you hear me? The rule is, pay when you pick up, he repeats. And she says, Yes, but when did that rule begin? Her friend Kate assured her that he need not be paid right away, in fact, her friend said she still owes him for last year's tax return and he'll understand, and he says, That's always been the rule here. And she says, Maybe, but not with my friend, you—, and he says, Nonsense, and she says, I couldn't agree more. I apologize. It's just a little unusual to have to pay cash, but if that's your rule, then we would-n't want you to break your rule, would we? And he stares at her, sitting back in his chair, holding a pencil above his chest.

She stands, fumbling with her purse, and says, I'll run to the cash ma-chine in the lobby, if you need cash now, and he says, Don't bother. She says, If that's your rule, just let me run out—, and he interrupts her and says, I said don't bother. I said no need, didn't I? I seem to remember saying— Then she interrupts him and says, First, you say it's the rule, when it's not, or at least it's not the rule for everyone, and then when I offer—, and her accountant stares at her and says, Get that look off your face, and she says, What look would that be, Klaus? Then he says, Don't give me that lip, and she says, You don't want the lip, you don't want the look, what do you want, Klaus? Please, tell me now so we can get it out of the way.

He says, Quit fussing yourself, girl. And she balks and says, Don't ever call me girl. Don't *ever* . . . Don't, she says, shaking her head. And he stares at her and then she says, Why don't you let me do as you ask, and we can be done with this now? The only reason I didn't bring cash was because I didn't know you needed to be paid in cash. I don't know many people who insist upon cash in these situations, besides which, my friend said you could take a check. But now you say no check, no credit cards, so why don't you let me—, and he says, Take it and go. Just take it and get out of my face. Git.

She sits and stares, and he says, I said, Git, go. Then she says, Fine, and she stands and takes her two envelopes and her bag of receipts, and leaves without saying good-bye, or maybe she says good-bye, she doesn't remember anything but slamming the door behind her. She presses the elevator and she waits in the hall, shaking, trying not to cry, thinks of secretary and git and that look on your face, etc., etc., gets in the elevator, the elevator stops, more people, more people, gets off, leaves the building, what look? Returns home, calls friend. Then her friend says, He was just trying to be funny. And she says, No, he wasn't trying to be funny. He was trying to be an asshole, etc. They talk some more, she hangs up, thinks, Some friend, etc.

Her phone rings and she thinks about letting the machine pick up, she's too exhausted to talk. Then she decides to answer, because it might be her assistant, and there might be a problem at work, so she answers the phone and hears Klaus's voice and wonders, What the hell do you want, you sick fuck? And she says, What can I do for you, Klaus? Then he asks how she knew it was him and she thinks of telling him what her friend originally told her about his Barry White voice, and she says, I'm very good with voices. Now what can I do for you?

Then he says that he's surprised she knows his voice that well, since he's only spoken to her twice in person and once on the phone, and she thinks, Plus the obnoxious secretary message. She says nothing in reply and thinks, Fuck you, Klaus. Fuck you, and then he says, I'm calling to apologize for earlier today. And then she says, What about it? And he says, For how I spoke to you in my office. I feel bad. I'm under a great deal of pressure right now. I haven't slept in days. It's a terrible week for me, and I'm sorry about what happened earlier. And she thinks, You have no idea. And he says, I wanted to apologize, and— Then she interrupts him and says, Don't worry about it, and he interrupts her and says, No, really, I . . . and she thinks, Stop. Just leave it alone, and he keeps talking, and she thinks, and she thinks. She wants him to stop talking, she wants him to leave her alone, she wants him to shut up, and she thinks, Yes, say it. Say it now, tell him, give it to him, and then she says, Thanks for calling, I appreciate it, and she hangs up the phone. Etc.

Reference
#388475848-5

by Amy Hempel

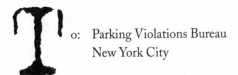

To: Parking Violations Bureau
      New York City

I am writing in reference to the ticket I was issued today for covering
"The Empire State" on my license plate. I include two photographs I
took this afternoon, which show, front and back, that the words "The
Empire State" are clearly visible. I noticed several cars on the same block
featuring license plates on which these words were entirely covered by the
frame provided by the car dealer, and I noticed that none of these cars had
been ticketed, as mine had. I don't mean to appear insolent, but I am

wondering if the ticket might have been issued by the young Hispanic guy I sometimes see patroling the double-parked cars during the week? I ask because the other day, my dog yanked the leash from my hand and ran to him and jumped up looking for a treat. He did not appear to be comfortable around dogs, and though mine is a friendly one, she's big, and maybe the guy was frightened for a moment? It happened as I was getting out of my car, so he would have known it was my car, is what I'm saying.

"The Empire State"—it occurred to me that this is a nickname. I mean, police officers do not put out an all-points bulletin in the Empire State; they put out an all-points bulletin in *New York*, which is also clearly visible on my license plates. In fact, there is no information the government might require that is not visible on these plates. You could even say that the words "The Empire State" are advertising. They fit a standard definition: a paid announcement, a public notice in print to induce people to use a product or entity, the action of making it generally known, providing information of general interest. Close enough.

I have parked my car with the plates as they appear in the accompanying photos on New York City streets for five years, since I drove the car out of the dealership on the Island five years ago; it has never been a problem until now. (I bought the car without ever reading *Consumer Reports*. I checked with a friend, who said the price I was quoted was a reasonable one, but I should refuse the extended warranty the dealer was pushing. "I'm trying to do you a favor," the dealer said, pissed off.)

At the time I bought the car, I didn't know I would soon be back living in the city, and hardly ever needing it. I had thought I would stay the two-hour drive east. What is the saying? "If you want to make God laugh, tell him your plans."

I have kept track of everything I'm supposed to do with the car, but your records will show that I paid the ticket for my expired registration the same week it was issued. I did better with the safety inspection, and FYI, I'm good through November. It's not really about the money, the seventy-five dollars the ticket would cost me. I wouldn't mind writing a check for that amount as a donation to a Police Athletic

League or a fund to help rebuild the city. I'm not like the guy at the film festival yesterday who asked the French director in the Q and A after his film was shown, "Are we going to get our money back?" I hadn't even wanted to see the film; before we went, I told my date what I did want to see, and he said, "They stole the idea from that other one, the one where they ate each other," and I said, "No, that was the plane crash; this is the two guys who had the mountain-climbing accident. It's a documentary." And he said, "What isn't?"

Then, after the French film, after the audience applauded for this major piece of crap, the date and I cut out and went to a place he had heard about in the East Village for tea. It turned out to be someone's exotic version of high tea, so instead of scones and clotted cream and cucumber sandwiches, we were each served a teaspoon of clear, rosemary-scented jelly with a single pomegranate seed inside! What came after that were these teensy cubes of polenta covered in grapefruit puree, all floating in a "bubble bath" of champagne. Then came a chocolate truffle the size of a tooth. The fellow and I were giddy. When we left, after the tea ceremony, it was pouring outside, and we didn't want to leave each other, so we walked another couple of blocks to see a second movie, one he wanted to see, and I didn't tell him I had already seen it because by that time I just wanted to sit next to him in the dark. "I wonder who that is singing," I whispered at one point in the soundtrack. He didn't know, but I did from having read the credits the first time I saw the movie. "Kind of sounds like Dave Matthews," I said, knowing I was right. "Let's be sure to check at the end," I said. "I'd like to get it for you."

Music keeps you youthful. Like, I'm not the target audience for The Verve, but this morning I put on that song that goes, *I'm a million different people from one day to the next—I can change, I can change* . . . and— what's my point? I was in a really good mood when I found the ticket on my windshield. Then how to get rid of the poison, like adrenaline, that flooded my system when I read what it was for?

There is a theory of healing based on animals in the wild. People have observed animals that barely escaped a predator, and they say these animals lie down and shake, and in so doing, somehow release the trauma. Whereas human beings take it in; we don't work it out, so it lodges in us where it produces any number of nasty effects and symptoms. If you follow a kind of guided fantasy, supposedly you can locate a calm, still place inside you and practice visiting it over and over, and that's as far as I got with this theory. It's supposed to make you feel better.

Maybe I should sell the car. But there is something about being able to get in a car and leave when you want to, or need to, without waiting to get to a car rental agency, if you even know where one is and if it is even open when you get there.

Like last week, after a guy grabbed my arm when I was running around the reservoir, when he was suddenly in front of me, coming from the trees on the south end of the track, and no one else was around just then and I couldn't swing around wide enough to get completely past him, and he grabbed my arm. I think it was my anger that made him finally release me, because that is what I felt, not fear, until I got back home with a sore throat from yelling at him to leave me the fuck alone. I was shaking like crazy, and it wouldn't stop, so I walked a block to where my car was parked, and I drove for a couple of hours toward the ocean. My right leg was bouncing on the accelerator from nerves for much of the way, but I stopped for coffee, and when I started up again I steered with my knees, the way real drivers steer, with a cup of coffee in one hand, playing the radio with the other. So maybe I am a wild animal, shaking off the trauma of near-capture.

There were actually two men at the reservoir. And I thought it was odd that when the first one grabbed me, and I reflexively swung my free arm around to sock him in the chest, the other man didn't stop me. Because he could have. He watched, and listened to me yell, so I don't know what the deal was. But I think it was worth paying the insurance and having to park the car and get this ticket to have the car there to use that day.

You could accuse me of trying to put a human face on this. And you would be correct. But is there anything wrong with that? Unless the ticket was issued by the guy my dog startled, I know it isn't personal. But I'm not a person who can take this ticket in stride with the kind of urbanity urbane people prize in each other. I feel I must question—and protest—this particular ticket.

I want what is fair. I don't want a fight. But the truth is, I'm shaking—right now, writing this letter. My hand is shaking while I write. It's saying what I can't say—this is the way I say it.

I'm Happy, You're Happy, We're All Happy

by Colette Paul

Oliver did this thing with his eyes. You know how you sometimes see pictures of saints or nuns with blurry, soft-focused pupils looking heavenward, well, it was like that. When he did this, I always wondered what he was thinking. He had another pose, too. Head down, eyes shut. He had the darkest, gravest eyelids I'd ever seen. The first time we went out for a drink together, he told me he had one blue eye and one green eye.

"Does it bother you?" I said. I was amazed I'd never noticed.

"If it's fine by David Bowie," he said, "it's fine by me." He was playing with a butt in the ashtray. After a few minutes, he said, "You've got nice eyes, too."

I said I'd always thought so, but no one had ever confirmed it. It was a joke, but he didn't realize, or if he did, he ignored it.

"You've been hanging around with the wrong people then," he said.

I first saw Oliver in Burger King. He was new, so had been put on broiler duty. He was feeding the machine with frozen discs of meat, and then sandwiching them between rolls as the burgers came flopping out the other side, bubbling fat and blood. It was the worst job. The grill dripped strings of yellow grease, which sizzled off the boiling metal; the whole machine trembled and steamed. Your face went blotchy after a few minutes beside it. Sweat glistened in your hairline, in the creases of your nose and chin. But Oliver was looking very cool about it. He had a nonchalant way of doing things. He gave the impression that he could saunter away at any moment, like he was only exerting the minimum of effort, and that's why he stayed.

None of the staff liked him. They thought he was arrogant, and too big for his boots. They had a field day when he slid on a french fry and had to be taken home. It was his own fault, they said. Those daft boots. He just had to be different, and look where it got him.

His cowboy boots were regulation black, so the manager couldn't tell him to change. They had silver stars on the side and heels that tip-tapped on the floor. I wasn't there when he fell, and can't imagine it. Can't imagine him having to be helped up, supported between two people, dependent.

Don't get me wrong. It wasn't that Oliver was handsome or anything. In fact, he had two of the pointiest incisor teeth I've ever seen. He wore his hair ridiculously greased up, matador-style. It was the way his face changed all the time. I watched for its alterations. I couldn't decide if he was ugly or handsome, so kept studying him to see.

I was too shy to sit in the staff room and would sit by myself in the dining area. One afternoon, he came over and sat down. He didn't look at me and sat eating his Whopper. Then he said, "What are you reading?"

I held up the front cover, embarrassed, and angry with myself for being embarrassed.

"Egon Schiele," he said, leaning back on his chair. "It's pretty obvious what his paintings are about."

"Yes," I said, although I didn't know what he was talking about. It was just a book I'd picked up in a jumble sale and had liked the look of.

He said he was a painter himself. He was trying to finish his portfolio for September. He said that every year, he went off to a remote Scottish island where he drew and painted by the sea. He said how strange the people were up there. How none of them had driver's licenses, but flew around in their cars like bats out of hell. They knocked down squirrels and grouse and retrieved them from the road, cooked them for dinner. He described red-nosed men slumped paralytic outside the weekly ceilidhs.

"Lot of queer hawks there," he said. "I was in good company."

Surprising myself, I said, "It can get lonely with normal people," and Oliver said, "Darn tooting." He said he liked my style.

We never really went out. I was unsure of where the boundaries lay, what could be said and what could be assumed. It was ages before I plucked up the courage to invite him to my flat. For weeks, I'd imagined making a meal, thinking about what I'd cook, how I'd throw it all together in front of him, drinking red wine from a mug. There would be candles, and chiffon draped over my lamp. The squalor would be beautiful. We'd look at my books piled carelessly along the walls. Imagining this night was one of my favorite pastimes. As it was, he came up one night after work. There was a thunderstorm on the way over, black clouds sank forebodingly over the streets, one bruised strip of light above us. We were soaked by the time we got home. My flatmates were in the kitchen, so we went into my room. The window was open, and cold air and rain were pum-melling into the room.

"It's freezing in here," Oliver said. "Can you not shut that thing?"

I told him it was jammed, but I'd put the fire on. It wouldn't ignite, and the room stank of gas and burnt matches. Oliver sat on the bed with his arms wrapped around himself. He prided himself on his thinness, how his hands could meet round his back. I could tell he was annoyed at the cold, and that annoyed me, so we both said nothing for a while.

"Why don't you come and lie down," he said at last. "You've nowhere to sit over there."

"Yeah, okay. It's quite uncomfy down here."

I undid my trainers and put them to the side, eased myself on top of the bed. I tried not to look at his boots dripping mud and dirty water onto my sheets. We lay side by side, and after a while I said, "I saw that girl you used to go with today."

"Yeah?" He turned to face me. "What was she doing?"

"Shopping, I suppose. It was in the St. Enoch Centre."

He wanted to know who she was with, so I described the girl.

"That'll be Anna," he said. "I can't stand her. She was never a good friend to Catherine." Then he said, "How did Catherine's skin look?"

"A bit sore. Is it acne she's got?"

"Catherine's got terrible problems with her skin."

He said this to himself, just loud enough for me to hear. He had his head down and looked so sorrowful I wanted to reach out and touch him.

"Do you think you'll ever get over it?" I said, casually.

"Yeah," he said, "but I don't know about Catherine."

He looked straight at me and said he wasn't looking for a relationship just yet, though.

"I want a bit of fun first," he said.

"Yeah," I said, "you don't want to be tied down or anything."

He began to stroke my ribs and I listened to the rain pound outside, dropping onto the floorboards under my window.

Sometimes, before work, we walked through the park together, or down Allison Street into town, or we picked a street we didn't know and followed it to see where it ended. Oliver liked the early morning. The streets were always long and bright, with unbroken shadows. It was December, just before Christmas, and the trees had been stripped bare, the pavements glistening with ice.

"Clears the cobwebs," said Oliver when I complained about the cold. "Feel that air," he said, and he abandoned his face to the wind. His hair came loose and flapped off his forehead until he smoothed it back. He looked out of place everywhere. His funny clothes, his lean, ravenous face. Too fragile for all his swaggering, and that's why it was attractive, because it was a stance, it was striven for.

"If people are going to think you're odd," he said, "you might as well go the whole hog."

I felt closest to him on these walks. Oliver talked about his dreams, which fascinated him. He had one where T. S. Eliot phoned him and introduced himself as Tom, and Oliver asked him how it was going, and they had a chat. He recited Oliver's favorite poem, the one that goes:

> O dark dark dark. They all go into the dark,
> The vacant interstellar spaces, the vacant into the vacant.

Oliver said the poem was the funniest thing he'd ever heard, he said it pretty much summed up his life view. I said I preferred Stevie Smith's *Smile, smile, and get some work to do*, and Oliver said that was a good one, too.

We played games where we imagined what people around the world were doing at that very moment. Olga in Moscow, famous for her sweetmeats, was decorating a cake that depicted the fall of the Berlin Wall; Pierre, a fraud inspector in Nice, an apologetic man who perspired a lot, had just found his wife in bed with his brother. Millions of births and marriages and divorces and people getting it on. People discovering they had cancer, breaking up, making up, getting drunk, sleeping, eating. A couple in this street, Mary and Brian, arguing about a basil plant Brian chucked out because it was cluttering the place.

I asked Oliver his favorite color, favorite song, favorite anxiety.

And all the time I could feel my blood move around my body, feel the electricity in my brain, I could feel and hear and see everything. All the life in everything was pulsating and alive and growing and enriching. The sky was more blue, the grass more green, noises were truer, human beings were nobler and greater and more beautiful than they would ever know. But it was only because Oliver was there with me. The mornings settled in, people made coffee, stared, thought about the day ahead. We wandered aimlessly. It was a conspiracy of sorts: nowhere to go, no one to go to.

"We're both solitary creatures," he said one morning. "People who are meant to be alone."

I was horrified, and said that I wasn't, or I hoped I wasn't. "Speak for yourself," I said.

"I mean, *I* don't need anybody," he went on. "Sometimes knowing that makes me feel guilty, and sometimes I think, Well why should I? What good does it do you? Sometimes I think, More fools them. I wouldn't give up my freedom for all the tea in China."

Oliver was always talking about his freedom like it was some physical attribute you either had or you hadn't, something you could lose or misguidedly relinquish. He said he'd sacrificed it for Catherine, but never again.

"You wouldn't give up your freedom for all the farms in Cuba," I said.

"Nope, not for two birds in one hand."

"Not for a cloud with a silver lining," I said, "or the crock of gold at the end of the rainbow. Red sky at night, shepherd's delight," I said. "Too many cooks spoil the broth."

"I think you're taking the piss now," said Oliver.

I told him to listen to Janis Joplin: *Freedom's just another word for noth-*

ing left to lose. I said what if chasing freedom's another form of being
unfree, of being trapped?

"You could have a point there," he said.

I had made friends with a girl I worked with at Burger King. Before I met
Oliver, Clara and I had started going to pubs together, sometimes to
nightclubs. She was the only person I'd gotten to know in Glasgow. I
didn't make friends easily, not even acquaintances. Oliver said it was
because I didn't smile much. Like Russian prime ministers in the old days,
he said. They didn't feel the need to grin all the time. He said it was
what had attracted him to me.

Clara laughed like there was no tomorrow. Her teeth were too big for
her mouth and made her lips stick out, obscuring everything else about
her face. Her skin was ragged and coarse like it'd been raked over, but she
didn't cover it up with makeup.

"This is me," she said, "the whole woeful package."

Everything Clara did was accompanied by noise. She talked as fast
as she could get the words out, she roared with laughter, she exclaimed
loudly, she dropped things, she was always tripping over paving stones or
jamming her fingers in doors. It wasn't ostentatious, intentional noise, but
a kind of edgy, desperate nerviness that she was always trying to beat back.
We spoke about our parents and our trials and tribulations at school, and
how we hated Burger King, and our money problems. We talked about
boys we liked, and how we didn't know why we liked them, and wondered
when any of them were going to like us back. Clara was in love with a boy
who worked at Safeway, and she'd make us walk down there and buy
something so she could see him. We always went to the cashier three tills
down from him because Clara was scared to talk to him. She'd wave, and
he'd smile bewilderedly back.

"He thinks I'm a nutcase," she'd say, "but I can't help myself. See that
lazy eye he's got, I just love him for that. He looks so sad, I'd just like to
cuddle him up to my bosom."

"Clara, you *are* a nutcase," I'd say.

I saw Clara less and less when I started going out with Oliver. I liked to be available in case he wanted to see me. One Saturday, when Oliver hadn't phoned, I called her and we arranged to meet in a café. She had dyed her hair a funny red color and was wearing a brown-checked bonnet of her dad's to hide it. She was upset about a boy who'd said he'd phone her, but hadn't.

"I even slept with him," she said, and I said she should know by now that that didn't guarantee anything, far from it.

"What is that supposed to mean?" she said.

"None of these boys ever phone you," I said. "I'm scared you're getting a reputation. And I hate seeing you do this to yourself when you're better than the whole lot of them."

At first, Clara didn't say anything. She sat still with her shoulders drooping, and the silly hat on, and I said, "Clara, I'm not trying to hurt you," which I wasn't. I just thought I was being honest, like friends should be.

Then she said, "You're jealous."

Her voice was getting louder and louder, and the conversations around us were dropping off.

"You're jealous," she repeated, "because boys want to sleep with me"—she put her hand to her chest like a damaged bird—"and not you. Because you're stuck with that nincompoop who couldn't give a bat's fart whether you live or die."

"Listen," I said, "forget what I said. Maybe you're right just having fun. Clara," I said, "just calm down."

She stood up and said, "If you want some honesty, let's start with you. Everyone but you knows you're making a fool of yourself. You love him all right, but does he love you?"

"I don't know," I said.

"Well, that's fine," she said, "but you should sort yourself out." She said, "I don't want to be your friend anymore. I don't think I need friends like you."

I went straight round to Oliver's flat, uninvited. I'd never done that before.

Oliver was a minimalist. He said he liked knowing that he could move on anytime he wanted. In his room, there was a single mattress on the floor, a chair beside a desk, and a chest of drawers, and that was it. I sat on the edge of the mattress. I told him Clara and I had fallen out and that I didn't think it was my fault, but maybe it was. Oliver didn't say anything. I said she was my only friend and I'd blown it, and she hated me now. Pitied me, which was even worse. I didn't tell him what she'd said.

Oliver sat down beside me. "She's not worth a hoot," he said. "There's other fish in the sea. When one door closes, another one opens. If you don't laugh, you'll cry," and he got me to wipe my face and stop crying.

He put his hand, just quickly, on top of mine, and said, "Just you and me against the world, eh?"

His hand on mine. I couldn't think anymore. I wanted to kiss every freckle on his skinny arms and say, Thank you. Thank you, thank you.

We started going to Queen's Park, where Oliver sketched and took photos of swans for his portfolio. He never finished anything, because he kept tearing the sketches up in moments of frustration.

"That tree was all wrong," he'd say, or, "I've spoiled that cloud that was meant to pull the picture together." He was ruthless.

He only painted swans. He started a new one just before he left. Two of them in the park, the taller one nestling the other in the crook of its curving white neck, protectively. They were as white and still as unmarked snow. He had ten in all. Swans in various settings. Untouched and untouchable white necks, like they'd just been cracked open from alabaster molds. Some flamingo pink, floating in murky rivers, one on a window ledge looking down on urban decay. I laughed at him choosing something as genteel, as decorous, as swans, and Oliver, annoyed, said they were beautiful, with a huge capacity for viciousness. He said he wanted to be a swan. They didn't get concerned about anything, just did their thing. He said maybe he'd live somewhere far away, with a whole gaggle of them doing their thing and he'd do his.

"What would that be?" I said, and he said he didn't know.

"You're more like a walrus than a swan," I said. "Walruses are sort of grand because they're so foolish-looking, but don't know it. They're never going to be what they think they are. Also, I imagine them to have independent spirits."

Oliver laughed. "If you had to be any animal," he said, "you'd be a baby elephant."

"Thanks very much."

"They're gentle and very loyal," he said, "like you."

"Loyalty's not much to have going for you," I said.

At the start of May, both our leases ran out, and Oliver said it would make sense to get somewhere together.

"It'd be cheaper," he said. "It'd be okay."

We found a room, a converted roof space, at the top of an old house on Joy Street. The name appealed to me, although there was nothing joyous about the place. Rambling old houses in various stages of dilapidation lined the street like rotten teeth that refused to budge. Next door to us was a derelict old folks' home, half the windows smashed, a pram and discolored mattress in the backyard. At night kids would congregate there, smoking and drinking cider. One morning, I woke up and they'd graffitied the side of the building next to our window: ARMS ARE FOR EMBRACING, and below, WE DON'T WANT YOUR BLOODY WAR, and then, obscurely, poignantly, JOHN F LOVES ME.

The landlady, Mrs. Reilly, lived downstairs with her husband, Stan. Oliver and I shared a bathroom on the second floor with the other lodger, a man called Mike who never spoke to any of us. Sometimes he put his hand up in a gesture of hello, and sometimes he didn't. When he had a shower, he always left a note on our door: *Please don't enter the bathroom for the next fifteen minutes as I will be showering and naked. Thanks.* He wore tight leather trousers and a biker jacket, and he played Morrissey and The Fall and opera music all night long. Oliver said he seemed like the type of person who might have scrapbooks full of movie stars' pictures. We invited him up to our room a few times, but he never came, and soon we stopped asking him.

Downstairs, where Mrs. Reilly lived, was like a war zone. The mess was awesome—a door propped against the wall in the kitchen, welts of brown sludge running up the bath and down the walls of the bathroom. There was fusty wet washing lying in the crook of a dirty velvet settee, old cat litter piled in the hall, a splintered church pew, seashells, stacks and stacks of dusty *Daily Record*s, plastic carrier bags. The house smelt of old vegetables and animals. I counted ten cats at one point, although they were always coming and going, some being reclaimed, others disappearing, new strays arriving. They darted about, tense-backed and wary, scratching at doors and walls and each other. Mrs. Reilly left bowls of food and water all round the house for them. She told me she was a sucker for strays.

When we first moved in, we made up fanciful and unreasonable stories about Mrs. Reilly. We imagined her the rich, pampered daughter of a textile mogul, fallen on hard times. Mrs. Reilly had inherited his crumbling empire, had been left all alone in the world with only her dreams and her charm at her disposal. She had been jilted once, and terribly, had married Stan on the rebound, a man who knew how to be restrained with his words, who loved her grandness, her excess. We could talk like this for hours.

"One day, there'll be no more stories," I said to Oliver one night. I put on a mock-sad voice. "And what then? What shall we do then?"

"There'll always be stories," said Oliver.

Oliver didn't like Mrs. Reilly, and he hated the cats. He said they made his allergy bad, and gave him the creeps. He had quit his job at Burger King and was staying at home, trying to paint. I was finding it hard living with him. Some days, he hardly spoke. He said speaking was a waste of time.

He said Kierkegaard gave up talking when he realized how meaningless it was. Oliver was going one better. He gave up movement, never mind talking. He said it was a political decision.

"If you don't move," he said, "you can't affect anything."

I asked Mrs. Reilly if she'd mind trying to keep the cats away from our room. "I would if I could," she said, "but it's their house, too."

She kept leaving bowls of cat food on our landing, and Oliver would grimly empty them out of our window. After a few weeks, the cats stopped coming near our door, and I suspected Oliver had been kicking them. I thought he was capable of that.

Mrs. Reilly, I soon realized, told lies. Not big, important lies, not even lies that made her look better, but the kind that made you wonder why anyone would waste her time telling them. Once, she told me that she'd been followed home from the shops by a man wearing a trilby, although I'd heard her in the kitchen all day. Another time, she said a baby chicken had fallen into her plate when she cracked her egg. I told Oliver to listen to her for sheer entertainment value, her whole theater of emphatic gestures and flourishes when she told her stories. Her eyes would dash around, searching for a wider audience, even though there was just me and Oliver in the room, and Oliver would turn his back on her, or pointedly read a book. She wore wigs—blonde, brunette, or red—and depending on the color, she would say that she'd always thought, really, that she should have been a blonde. She'd put her hands to her face coquettishly and ask me what I thought of it, and I'd say it suited her.

"Monroe, eat your heart out," she'd say. "There's a new girl in town."

One afternoon, she confided in me that she wore the wigs because her hair was falling out, and it distressed her. Bald patches the size of plums all over her head. I knew this wasn't true because I'd seen her coming out of the bathroom one day, and her hair was wet and streaming down her back. Black, and no bald patches. What was funny was that the wigs weren't even glamorous, but old-fashioned, brittle, and imperturbable. They were shaped into bouffant styles that wartime mothers might have worn, perched at a jaunty angle, like tea cozies, on top of her head. Also, I only ever saw her in slippers, pale pink, spiky-heeled ones, with tufts of marabou at the front. Drag-queen slippers, Oliver said.

We'd hear her stomp around restlessly downstairs after Stan had gone to work. And then, the creaking of the stairs.

"Here comes the Madam," Oliver would say. "I'm out of here."

And I'd sit and listen to them pass each other, in silence, on the stairs.

"Hello, dear, I'm just up to see how you are."

"I'm fine, Mrs. Reilly, and yourself?"

This was her cue to tell me exactly, and with great detail, how she was. "Well, you know how it is," she'd start off, touching the corners of her mouth with her great sausage fingers. "They think it's down to the surgeon's knife now. A h-y-s-t-e-r-e-c-t-o-m-y. I will just sit down for a minute . . ."

I came to dread hearing her knock because it meant Oliver would go out, sometimes not coming back for hours, or else he'd be in a bad mood all day. We'd stop what we were doing and sit very still, or I'd peek my head out of the door, doing as much as I could to bar her. But nothing put her off. She sat heavily on our bed, her cigarettes and ashtray balanced on one knee each. She told me true-life stories she'd read in a magazine (a woman whose sister bit off her ear; a woman whose husband was actually a woman; a woman addicted to Spam), and how she liked a cracker with pâté at eleven o'clock every day, wasn't that funny? and that the couple at number twenty were breeding rabbits just so they could watch them copulate.

"Maybe they're pets," I said, enjoying the ridiculousness of it.

"When you get to my age, love," Mrs. Reilly said, "you get to know a pet lover from a pervert. No," she said, "you just keep to the other side of the road from them."

Oliver got into terrible moods. He would cry for days and days, sitting on a chair and letting the tears fall until his eyes were raw. It distressed me more than him, I think. I begged him to tell me what was wrong.

"Nothing," he would say. He said he didn't want my help, he wanted me to go away.

"But I've nowhere to go," I said.

"Just go away and I'll be fine."

I put my hand on his back, and he shook it off and told me not to fucking mother him.

"If you don't want me to mother you, then don't act like a fucking baby."

Sometimes I'd storm out, but once outside our bedroom, I realized that I really did have nowhere to go, no one to go to. Clara was still ignoring me at work. So I'd go round the block and then back in. One time, he apologized. He said he should treat me better, but that he was a depressed person, he was never going to be happy.

"Don't look at me like that," he said. "Don't look at me so pitifully. It's chronic," he said, "not terminal."

A day later, or even a few hours later, Oliver would be in a good mood. His face would be animated and jumpy, as if someone were pulling strings connected to pulse points behind his bones. Then we could talk all day. We spoke about our futures, but always solitary futures that didn't involve each other. That made me sad. Oliver wanted to own a traveling library that he'd drive to a new place every day. He would live in the library, and everything had to be wiped clean, and able to fold away entirely. That was important. I said I'd grow massive, prize-winning marrows, and Oliver said forget the traveling library, he'd be a famous artist. There'd be spoons given out on national holidays with his face on them.

"No," I said, "I think you'll just become a common pedestrian little human being. You'll get fat, and have a mouthful of bad teeth, and be unashamed."

"Common!" Oliver said. "I'd rather die."

He ran over and pulled me into his arms, into a Hollywood romance pose.

"We'll have no more of this talk," he said. "Okay?" he said, and I said I couldn't speak, I was swooning.

"Quite right," he said. "Carry on."

We stayed in our room almost all the time. Twice a week, I worked double shifts at Burger King, starting at seven and ending at midnight. On those mornings, I would wake up early, about half past five, and lie in bed, looking out of the window at the sky, clay white, violet-streaked. I'd stare for ages at the ARMS ARE FOR EMBRACING graffiti, the only bit of the wall I could see from our bed. Such a strange feeling came over me those days, a feeling that was oppressive and overwhelming, sorrowful and buoyant at the same time. I still can't describe it.

The room was dusty. There were gargantuan roses crawling up the wallpaper, a tiny sink, a hob, a chair with the telly on it. The brown, singed carpet stopped a few inches short of the wall. Everything we owned was on the floor. We fought about the mess, but then we fought about everything. I remember one argument about Melvyn Bragg's hair. It escalated so suddenly, violently. I remember Oliver saying that was it.

"Fuck this," he said.

He ran over to the telly and shoved it as hard as he could off the chair. The telly was especially important to me because I watched it all day when Oliver wasn't speaking to me. In a kind of blind rage, I grabbed his special Elvis record and tried to bend it. He ripped my Bob Dylan poster. I chucked his boots out of the window. Oliver said I was pathetic, always wanting people to like me, and it made him ill.

"You're the one with no friends," I said, and Oliver said he didn't see people queuing up to talk to me.

"Only that mad hatter downstairs," he said. "And you're so grateful.

Slobbering like Pavlov's dog when she says she'll show you how to make soup. You're just another one of her strays," he said.

I called him selfish, a big baby. I said he always felt sorry for himself and it was pathetic. He couldn't stand to be denied anything. He couldn't take responsibility for himself, for anything he did. Oliver said at least he was honest.

"Well, you," he said, "you thinking you're such a nice person when you don't even like people that much. You just want them to like you. That's fraudulent. You've got a bullying streak. That's why we're in this shithole," he said. "Because you were going on and on, you thought it'd be a good idea. I had no choice."

And so it went till we were both crying, both out of breath, spent, looking round at the mess. And we said truce. I went out to the back to find his boots, and when I came back, Oliver was huddled on the bed.

"I don't know about you," he said. "You don't anchor me in reality."

"What d'you mean?" I said. "What does that mean?"

He said Catherine had been like a reality check for him, like the canary you take down the mine with you. She let him know when he was in trouble, when he was getting too crazy.

"But you're crazy, too," he said.

I said everyone was crazy in their own way, he shouldn't let it bother him. We went for a walk, and I put my arm through his. We walked for hours, no moonshine, the streets getting darker.

At times, yearning for Oliver made me almost weak. I wanted to touch him, but was afraid to, like a light switch I knew would give me a shock. I named parts of his body as mine. A hairless strip of skin on the back of his shin, one stray black hair coming out of his sharp shoulder blade.

"You're going to make me loathsome when you go," I said.

Rain began to batter against the window. I thought he'd gone to sleep, and was watching him, a little bit asleep myself. Suddenly, he asked me if I loved him.

"Yes," I said. "Do you love me?"

"I think so. How much do you love me?"

"Till the ocean is folded and hung up to dry."

"That's okay then," he said, and shut his eyes. Soon, he was asleep, and I, still a bit asleep myself, continued to watch him.

About two months before Christmas, almost a year since we'd first known each other, Oliver didn't come home. It wasn't until the next night that he turned up.

"Before you start," he said, "I've got something to tell you."

He was going to Grenoble to work in one of the ski resorts. They were desperate for staff. Good wages, and a beautiful place to work. They were going to pay his flights and everything. He could be away before Christmas. He hated Christmas.

"Where did you hear about this?"

"From Catherine," he said.

He'd met her the other day on his way back from the library. They'd gone for a drink, and started talking about things. He didn't tell me, but I knew he must have spent the night with her.

"And is she going? Are you going together?"

He said there was a bunch of them, all friends from school. He was leaving five weeks from Monday.

"Hey, don't cry," he said.

"I'm not crying."

He said he was sorry. He thought I knew the deal.

"The no strings attached idea?" I said, and Oliver said yeah.

"I like you a lot," he said. "I might even love you, whatever that means. But you always knew I wasn't over Catherine. I never lied to you."

I said I was actually happy he was going, and he was happy to be going. "We're all happy," I said. "Happy happy joy joy. So, why don't you just beat it."

Oliver said he wasn't going to leave it like that. He said, "Come on, it's late," and lay down on the bed.

"Come and tell me one of your stories," he said.

The next day, I told him to get out. I said not to phone me, not to come round. "This is our good-bye," I said, and he said, "Okay."

He said, "Take care."

The next night, I went downstairs. Mrs. Reilly was in the kitchen reading *Woman's Own*.

"What's wrong, pet?"

"Just left me," I said. "I don't know what to do."

Mrs. Reilly came over and smothered me in her arms. She said she'd known something was going on.

"Just left me," I said. "I don't know what to do."

Mrs. Reilly said it wasn't the end of the world, even if it felt like it. She said it happens all the time, all the time, and other people manage, and I said no. No, she didn't understand.

"Sit down," she said. "I'll make some tea."

She said I was too good for him, she could see that. There was no life in him.

"We understood each other," I said, and Mrs. Reilly said I'd find someone who understood me better. "Don't speak to him," she said, "don't talk to him. If you've got a cancer, cut it out."

She sat with me for hours, until I was worn out and could hardly lift myself from the chair.

"Scoot," she said and nudged me toward the stairs. "Get some sleep." She shouted up that I had to remember he was a fool.

"You don't get many of you in a lucky bag," she shouted.

———

For a week, I lay in bed, absorbed in my own grief. Everything in the room reminded me of him. I reran conversations we'd had, wondering if anything I'd said, or hadn't said, would have made a difference. I didn't eat, was sick, didn't sleep. I got sacked and didn't care.

Gradually, things started to get a bit better. I got a new job in Freezways. I worked with a fifty-five-year-old woman who sat in the back all day, smoking menthol cigarettes and thinking up things for me to do. I worked in a trance, puzzled that my body had not shut down, puzzled that I was still able to function, put on makeup, talk, eat, catch buses. I washed the freezer lids with water and vinegar, and mopped and buffed the floor till it gleamed. I listened to the steady buzz of the freezers all day long, and was sullen and disagreeable to customers. Oliver would've approved. I managed to get through days, and then weeks.

The Monday when Oliver's plane was leaving, I couldn't sleep. I got up and dressed and took the earliest bus I could get down to the airport. It was three days before Christmas, and the place was decked in tinsel. There was a massive tree covered with glass baubles, and hundreds of people moving all at the same time in different directions. I suddenly felt dizzy, as if I were about to faint. I made my way forward to read the departure board. A plane for Grenoble had already left, but there were more throughout the afternoon. I sat in one of the visitor lounges. If they passed, I'd see them, but they probably wouldn't see me. That's what I wanted. By midmorning, the crowds had thinned out, and then it was busy again about lunchtime. Someone came and asked me if I needed any assistance, and I said, "No, thank you."

"Check the board," she said, "that tells you about any delays."

By five, all the lights were blazing and the plate glass reflected me back to myself. I thought, I'd better go home, but didn't have the energy to move. I thought, I'm not going to cry, but then I was.

Ten Thousand
City Nights

by Ariel Gore

As recently as my grandfather's time, unscrupulous ship captains who didn't want to pay their crews bought young laborers from backrooms and underground cities on the West Coast of America.

One moment, a man would be sitting on a cracked barstool in a smoky saloon on the western side of town, drinking Johnnie Walker and arguing about politics; next thing, he'd wake up in a damp tunnel, or already onboard some gray ship bound for China or Australia.

His fate sealed, he had no choice but to work.

Of those who made it safely to Shanghai—a city that required neither visa nor passport for entrance—some, at once sea-weary and enamored by the city's magnetic beauty, managed to stay.

141

In fact, so few sailors ever wanted to leave Shanghai that when it came time for ships to set off again, new crewmen had to be kidnapped from the bars on Blood Alley or in the French Concession.

Down-and-out or on-the-run, hiding from the past or running toward a future, they were held by Shanghai, city of dragon-horse dreams.

This is why I have Western eyes and a stranger for a great-grandmother. Her ghost still roams the tunnels under the city of Portland. She clutches a single shoe, searches night and day for her lost son.

Sometimes, just as I'm falling asleep, a damp chill comes over me and I swear I can hear her crying out for him. On those nights, I want nothing more than to call back to her through those dark tunnels: "Your son arrived safely." The message he could never send home. But just as I open my mouth and begin to form the words, I'm wide awake again. I've lost her to the distance. The neon lights shine in through my uncurtained window, bathing my one-room apartment in a strange tangerine glow. I sit up in bed then, but only the refrigerator hums. The muffled sound of lovers arguing in the apartment next door, their voices pitching up and down. An intermittent drunken shout in Chinese or English from the street below as the last partiers tumble out of the clubs and head home.

I often muse that all times exist simultaneously—it's just that we, like fireflies in a fog, trapped by the limits of our own perception, can only see and feel that tiny realm of experience we manage to illuminate with our own feeble light. I'm convinced that if I could just concentrate hard enough, I could locate secret passageways between our times and the past.

I remember feeling this way even as a small child. At eight, I'd lay awake nights, looking out the window at the giant dusted moon, and imagine slipping back to meet a younger self. I'd relay some urgent message to her: *Don't trust Teacher Wu*, or *Compliment mother's cooking tonight*. At sixteen, when I first smoked hashish behind the foreigner's hostel on Nanjing Lu, I walked alone to the bank of the dirty Suzhou River and sat there on the wall, my feet dangling over the edge. I closed my eyes and willed my consciousness to break through the divides.

But it's all gotten so much more intense since I moved into my grandmother's apartment. She lived here most of her adult life—even managed to keep the place through the Revolution and the cold years because of a mysterious connection to a local party leader. That connection became both the subject and the fuel of many rumors, but my grandmother had long since grown immune to rumors.

I moved in here just a few weeks after she died—an anticlimactic end to five years of bed rest. The move seemed only logical at the time. I'd just graduated from university and taken a job as a bookkeeper at the Butterfly Internet Café several blocks away. It didn't make sense to stay in my parents' apartment out in the suburbs and throw myself into the hours-long daily commute.

I didn't have to beg for too long. My parents never learned how to tell me no, and when I told them in the morning that I'd like to discuss my future that evening, I think they prepared for the worst: The Lees downstairs hadn't heard from their son in six months, and Lui Di, my childhood playmate across the hall, was packing up to go to graduate school in America. My parents knew I'd always kept an eye focused on the Pacific horizon. Still, I was disinclined to long journeys. I never wanted to cross that water. America? What a cold and ruthless place! No. It was the hot rhythm and bustle of Shanghai that called me like a lovesick songbird.

There were reasons to leave home I didn't mention, of course. I'd started sleeping with my college boyfriend, Hai Ying. Our own apartment was the obvious way to house our secret. When we moved in, the first thing Hai Ying and I did was to push onto the Metro train and head across the Huang Pu River to IKEA. He spent his savings on a bed that came in a box. I watched him assemble the thing and imagined the life we'd have here: Free from my parents' constant surveillance and inquiries, I saw myself bursting upon the city like a butterfly from her cocoon.

I didn't blame my parents for being old-fashioned, even then. We're all products of our limited perception and of our times, and even though the topic is keenly avoided in my family, I know that my grandmother's reputation caused my mother—and even my father—a great deal of shame.

No, my mother did not inherit my grandmother's thick skin.

Even when people are busy calling each other "comrade," they remember who's who. How could my mother disguise the fact that she was the daughter of a white devil's whore? If the whispered rumors weren't enough, the slight curl of her hair served as a continuous reminder.

The first morning in my new apartment, I woke to the almost deafening sound of jackhammers and earth-moving machinery. "We're really here," I squealed, shaking Hai Ying awake.

"We're where?" he grumbled.

"The city!" I bounced up and down on our new bed. The smell of salt fish and espresso drifted up from the street.

Hai Ying rubbed his eyes, smiled at me.

I grabbed his face and kissed him hard, running my hands down his soft back.

When his mobile phone rang an electronic rendition of an old song by The Clash, he pulled away, answered hopefully. He frowned as he hung up. "I'm sorry. I have to go to work." He had a job fixing computers for a small foreign company. The pay was good enough, but the hours unpredictable.

"Can't you tell them you'll come in an hour?" I whispered, hoping to seduce him, but it was no use.

"I'm sorry," he said, then kissed me quickly on the cheek.

I lay in bed, taking in the city sounds. The honks and the yelling, the construction and music from passing cars. I didn't have to go to work for another couple of hours. This was the first day of the rest of my life, I thought. City girl. But I hadn't banked on all the ghosts in that apartment: near enough to hear, but still too far away to call out to.

After washing my face in the building's shared bathroom down the hall, I made myself a cup of coffee and a steamed pork bun in my kitchenette. My own kitchenette! I had the sudden urge to put a jazz CD on my little player. Far from being embarrassed by my grandmother's past, I'd always secretly romanticized her prerevolution life. A flower of Shanghai. When I was cleaning out the apartment after she died, I found a long-hidden black-and-white photograph. She must have been about my age—sexy in her tight-fitting silk dress, she looked coyly up at the cameraman. I taped the picture to the grease-stained wall.

"It's dangerous for a woman to be too beautiful," they say. But I hungered for a little taste of danger.

I finished off my coffee and crawled back into bed, masturbated as I imagined myself a gorgeous little flower of old Shanghai. As "Mack the Knife" wailed from my CD player, my body shook.

Out on the balcony—just big enough for a single metal chair—I lit a cigarette. As I blew the smoke into the damp city air, I had the urge to do something drastic in honor of my new life.

My day at work was unremarkable. All finances accounted for. There were whispered rumors that one of our regular bloggers had been arrested for posting antigovernment stories on her site, but my coworker Mei insisted that she'd just gone to Beijing for the month.

I left at dusk, joined the throngs of people all in a hurry to get somewhere. *Oh, Grandma, you wouldn't believe it. Old Shanghai pushes up through the cracks in the cement. The child beggars dressed in blue rags, the prostitutes in their stilettos.* A short detour to the shopping plaza. I took the elevator up to the eighth floor, grabbed the cheapest bleach kit. After I paid for it, I lingered at a high glass wall, watching the neon lights flash on, one by one, until the whole city glowed and pulsed like some science-fiction fantasy. The glass and steel skyline of Pu Dong across the river filled me with a sudden terror that vanished just as quickly, before I could put my finger on it.

"Holy shit, Lili!" Hai Ying sounded like he feared for my sanity when he opened the door and got his first look at me.

"It's only hair," I tried to reassure him, but I couldn't hide a tinge of disappointment. "I thought you'd like it."

He nodded, taking it in. "You look good blonde," he finally said. "Kind of like a Chinese Uma Thurman. It just surprised me." I wasn't sure if he was telling the truth, or just trying to make me feel better. Hai Ying was sweet, but his appetites were simpler than mine. He did not smoke, preferred beer to liquor, and even though he always listened to my ramblings about time and the nature of the universe, I think he felt safer when he could imagine the whole world as small as a computer screen.

"C'mon, let's go out to the Coco Club." I tugged at his arm.

"Give me a few minutes," he said, setting down his bag and pouring himself a mug full of jasmine tea from my red thermos. "Anyway, I was hoping for a walk along the Bund. Something more romantic. What do you think?"

I sighed, but agreed. We had ten thousand city nights ahead of us.

I wanted to let the flow of the crowd carry us like a river. The trendsetters and the travelers, the businessmen and the druggies. Everyone at home here. Everyone moving. The skyscrapers and the fantasies. I had the feeling we could be a part of something.

"The city wears its history like a scar," Hai Ying said. "Cool and dangerous."

"And hurt."

146

———————

"What do you dream about?" I whispered in Hai Ying's ear as we strolled next to the river, giant ships crawling toward the port.

"I hardly ever remember my dreams," he admitted. "But just last night, a terrible brawl between two men startled me awake. I wasn't one of the fighters. I just observed the scene. But it felt so real."

"Who were they?" I wanted to know.

Hai Ying shook his head. "That's the weird part. I didn't know them. In the dream, I think I knew them vaguely—the way you know someone you see every day but rarely speak to—but I've been wracking my brain all day, those faces are completely unfamiliar to me. They were dressed in old-fashioned clothes, one like a gangster, the other more casually, but strange-looking. He might even have been white. In any case," he said, "they were fighting to kill."

"How did it end?"

"The gangster knocked the strange-looking one down. Blood gushed from his head onto the cobblestone street. That's when I woke up."

"Was he dead?"

"I don't think so."

I pulled Hai Ying's arm tighter around me. I could smell the rain creeping in from the ocean, but couldn't hear it yet. "Why didn't you tell me this morning?"

He shrugged. "It didn't seem that important. It wasn't until midday that I realized the whole scene seemed to be haunting me. I couldn't get it out of my mind."

We walked in silence for a long time, stepped into a quiet bar five minutes before midnight. A single lit blue bulb hung from the ceiling, a string of red Christmas lights. "I'll have a shot of Johnnie Walker," I told the young guy behind the bar.

Hai Ying tapped the edge of his stool, hesitating. "I'll have the same," he finally said.

———————

That night we made love the way they do in old movies, shy and seductive, wrapped in damp sheets. But after Hai Ying passed out, I couldn't manage to quiet my mind. A siren wailed in the distance. It must have been about three o'clock in the morning when I finally gave up and got dressed, tiptoed out the apartment door and downstairs to the street. I pulled my black wool sweater tight around me as I stepped into the alley.

I could hear some commotion around the corner—voices arguing in Shanghaiese. I strained to make out their words, but could only understand bits and pieces. Something about a Green Gang, a last hope. I took a few steps closer, peered around the corner through the drizzle.

Try to focus on the scene: a woman in a tight dress and high heels, her powdered face glowing pale in the moonlight, long black hair piled in a bun on her head; a man standing too close to her, gesturing in her face, yelling. Suddenly, she pulls back, slaps him across the cheek, then freezes. Immediate stone regret.

"You little whore!" He grabs her by the shoulders, shakes her hard. She lets out a snarl as he pulls her forward, this time like he's about to slam her into the brick wall behind.

I think, "Hey!" and am surprised when I hear myself say it.

The man loosens his grip just enough for her to pull free.

She knees him in the crotch, rushes away, past me, tripping over her heels.

I follow even though she doesn't motion for me, steam rising from street vents.

My heartbeat sounds like footfalls behind me as I run through the mossy and rain-wet cobblestone alleys, around corners.

The woman only slows down after we've ducked through what looked like a doorway but turns out to be a quick passage to the riverbank.

"What do you want?" she gasps, turning to me, long strands of wet hair loose on her shoulders now.

The question takes me by surprise. I don't know how to answer.

When I'd seen the two fighting, I'd felt like I was watching a movie, but now the heroine has stepped off the screen—or I've stepped on. *What did I want?* We walk quickly along the waterfront.

"I thought he might hurt you," I try.

And the woman nods.

Clip-clop. Clip-clop.

We've been walking a long time when I realize everything but our footsteps has gotten heavenly quiet. A ragged child sleeps in the shelter of a doorway.

"Well, I'm all right now," the woman says, then sort of shoos me away with a flick of her chin.

I slow my pace.

She walks on.

Where am I? It's raining now, but it's a warm rain. The smell of fry grease from somewhere. The sound of a single car in the distance. The hiss of a wok. Narrow street. Maybe Old Town. Did we walk that far south?

Suddenly, I'm standing over a body. Is it alive? As I kneel down next to it, it comes into focus: a man, white, but small. I have the distinct sensation that I know him—I know the face—but I can't place him. A customer at the Butterfly Café? An old English teacher from university?

He moans helplessly.

I can hear yelling—the voices pitching up and down, getting closer. That same clipped Shanghai dialect. "He's dead!" brags a gravelly voice.

I panic, manage to scoop my arms under the body, pull it in through an arched doorway.

The smell of jasmine incense. We're in a stone-floor temple. The rising sun through a gilded window makes the whole room glow the color of lit jade.

Blood gushes from the man's head like thick wine from a faucet. I rip the T-shirt I'm wearing under my sweater, make a quick bandage. My heart is beating crazy red. The man coughs, more blood pours from his pale lips.

The voices are right outside the door now, loud and accusing.

I hold my breath, press the makeshift bandage to the wound,

concentrate on our hiddenness, invisibility. We're ghosts, I tell myself: undiscoverable. Hush. His breathing steadies. *Shhh.* He opens his eyes, just for a moment, and I know the way he looks right now will stay with me.

Will it? By the time I found my way home, I could no longer recall the exact curve of his brow. Hang on to it, Lili. But it was already gone. I boiled water for coffee in my new kitchenette.

Hai Ying stirred under the sheets. "You're up early," he hummed.

The following Sunday, as promised, I pushed onto a crowded Metro train, then took a series of buses out to my hometown. Stepping onto those empty streets of my concrete suburban childhood, the week I'd been gone felt like lifetimes. Suburbs. It even seemed laughable that I'd always thought of this place as a suburb of Shanghai. It was halfway to Hangzhou!

The creek that ran in front of my parents' apartment building looked almost clean compared to the brown filth of the Suzhou.

"Aya!" My mother howled as soon as I walked in. "You look like a ghost!"

I blushed. "It'll grow."

She shook her head, tugged at my hair instead of hugging me. *"Aya."*

The smells floating from the kitchen made me homesick in the worst kind of way. Crab and pork meatballs. Steaming rice. Sweet chili sauce.

My father, already sitting at the round black table, looked me over, said nothing.

I plopped myself down in my chair—*my* chair—so familiar, but was it still mine? I felt self-conscious, like my parents could smell the cigarettes and sex on my body like a perfume.

"Big city girl now?" my father scoffed. His own hair had finally gone white.

The rice wine I'd brought in my new black-and-red fake leather bag felt suddenly inappropriate, but I offered it up, and both of them seemed relieved. A strong, bitter brew to take the edge off. My mother warmed it on the stove, served it in the giant blue mugs I'd bought her for her birthday. She hadn't seemed to like them at the time. "So big!" But sometimes a big mug is what's called for.

The meal was like some kind of heaven. Piles of savory and hot. Fried river fish in sauce thick enough to hide a dagger. I felt like I hadn't eaten in months. Had I?

A second mug of wine. I must have been getting drunk when I thought, "Why didn't my grandfather ever leave Shanghai?" and was shocked to hear myself say it.

Both of them stared at me from their places, chopsticks frozen between food and mouth.

I wanted to take it back, didn't know how.

My father spoke slowly: "Why are you so concerned with that man?"

My mother stared up at the ceiling.

I wanted nothing more than to know what was going through her mind. Hurt? Anger? Regret? It was she who had rejected him, after all, not the other way around.

After the revolution, when most foreigners fled the country, he'd had to keep a low profile, but he'd managed a living in the bootlegging business that still thrived in underground halls along the Suzhou River. To the extent that history would allow, he took care of his new family. But when the Cultural Revolution swept through the city, my mother stopped speaking the English she had used with him as a child, and soon refused to acknowledge him at all. It didn't matter that he'd been dragged here against his will; to her, he represented the foreign imperialist. She was away at a work unit in the countryside when he died in his sleep, and by all accounts, she never shed a tear.

She polished off her rice wine, poured herself another mugful. "Probably opium," she said gravely. "What else?" She sipped her bitter drink, closed her eyes and rolled her head from side to side. "Why don't you put on that new cassette Liu Di sent?" my mother told my father. She hummed along with Norah Jones. Was my mother getting tipsy? "He always claimed he'd been attacked by a gangster." She looked down, let out a low, incredulous chuckle. "His attacker had left him for dead, but he was pulled to safety by a white-haired angel." She gazed out the window over her concrete suburb. "The angel didn't say a word, but he woke up in a jade temple, convinced that his destiny was in Shanghai. Destiny." She shook her head. *"Aya."*

My father chuckled, nodding. "Sounds like opium."

My mother shook her head in disapproval. "He never even sent word home. He thought his choice would break his mother's heart." She looked directly at me then, her black eyes trying to pierce through me. "What breaks a mother's heart is *not* knowing."

A clanging sound in the distance, like demolition machinery.

"You haven't told us about your new job, Lili," my father offered, changing the subject.

"All alone in the city," my mother frowned.

"I have a few friends from university who are living in Shanghai now," I promised. "I'm not lonely, but I miss you both." I meant it, too. The part about missing them. It's such a strange, sad feeling: to love the safe cocoon of your home with all your soul—its sweet smells and stiff silences—but to know, too, that your destiny is pulling you to another home on another river.

From a yellow pay phone at the bus stop, I called Hai Ying's mobile phone.

"Wei?"

"Where are you?"

"Sitting on the river wall, watching the levitating train. Where else?"

"I'm coming home now." I felt drawn to him, drawn to my new city, like some kind of electromagnet.

"What do you say we go out to the Coco Club? That band Funny Love is playing."

What Kind of Boy

by Elizabeth Graver

began the year my family spent in Boston as an awkward girl of twelve who still played with dolls. Now (I blinked and it happened), I find myself back in the same city, a woman of thirty-five with a husband and two kids. In a picture from early on in seventh grade, I am a little girl still, dressed in a terrible green dress with puffed sleeves and a pattern of blue and white balloons. Fat, gold barrettes clamp back my hair on either side of my thin face. My mouth smiles, but my eyes challenge. My mother did not force that dress on me. We bought it, I remember, at JCPenney, and I wanted it because it looked too young for me. I picked that dress myself.

In other, later photos from that same year, I have changed a little—I am trying, anyway. There I wear Levi's corduroys and pastel shirts with long collars, or red and yellow smocks. My hair has come down from the barrettes and curls away from my face in stiff wings. I hunch my shoulders beneath the fabric of the shirts, but my forehead is scrubbed and exposed, and my mouth pale pink with the most invisible color of lip gloss and the vaguest sort of longing. In one photo, Charlotte leans over me holding a big plank, and I cower beneath her, my mouth in a twist of mock maiden terror, my eyes rolled back. I remember how we asked my father to take the picture; how afterward, she and I collapsed laughing on the sun-warmed brick patio, knowing it was funny, not knowing—quite—why.

Charlotte lived in a big, brown, shingled house next to the one we rented. My family was in the area just for the year; we had come from our college town in upstate New York so my parents could do research at a lab at MIT. I did not know how to live in a city or even the suburbs, and I did not know how to manage a big middle school, and—mostly—I did not know how to make friends. For most of my childhood, I'd had only one friend, Nicola. Together we had lived in a fantasy world so thick and complex that emerging from it into this new place left me feeling at once sad and relieved, practically gasping for air.

In my lime-green diary with its gold lock, I recorded certain vows at the beginning of that year:

1. STOP Playing with Dolls
2. Get better Clothes and do better in Math
3. Come back home and be Friends with the POPULAR kids
4. Stop Smoking (ha ha just kidding!!!!)

And yet this was only half the picture, for then there is the fact that my mother, with my older cousin as a guide, offered to get me all the right things: blue jeans, Fair Isle sweaters, velour. And in an act of perverse stubbornness, I bought that dress with its ludicrous balloons. I bought that dress and wore it to school on the very first day, knowing it would get me nowhere. I stopped playing with dolls and forced my mind around math problems, but in the afternoons, on the leafy streets of Belmont and the sidewalks of Harvard Square, and in her gabled room, I found Charlotte.

A month after my thirty-fifth birthday, this—the stubborn, odd one, the girl who spoke in many voices and made a friend like Charlotte—is the person I am afraid I have lost track of. There she is—there I am—crouching in the photo, all play and mockery and dusty, brick-colored laughter.

Charlotte wore—every day, without fail, unless her mother was doing laundry—tan or green corduroy overalls and one of several button-down paisley shirts. Her hair was black and curly, her skin still childlike in the smoothness of its whites and pinks, her eyes a brilliant, staring blue beneath thick glasses. She walked and ran with an overgrown clumsiness, her gestures wide and unapologetic, her laughter loud. I do not remember how I met her—or if, the first time I saw her, I found myself uncomfortable before her frank blue stare. I imagine she came over on the very day we arrived, stood balancing on the railroad ties that hemmed the garden in the front yard, a little hesitant, mostly quite determined to be there. In her mind, it was predestined. We were to be friends because her best friend Erika had lived in my house; my family was renting it from hers. That friend was away for the year; I had arrived, the proper age and sex, to take her place.

The first time we went to Harvard Square, we took the bus. I remember the smooth brass token Charlotte gave me, warm from her fist, remember standing next to her holding on to a silver pole, and the deep sigh the bus made when it started up. I came from a town with ten stores and no buses; I had played, for most of my life, in the woods. When we got to the square, the bus slid into a tunnel and lurched to a stop, and I stepped off and tasted the city on the back of my tongue.

"Come on," said Charlotte, and she led me up the escalator and through the crowds.

On that first trip, we smelled scented candles shaped like owls, tried on hand-tooled leather bracelets. We stood on a street corner and listened to soap-box preachers predict the end of the world. Later, on other days, we grew braver and went from deli to deli asking for samples of salami and cheese.

"A little sharp," Charlotte would say, wrinkling her nose. "Do you have any that's milder?"

Slowly, we made the rounds, getting our afternoon snack that way; then we tried on clothes in boutiques, not kids' clothes, but women's, tried on silk shirts and straw sun hats and stood outside the jeweler's window, watching as a girl on a tall green stool clutched her boyfriend's hand while the jeweler raised a gun to her head and pierced her ears. The people who worked in the stores were patient with us. At the time, I half thought they took us for adults, that they believed us when we said we were interested in buying the blue silk dress and needed to try it on. Looking back, I know otherwise. Some girls might have pulled it off— those with poise, or those who had grown up rich. But Charlotte and I were so clearly playing dress-up, and yet still, somehow, the women ushered us into the fitting room, handed us the slippery fabric, closed the door. Our desire—for the city, for the fabric, for a life we thought lived inside these stores and on those streets—must have been palpable. People were nice to us; no one told us to get lost.

We spent months that way, taking the empty bus to Harvard Square in the afternoons and riding home with the rush-hour crowd at dinnertime. I began to wear my house key around my neck the way Charlotte did, and soon I could reel off the numbers of the buses and provide an exhaustive list of the stores in the square and what each sold. Some afternoons, if it was raining or one of us had a test the next day, we stayed in, up in her room usually, which was a converted attic. Her mother had covered the slanted walls with cork and Charlotte had pinned up advertisements for trips to Australia, an Escher print of geese and fish, pictures of Tatum O'Neal and Peter Frampton.

Just as I am not sure exactly how and when I met Charlotte, I do not remember exactly when things began to change between us. I lived in a sort of blur that year, unsure, I think, of both who I was and who I was becoming, tracking nothing but the uncomfortable swellings of my breasts (which I tried to hide under little-girl dresses or loose peasant shirts), and the terrain of the city I explored. Yes, I had my goals, written so bluntly in my diary. I knew I should make more effort with the kids at school, try to groom myself in their image so that I might fare better among the rigid cliques of my town when I returned. But I could not be bothered, quite. At home, I'd had Nicola, who now sent me letters in Boston in which she wrote, "Don't change." I was changing, in love with the city, my dolls sitting neglected at the bottom of my bed. But for most of that year, I simply replaced Nicola with Charlotte and forgot about guiding my own refashioning. The months stretched before me; a year is a long time to a twelve-year-old.

I do know that first we tried on dresses in stores and then we did not; that first we were polite and a bit formal with each other, the way new friends are, and then we began to tease, play tricks, ask questions. That first she was Charlotte, and then she was Charlie.

This did not seem strange to me. I had lived most of my childhood in the pretend. I had been chased by packs of hounds and had my blood sucked by leeches, had spoken in the voices of farmhands, princes, executioners. Nicola had done some of the voices in our games; I had done others. We never decided beforehand; when the spirit moved us, we spoke. When I arrived in Boston, my body felt stiff and unhappy, but my mind was wide and mobile, still a child's. And so it did not seem strange to me when Charlotte said, "I'm going to tell the lady in the store I'm your brother and need to help you pick out a dress to go on a cruise." Or "Let's go see the newsstand man who called me 'sonny' last time." Or "Pretend I'm your boyfriend, Becca. Let's hold hands."

One day, we got off the bus at Harvard Square as usual. Charlotte was wearing what she always wore—her overalls and paisley shirt, covered by a red down jacket because it was mid-December. I was wearing jeans, a smock, and a blue down jacket, my hair pulled back in a long ponytail.

"Your turn," said Charlotte. We took turns deciding where we would go.

"Um—" I swiveled in a full circle and surveyed the square. It was a Saturday, the street full of Christmas shoppers, everything crowded and hurried, not like it had been in the early fall when people wandered and musicians played on every corner. "I don't know," I said. Christmas always made me feel crabby and left out. "You decide."

"Me decide? It's your turn."

"I don't care."

She thought for a minute, then pulled her jacket hood up around her face. "Okay," she said. "We go to the record store, and I'm your brother, and while I'm looking at stuff in the back, you say to the cashier that you want to get me something for Christmas, but you don't know what kind of music boys like."

I shot her a look. "I don't celebrate Christmas."

"Or whatever. You want to get me something for whatchamacallit—Hanukkah."

"It's already over. It came early this year."

"Come on." She took me firmly by the arm. "For my birthday, whatever. Who cares, Becca. It's to trick them. Don't you want to play? Come on, I dare you."

We had played these tricking games before, but she had always been the one to approach the storekeepers. I could be terribly shy; it was hard for me to predict when timidity would overtake me, leaving me dry-mouthed, my eyes blinking furiously. With Nicola, at home, I had pretended all sorts of things with the trees as my audience, but for Charlotte, pretending meant fooling other people, moving through the city in a pose.

When we got to the record store, she went straight to the back, where she jammed her hands in her pockets, put her feet about a foot apart, and stood straight-kneed, flipping through some records. Her dare hung over me as I hovered in the middle aisle, looking down at an album cover of the devil riding a pig. Finally, I went back to her.

"This is stupid," I whispered. "I can't do it. Anyhow, who cares what he thinks? It's a dumb game." I looked over at the man behind the counter, who was middle-aged and overweight, with a purple sweater stretched tight across his belly.

"I dare you," she whispered. "Chicken."

"Cut it out," I said.

"If you really don't care what he thinks, then just go ahead."

"Why?"

She looked at me, and something in her blue eyes magnified by her glasses was so serious and intent that I had to look away.

"To see if it works," she said. Then she shrugged and laughed. "To see if he's as stupid as he looks."

"What do I get?" I asked.

"Grand Prize Numero Uno—me as your brother."

"Big whoop."

"Go on," she said, pushing me gently toward him. "And make sure you let him know it's me who's your brother, that I'm here."

I walked up to the counter, waited while someone else was being helped; then my turn came and I cleared my throat. I could feel Charlotte watching me from the back of the store.

"Yes?" said the man.

"I wanted—" my voice came out too soft. "I wanted, um, to get my brother back there, the guy in the red jacket, a present, but I didn't know, I mean I wasn't sure what kind of music boys liked."

The man glanced at the back wall of the store. "That," he said, "is an elusive, difficult question." He sounded like a teacher, and I was afraid he could see that I was lying. "What kind of boy is your brother?"

I shrugged.

"Well, is he a heavy-metal kind of boy or an operatic sort? Does he spend a lot of time in the basement, or in the woods, or in the alleyways of our fair city with a rat on his shoulder?"

"I don't know," I said. A line had formed behind me and I could feel someone pressing up against the padded tubing of my jacket. "Forget it. Sorry."

"Oh no, miss," he said, in what I was sure was a mocking tone. "Don't be sorry. I am here to serve."

"Sorry," I repeated. I wanted to tell him I was lying; she was not my brother, she was a girl and not even my sister. I was sure he knew all that, was sure he was darting glances at the people behind me, laughing at the pointlessness of my lie.

"Do come again," said the man.

Outside, Charlotte was gleeful, jumping up and down. "Did he buy it?" I nodded.

"What'd he say? What'd he tell you to get me?"

"We didn't get that far. He asked what you were like."

"What'd you say?"

"Nothing, really." As I leaned against the cold brick, I felt suddenly relieved and happy, watching my breath puff out in front of me, seeing how pleased she was.

"I said you were a guitarist yourself," I lied, and then felt even happier. Tricking people, I was beginning to realize, was as easy as playing pretend games.

She shook her head. "A guitarist? You wouldn't need to ask him then. You'd know what kind of stuff I liked. I can't believe you."

She turned away from me and scanned the crowd, and my good mood vanished. Don't be mad, I wanted to say. Don't look away like that.

"Come on, bro," I said loudly, turning to see if anyone was listening. "Mom'll be waiting."

It worked; she smiled broadly. "Yeah, Mom gets so uptight when we're late. Remember the time we stayed in the fort?"

We knew that no one was listening, and that even if they had been, they couldn't have cared less whether or not we were brother and sister or dog and cat. Still, we spun our lies out loud, for the street to hear. Charlotte swaggered next to me, and I found myself trying to be more girl-like to play opposite her boy.

"I might have had a brother," I said to her after a while. "My mom couldn't decide whether to go back to school or have another baby when I was five, but she ended up going back to school."

"I'm your brother," she said, and slapped me on the back. "Did you ever have a boyfriend?"

"No, not really. Did you?"

"Sort of," she said. "Not really. Okay, so I'll be Charlie your boyfriend till we get to the bus."

She slipped her hand through mine and we walked for a block or so that way, first palm to palm, then with our fingers entwined. I wondered, as I walked, if people thought she was a boy, and the possibility sent a shudder of pride through me—that I might be walking hand in hand through the streets of a city with a boy. But then I saw a woman stare at us, her head cocked. Now, thinking back, I am sure I was imagining it, or that she was looking because we were two antic girls, two girls with bright cheeks and uneven gestures, posing in the street. At the time, I don't know what I thought, only that I dropped Charlotte's hand and ran in front of her, making her chase me to the bus.

"Why'd you take off like that?" she said when we arrived at the stop and stood panting.

"I don't know. I felt like it."

"You're weird," she said.

"You're weirder."

"Maybe you can come for dinner," said Charlotte. "I'll ask my mom."

Soon after that, Brother Charlie dropped out, and Boyfriend Charlie pretty much took his place. He was a laconic, tough boy, one who swaggered and told occasional hilarious jokes—and who became, in his weaker moments, terribly, heartbreakingly sweet. And I, I was not the Becca of real life, but someone else, a giggler, a hair tosser, a flirt. A seventh-grader with a boyfriend, one of the precocious ones. A popular girl, so that in a funny way, the goal I had written in my diary was working out. I knew the whole scenario was not true, and yet it felt true in a certain way, the way the dolls Nicola and I had played with were at once plastic and flesh to me.

My boyfriend Charlie left me presents, things he found on the street and slipped into my coat pockets. A rock, a bottle cap, a golf ball, with notes: Let's Go Steady When You Are Ready. Becca Becca Is A Mecca (a word I had to look up). He stammered and blushed and confessed his crush on me, in high movie fashion: "My heart just, um, can't stop thumping over you." Usually, when the drama reached its peak, the spell would break and we would become two girls again, laughing at ourselves.

"Pretty good, huh?" Charlotte would say.

"Your heart can't stop thumping? Like if I wasn't around, it'd stop and you'd have a heart attack and croak?"

"I heard it someplace," she said. "In an old movie my mom was watching, a Western or something."

"I don't think you got it right."

"Thumping," she said. "And then the horse thumps its hoof on the ground. It wasn't a joke, I swear. The lady swoons after that."

Most of our play took place outside in the square, or on the streets of our suburb, where we looked at people's houses and lawns and made up stories of who they were. At first, Charlotte was only my boyfriend when we were outside, but one day we were up in her room, lying on her bed listening to David Soul sing, *Don't give up on us, baby.* It was freezing cold out; a late February storm had offered us five snow days in a row. For the first few days we had run up and down drifts and gone sledding on the golf course, but by the fifth day I had a cold and Charlotte was tired, so we stayed in her room.

"I love this song," I said. I had just discovered pop music and had decided to make David Soul, with his blond hair and high cheekbones, my idol.

"It's okay."

"He's so cute." My voice sounded a bit false to me, but I did mean it; he was cute on the record album, dressed in worn jeans slung low on his hips and a soft blue denim shirt.

"Do you wish he was your boyfriend?"

I laughed. "David Soul? I bet he's in his twenties. But I guess, if he was younger. He could sing to me."

"You like him better than Charlie?" She studied the album cover, ran her finger over its rim.

"Maybe." I tossed my hair back.

"Okay, shut your eyes," Charlotte said, "and put your hand over his face."

She turned down the music a little, put the album cover in my lap, and placed my palm on David Soul. "Okay," she said, making her voice deep. "I'm going to hypnotize you. I am David Soul. Don't give up on me, baby."

I sputtered with laughter and opened my eyes.

"No," she said. "Lie down. I'm going to hypnotize you. My uncle did this once to me, it's really cool. Stop laughing. Shut your eyes."

I lay down on my back and she put the album on my stomach. "You are walking down a long, long staircase," she said, her voice slow and even. "You go down one stair, and your toes relax." She nudged my toes, and I tried to make them limp. "You go down another stair, and your ankles and knees relax. . . ."

She talked me all the way down the staircase and up my body: thighs and butt, stomach, neck and head. Her voice was soothing and her bed soft, and though I had started out all giggly, by the end I thought I might fall asleep. "At the bottom," she said, "you go into a big field and there's David Soul, all blond and whatever. Don't open your eyes. He looks at you and says hi and he's just like on the album—" I felt her press it against me.

"Just picture him," she said. "Just let yourself see him."

The record played on, and I saw David Soul's blond face, right up close to me like he was singing in my ear.

Charlotte was silent for a few minutes, and then she had her hand on my forehead as if she were checking for a fever, and then she was kissing me, the first real kiss I ever had. I kept my eyes shut for a minute and kissed her back, not awkwardly—that is the amazing thing. I put my hands on the nape of her neck, under her thick hair, and kissed her, a little tentatively at first, but then it really was as if she had hypnotized me, as if I had found myself in some spacious, sleepy field where sensation was everything, her mouth (his mouth? I had my eyes squeezed shut and David Soul perched upon my stomach) the softest, wettest thing I had ever tasted.

When the record ended, the needle arm clicked back into its holder. Something clicked in me as well, and I pushed her away and sat up. "What time is it?" I asked.

She peered at her clock radio. "Five-thirty-two."

"Oh my god," I lied. "I told my mom I'd be home."

After that, we forgot about David Soul. We still went up to her room and kissed—not as girls, but as Charlie and Becca usually, and then sometimes we didn't kiss at all, but just lay curled together under her red plaid quilt, gave each other back rubs, and napped. I waited all morning for those long, blurry afternoons. Her mother never seemed to pay much attention to us, and I don't remember worrying that we would get caught at anything. I don't even think I knew that girls could have sex with other girls. I'm not sure what I knew; it's hard to remember, looking back. I know I loved the rise and fall of her breath when she fell asleep next to me, and that the smell of her shampoo—like green, soapy apples—made me ache in my wrists and hips and temples. Once, Charlotte touched my nipple under my shirt, and I moved away. I'm not sure if I did it because she was a girl or because they were still so new, my breasts; I was so uncomfortable with their small mounds, their growing, wanted to push them back into my chest where they had come from.

"I've got to go," I said, then, and I went home and watched TV by myself until my body no longer felt flushed.

And then it was spring, the year that had begun so slowly suddenly galloping by. I realized I would be going home soon, looked back at my resolutions, and saw I had done little to transform myself during my time away. My mother took me shopping, and I picked out the pastel shirts, the corduroy jeans, even a training bra. I got my hair cut and struggled to curl it into wings on each side of my face. At school, I tried to talk to Ginny Bounty and Patty Santamaria, two popular girls who had been vaguely nice to me in the fall, but too much time had passed and they had no interest in me now. I still saw Charlotte most afternoons, but we did not go to her room as much. Bit by bit, Charlie dropped away and we stopped kissing, and one day, she snapped at me over something stupid and I realized she was mad at me.

"What?" I said. My family was leaving in two weeks; the front porch where Charlotte and I sat was stacked with cardboard boxes my father had brought home from the supermarket.

"Nothing." She kicked the porch step.

"What?"

"You'll go home and totally forget about me."

"No I won't."

"You will, too."

She turned a cardboard box upside down and put it over her head. I slid closer to her, knocked on the box.

"The doctor is out, Charlie Brown," she said.

I peeked under the edge. It was dark in there, but I could feel her presence, her tense shoulders and held breath. Then she sighed, and in that moment I may have realized I was a little bit in love with her, if a twelve-year-old as immature as myself could be in love. I wanted to stay in that box, to inhabit its darkness—felt, I think, for a brief moment, what it is like to lie as an adult in a pitch-dark room with your lover breathing by your face.

Then a car drove by, its noise a quick swoosh as it passed the house. I had a vision of Patty Santamaria and Ginny Bounty sitting in the back seat and seeing me with my head stuck in a box with another girl. And for the first time, perched there in my new clothes, I felt an unfamiliar, sickening sense of shame.

"I'll write," I said, straightening back up.

"You'll forget about me," Charlotte repeated. She lifted the box off, and I found myself with my face peering at hers, both of us blinking in the sun.

Back home, I told people about a boy I had met in Boston named Charlie. That next year in eighth grade, I made new friends, not the popular kids, but the next rung in the hierarchy, the artsy, smart kids—a few of them boys—who might have been popular if they had tried harder. Among my new friends, I began to learn the careful dance of social games and fitting in. To my relief, Nicola had also changed that year, and both of us agreed, though with some sadness, that we were too old to play with dolls. I showed her the notes from Charlie, the golf ball, the stone— artifacts of someone loving me. I am not sure if she believed me; somehow I think she may not have, my sighs, my "I really miss him's" too insistent, my tone strained. But Nicola and I had spent years in make-believe with each other, and if she didn't believe me, she didn't push it.

"He sounds nice," she simply said.

For a while, Charlotte and I sent each other frequent postcards, then, for a few years, birthday cards. But by the time I graduated from high school, my body had become more graceful, but my mind had tensed up. I could not think of her without confusion and embarrassment, and we lost touch.

Now that we have moved back here, I imagine running into her in Harvard Square. She would have grown into her body as I have grown into mine; she might be humming as she walked, or joking with a friend. She is, of course, not the only such ghost from my past, but she is the first, and I am afraid she thinks I have forgotten her.

"Hey, Charlie," I might say if I passed her, and she might look at me uncomprehending and walk on, or perhaps she'd stop for a moment, drop the hand of a lover or child, readjust her shoulder bag, and peer at me. Laugh. We might drink coffee, or just stand there talking in the street. We might make love. Are you happy? she might ask, and I'd say, Yes, I am, I think I am, happy enough but still there are so many things I haven't done, but mostly I'm pretty happy, I've been lucky, mostly I'm okay, I think, are you?

Double Cutaway

by Gail Louise Siegel

When I first met Rennie, he had more guitars than pairs of pants. For our only anniversary, I bought him a hand-knit, amethyst blue sweater. Now I've got it and his chiffon yellow guitar, and I don't know what to do with them. They're leftovers. When my brother Luke died, his belongings were like flypaper. We got stuck to them. But Rennie's not dead, just gone.

Luke was another story entirely. Luke was on the verge of it all. Hungry to spend the summer mountain biking through the Northwest with his girlfriend, Barrett. About to record some new tunes with his band, Mugsy. Picking up cash doing studio work on commercial tracks.

He was twenty-two, four years ahead of me, a senior at Ann Arbor. Eight years younger than I am now.

A lethal hockey stick would have been the last danger to cross his mind. Yet that's what killed him. Luke didn't even play hockey. But when his roommates got a 4 A.M. ice time, he went along as the designated spectator. He sat in the stands, listening to their thick blades scrape up a new layer of frosting, watching the puck ricochet against the boards. He was a connoisseur of sound. He loved the whistle of a scrimmage in the midnight rink, aloft in the bleachers where everything echoes, even your breath. He called it *jock music*, the *other* athletic score.

That night, Luke brought along his gold-top Gibson Les Paul, the axe he called Patsy Cline. It's an electric with a warm gloss. He played it un-plugged, the crisp air and high ceilings amplifying each chord. His nose would have gone hard with chill, and he would have paused to rub his hands together for warmth or to tighten Patsy Cline's nippy strings. They played for an hour—the clashing skaters, the guitarist behind the Plexiglas—until the next round of graceful giants came gliding in.

Then the five housemates—Luke, Josh, Mario, Al, and Greg—scrunched themselves into Mario's pre-airbag Audi. Patsy Cline rode in the trunk with the knee and arm pads, to make elbow room. The hockey sticks didn't fit in the trunk. Instead, they lay propped between Mario and Greg in front, the handles resting on Luke's rear-seated lap. That is, until Mario collided with a sleepy milk-truck driver, and two of the poles ran through Luke like pikes at a medieval joust.

Everyone else lived, sort of. Josh lost the use of an arm, and Alan Elf-man gave up his NHL fantasies to enter veterinary school. I still see him; he's my vet. He bandaged up my cat when Hector got his tail caught in my neighbor's door.

Alan said that after the crash the street was strewn with shards, re-flecting the dawn like fresh-cut diamonds. Milk trickled everywhere, its smell mingling with the tang of blood, coating their winter jackets, painting everything a sticky crimson, and then drying to brown. It was as if they'd careened right into the dairy section at Jewel. Alan told me this more than once, shaking his head and resting his big hairy paws on his knees while a collie barked in the next examining room.

Unlike her namesake, Patsy Cline lived, too. Snug between skates and pads, she came through unscathed. I've got her here, in the next room. On a stand right next to Rennie's lemon yellow Japanese replica. If it seems like a morbid totem, it's not meant to be. I more than adored my brother. I spent years nestled in his shadow, a comfortable place to be. There I was, straggling along behind him like a puppy on a long leash, trotting off to grammar school, rocking to the beat of his high school band at our junior high dances, snooping around the top of the stairs while he smooched with nameless girls on the living room couch, a tangle of bent limbs and murmured giggles.

As much as he abused me—decapitating my Barbie dolls, and then making me pinky-swear that I wouldn't rat on him, banishing me from the room if he was playing with friends, and even locking me out of the house one night after I'd scratched a record—he also catered to me. Throughout my sickly, feverish childhood, he was my diversion, my keeper. He'd lie in a deck chair and let me paint and repaint his toenails Spring Violet, Pink Flamingo, and Ruby Heart Red. He'd let me cheat and win at games, from Candy Land to hearts.

Oddly, it took me a long time to feel his death. I was used to his absence. It wasn't until I went away to college the next September that it overwhelmed me. Each time someone new asked if I had any brothers or sisters I choked. I didn't know the true, the honest answer. The only answer I had was a throb in my head, an ache in my chest.

In those first months, he seemed gone, not dead. I'd waited years for him to leave home so I could abandon my nine-by-nine cell for his expansive bedroom. I hung my bike license plate, JULIA in big blue letters, on the door. True, he left parts of himself behind. His old baseball cards, his geode collection, his matchbox cars and pewter gnomes all lurked in the cabinet under the window seat. His leather mitt might still be there—tied over a baseball with an oversized rubber band, thirsty for Glovolium.

Mom stored his old clothes in the extra closet. Until he died, anyway. Piece by piece, they disappeared and reemerged on her back. One morning, when I left for school, she was wearing his shiny black soccer warm-ups and a foam green T-shirt. That night, his red parka was draped over the newel post, instead of her coat. I pictured her wearing it on errands to the grocery store, the post office, the gas station. Whatever she did, it was creepier to think of it transpiring within my dead brother's gym clothes, his fading scent against her skin.

At least she was getting out, Dad said. Luke's death had knocked her over like a bowling pin. It took her weeks to get out of bed, and then she would clean the kitchen for hours. Her eyes were spun over with spidery red webs. The lids were swollen and shiny, snailish. I'd come to set the table and she'd be stooped over the sink nodding, tears dripping off the tip of her nose.

One night, I heard her talking to a friend through the heating vent. "I can't get through this. It's terrible to say, but it isn't just that Luke was my son. I loved him more than my father, more than *his* father. He was the most fascinating man I've ever known."

I pictured her on the other side of the drywall, sunk inside Luke's blue-and-gray flannel pajamas. She quieted, and then heaved a final, resigned sob. "Yes, you're probably right. I suppose every mother thinks so."

At first, I tried to comfort her, leaning against her at the sink after dinner and kissing her cheek. Then months passed, and I was angry. Where was my affectionate, elegant mother? Shouldn't she be back by now, sweeping into the room in a soft silk dress on the way from some art board meeting? Or listening to me practice Mozart for my recital, reviewing my college applications? She had checked out, as if having kids was an all-or-nothing deal. She was nearly as absent as Luke.

Dad hardly made it up to me. He was always the cheerful parent, perpetually upbeat. Then, after the funeral, he hardly spoke expect to spit out something bitter. He called himself "Luke's ex-father". He called Mom his "partner in demise." Maybe being glib held the truth at bay.

Grief had kidnapped my parents and left these two cold shells in their place. They were hostages, and the only ransom I could pay was time. With it, Dad's sarcasm abated, as did Mom's weeping. But they never entirely recovered their vitality. Now that I've hit thirty, I sometimes think I owe them a grandchild; maybe that will bring them back to life. I'd like to know how to resuscitate passion for something that's gone flat.

Like work. I used to enjoy my job. Before Rennie. For three years, I thought I was the luckiest girl in Chicago, doing PR for the Field Museum. The hours weren't bad, which gave me plenty of time to teach piano. Plus, the old museum captivated me. When I got bored making press calls, I wandered down to the temporary exhibits: screaming red voodoo masks, paintings of the Haitian slave revolt, neon butterflies, or polished motorcycles.

I always ended up at the mummies and the Egyptian marketplace, browsing through the scarabs and hieroglyphics, reading and immediately forgetting the curatorial tidbits. Like this: Since their water stank, the Egyptians guzzled liters of beer each day. But I never could remember how *many* liters. It didn't matter. I loved the incongruity of that angular, mathematical society awash in beer. I decided *that* was the secret of the pyramids. The slaves were willing to haul those heavy stones because they were drunk.

Nobody missed me when I wandered off. I was just an underling at the Field; I still am. I don't conceptualize. I write my press releases, call culture critics and calendar editors. And I don't mind. If you work too much, or take too much credit when things go well, you risk getting saddled with too much blame when they don't.

———————

Now the event where I met Rennie—that's an example of what can go wrong. It wasn't as dramatic as dinosaur skeletons clattering to the floor in accidental disarray or lice infesting newly acquired puma pelts. It was a smaller scale disaster. About sixteen months ago, just after my childhood friend Kate moved to Peru in search of good alpaca yarn and Latin cowboys, my boss LuAnn decided there weren't enough twentysomethings coming to the museum. She wanted to branch out from our mainstays— young families and the society crowd. She plotted out a concert series and called it "Dinosaur Rock."

One Friday night in November, there was Rennie, right under the *T. Rex* bones in the Great Hall, all in black except for a thick shock of bleached hair. He was lazily plucking away at a chiffon yellow Ibanez double cutaway, a Gibson Les Paul replica. I liked the cutaway design. It was spare, especially compared to a traditional folk guitar, with its bosomy bouts intact—those rounded bulges on either side of the neck. In a cutaway, the lopped-off parts leave horns, which make for better reach. Everyone's seen it—one cutaway on a Telecaster, two on a Stratocaster. I approved of naming something after an absence. Almost like calling a guitar a single or double amputee, after its missing limbs.

Rennie's band was backing up a resurrected rock star that LuAnn had unearthed. The resurrection was a failure. The act had no more life in it than mummies or dinosaurs. Hardly anybody showed. LuAnn was fretting. I slipped behind a giant white pillar where I could avoid her rage and get a clear view of Rennie. Between the two halfhearted sets, I introduced myself to him. I said I liked his guitar, that I had an original Gibson Les Paul single cutaway myself, but that I'd never really learned to play.

I don't know if Rennie would have remembered me if it weren't for the guitar. It's like tracing a river back to its source in geologic time. Maybe I wouldn't have noticed him if it weren't for his double cutaway. Bleached blonds were never exactly my thing. But guitars were. They conjured up the times I felt closest to Luke—me huddled on his lower bunk, him on the window seat, fiddling with his strings. He'd dart around between tunes, playing a few bars of Hendrix or Robert Johnson while I leafed through his *Guitar* magazine and complained about my piano lessons.

"It's not fair. They won't let me quit."

"But you can't. You're a fucking *prodigy*." He was matter-of-fact, not jealous, mimicking my piano teacher's nasal French accent.

"A *fucking* prodigy," I'd giggle my scandalized twelve-year-old giggle, collapse into a pillow. "No, I'm not. That would be something else."

We'd laugh at our private joke. We were so young that just the idea of fucking was laughable. Even now, when it's not a joke, nothing's more natural to me than sitting on some boy's bed while he plays around with his distortion pedal.

So, I was enticed when Rennie took my number. He wanted to see the Les Paul, maybe buy it, add it to his collection. I had no intention of selling, but liked the excuse to see him. Just days later, he was ringing my buzzer, knocking the snow off his boots on my landing while I tried to wrap up a phone call with LuAnn. I waved him in and he poked around the dining room, inspecting the papers stacked around my laptop. I shrugged in apology, keeping the portable at my ear. In the window's harsh light, I saw I'd misjudged his age. He had eight or ten years on me, was maybe pushing forty. He roamed around the living room and mimed wiping off the piano bench with an invisible handkerchief. He performed. He posed, wrists flexed, head flung back, and then plunged into some passionate Rachmaninoff.

That did it for me. The showoffy wooing. The stormy chords. The contrast between his punk hair and his classical mastery. He seemed ardent, impetuous. I considered what he would be like to kiss. I hung up the phone and applauded.

"Well," I spoke over the sustain. "Want to see the guitar?"

He flipped up his tux's implied tails and bowed.

"Oh yeah," he said. "That, too."

Once I dragged it out of the closet and he set to tuning it, the flirtation stopped. The single cutaway hadn't been touched in years, and the strings were shot. It took twenty minutes to tune it, and then the wires slipped. I apologized.

"No biggie," he was unfazed. "I can run up to the guitar store. Or go back home for strings."

My heart tightened. I didn't want him to leave. "It's only ten-thirty. Nothing opens until noon." I improvised. "You can boil them. Luke used to boil his strings."

"Who's Luke?" he asked, loosening the pegs and uncoiling the wires. "Old boyfriend?"

"Older brother," I said. "He died."

He looked up and rubbed his forehead. "I'm sorry. That's rough."

"Yes, it was. Is." In that instant, I missed Luke fiercely. If life were fair, *he* would be sitting there, scandalizing me with his blues club worldliness, running through his riffs on Patsy Cline. Not Rennie.

Instead, Rennie and I sat on the radiator in the kitchen while a spaghetti pot full of water and wire tried to boil on my reluctant electric range. Our thighs grazed. I told him about Luke, impaled on hockey sticks. Did I want to tell the story or want Rennie to reopen that spigot of empathy or want him to kiss me? Probably all three, which I got. We made love in the cramped kitchen, Rennie pressing me against the radiator, steam fogging the windows, the air moist as our humid bodies, everything slick and satisfying.

For the next eight months, I was elated. Work crawled while I marked time between dates with Rennie. I hauled him to exhibit openings. At his gigs, I sat with Jennifer, his drummer Brian's pregnant wife. I kept my eyes on Rennie, half-listening to Jennifer complain about secondhand smoke and her tribulations as a clothing buyer for Marshall Field's. "Seams just aren't finished the way they used to be," she said.

Rennie had that overeager suburban zeal for the city that Luke and Kate and I always had, even as kids. He studied *Chicago Reader* for obscure spots to rendezvous midweek. For me, it was lunch; for him, breakfast. I taxied to the DePaul Music Center and we ate Thai food in the balcony, listening to the Hyde Park Children's Chorus. Or we wandered through the bowels of the Loop, following the Pedway Tunnels from City Hall to the Prudential Building. It was a concrete maze, stocked with glittery boutiques and sweaty beggars, deserted hallways and screeching trains. We came up for air to catch a reading in the Cultural Center's mosaic rotunda, or ate gumbo on the seventh floor of the Garland Building. I was burning through several lifetimes of good romantic karma. I'd taxi back to the Field humming with pleasure and give the cabbie a ridiculous tip, trying to prolong my luck a few dollars at a time.

Rennie's apartment on Diversey was an oversized 1BR w/DR+LR, done up in sound-studio decor. The walls were lined with shelves of records, tapes, and CDs. Computers, mixers, and amps cluttered the tables. A thicket of mike stands thrived in the corner, an electronic woods.

In the courtyard off the fire escape, there was a small grove, too. A stand of scraggly elms had escaped the city foresters' hacksaw and a band of black squirrels took refuge there. (The Field's taxidermist, Mr. Crosby, said their coat color was from age, not their species.) They were elegant, like little minks. Rennie and I spent half the summer on his "deck," luring our favorite squirrel, Bix, up the fire escape by scattering peanuts across the landing. Rennie batted at flies with a retro turquoise fly swatter, and I started (but never finished) letters to Kate in Peru.

There were also Rennie's occasional pranks, which took me by surprise. Most were harmless: food coloring or salt in the ice cubes, strange messages on my voicemail at work, incidents that I saw as affectionate, not malicious.

The phone rang and rang and I found it in the refrigerator, or the medicine cabinet, or once, my underwear drawer. It made me laugh. It was like having a big brother again. Like Luke, sneaking into my bedroom one April Fool's Day and dripping warm water on my wrist until I wet the bed. It was a cruel gesture of rage at my very existence—the way a brother has an irresistible urge to trip and kick you one instant, tickle and kiss you the next. I woke up cold and sticky and Luke was grounded in his room, which pleased me only until I wanted to play with him.

Like Luke, Rennie had tremendous range. His bands (he juggled three) favored grocery themes: Frosted Flakes, Aisle 10, and Fresh Ground. Tributes to an adolescence spent stacking the Happy Food aisles in Skokie. Each one had a different configuration. Fresh Ground was a small jazz trio hired out for background music at receptions; Aisle 10 was an R&B band with a monthly gig at Lily's; Frosted Flakes was a cover band, specializing in the party circuit.

Rennie was making a living—no small feat—but he wanted more respect for Frosted Flakes. He was writing serious music. He fired a string of vocalists and was auditioning new talent. That's when he launched a campaign to recruit me. We were tangled up on my couch.

"Why don't you quit that mausoleum? I could use a keyboard player."

"Thanks, but no thanks." I liked the quiet ease of writing goofy headlines for children's magazines ("Invasion of the Beetle-Snatchers!") and watching toddlers crane their necks at the Supersaurus skeleton. I enjoyed regular sleep. I didn't relish reeking of spilt beer like an Egyptian slave. My musical ambitions and training were classical. I knew my limits.

Rennie was tenacious. "You should perform. It would help you come to terms with your brother's death."

My scalp went hot. I unknotted my legs and sat up. "Don't blackmail me with Luke."

He threw his hands up in quick surrender. "Hey, it's just an idea. Just think about it."

A selfish idea, I thought. A way to divert my attention away from work and onto him. Next he'd be lobbying me to give up teaching piano so he wouldn't have to suffer through lurching renditions of *Für Elise* on Saturday mornings, when he wanted to sleep off the night before.

Rennie's next strategy was to take me to Brian's basement for their vocalist auditions. That's where I met Mona. Jennifer and I sat on the brown velour couch, its single wide cushion tilting precariously under her ripening belly. When Mona strutted in with her black fishnet stockings, a leather miniskirt, and a Morticia Addams hairdo, Jennifer grunted. Mona was an alluring Gothic door prize. She was not remotely pregnant. As she stood before a backdrop of old felt Cubs pennants in her spiked heels, I spied her necklace—a cartouche of hieroglyphic characters: a bird, a squiggle of water, a bent arm. I felt robbed. I was the amateur Egyptologist. What was she doing with that?

But as much as I yearned to scorn Mona, I coveted her voice. We all did. Brian and Rennie ran her through everything, from Sam Cooke to Janis Joplin to Ella Fitzgerald. She could warble, she could rasp, she could scat, she could croon. She had a sweet, unaffected vibrato. We were under her spell. There was no debate when she finished. Just a rustling of calendars to nail down club dates. Mona was on board.

With a new singer and original music, Rennie wanted a name change. That's when we had our first fight. Right here, in my dining room. Brian and Jennifer were here, and so was Mona. We were throwing around names. It was fun. A word game. Rennie kept a list. I suggested Manservant, Dry Ice, Suspended Animation. Rennie said they were too static. Brian had darker inclinations: Robber Barons, Epidemic. Jennifer offered clothing analogies: Aluminum Lace, Black Denim. Then I said Eye-Banana.

"Eye-Banana." Rennie was offended. "What the hell is that supposed to mean? Something like, I Tarzan, You Jane?"

"No," I said. "Like your Ibanez double cutaway. It's yellow chiffon. But Yellow Chiffon Banana doesn't quite cut it. Too retro, too psychedelic."

Heads bobbed—Jennifer's, Mona's, and Brian's. They liked it. It was a nod and a wink. It was Guitar with a capital G. It summed something up.

Except Rennie was glaring at me. "I hate it," he said. "It sucks." He pounded the table, rattling the half-empty Anchor Steams. "You just can't take my work seriously, can you? Don't you get it? I don't want to be a grocery clerk anymore. And what if I use your single cutaway? Patsy Cline? My Fender? Or my Martin? What then, genius? If you're so fucking smart, Ms. Julliard. What then?"

The beer curdled in my gut. Everyone hushed. Jennifer smoothed her sweater over her belly. Mona inspected her black nails. I found my voice. "It's just a name, Rennie. It doesn't matter what you play."

"Not to you, maybe," he spat out. "Maybe not to you."

"And I went to Indiana State, not Julliard." I was apologizing for my music education, waiting for *him* to say, "Sorry." He didn't. I left the room. I spent the rest of the night at the piano—doing scales and exercises. I played from my collection of cowboy tunes. I resisted tears. I thought back to an April afternoon at Rennie's. Waiting for pizza, he played his Ibanez for me, reciting her virtues like a love poem.

"Rule one, Julia," he pointed his pick at me. "You always stand to play an electric guitar." He stroked her contoured body, more curvaceous than a flat Fender slab. He hopped around the dining room to find a place to foil the feedback from the hulking transformer outside his window. He bent the superslinky wires into slow, melancholy vibratos. Then he coaxed out a nice, fat sustain, praised her humbucker pickups, and toyed with her harmonics. "Like bells," he said. "Not twangy."

I thought Eye-Banana was a tribute to his guitar, but Rennie was still living down his Happy Foods past. He wasn't stacking pyramids in the produce section anymore. By the time everyone left my apartment, they'd settled on The Voodoo Farmers, Mona's solitary idea.

———————

Our fight was nasty—not for its length, but for being public. In private, Rennie tried to make it up with romantic indulgences. The next day, he brought me yellow tulips. At every gig through September and October, he garnished our table with another sunny bouquet. Daffodils, yellow roses, sunflowers, black-eyed Susans, mums, marigolds, forsythia, even yellow begonias. In self-mockery, he began calling the double cutaway the Eye-Banana. I-ban for short, which sounded like a deodorant. We settled back into an ostensibly comfortable routine.

We had only one quarrel. Rennie was meeting me before a gig. I got home twenty minutes late. He was sitting against the mailboxes in my vestibule.

"Sorry I'm late." I meant it.

"Sure you are." He was tired. He was cold. His sarcasm stung like a whip.

"Really, Rennie. Have I ever stood you up? LuAnn was ranting at me. Traffic was horrendous. It was out of my control."

Rennie stood and dusted off his jeans. He held out a paper bag. "First, a present."

The bag was soft and wrinkled, like Rennie'd used it for a thousand lunches, carefully folding it up each night. He grimaced. I kept his peculiar expression in view as I unrolled the top. The light was too dim for me to make it out. Just something gnarled, hard, and musty.

"Goddamnit!" I threw the bag at Rennie. It bounced off his shoulder and hit the floor, dead squirrel spilling out. It was Bix. "You asshole! What's your point? Don't be late? Are you the time police?"

Rennie snickered. "I thought you liked old dead things. Relics. The museum and all. You can give him to that Crosby guy. The taxidermist."

"Oh, so this is a memento? To stuff old Bix for my cubicle wall?" My back tensed. My jaw clenched.

We glowered at each other, locked in a staring contest. Rennie blinked first. His pinched mouth slackened. He sighed and kicked away

Bix and then wrapped his arms around me. He was tentative. He knew he'd crossed a line. He whispered into my hair.

"I'm sorry."

"Sure you are," I said. I sighed. Maybe he was. I wanted him to be. "How did he die?"

He relaxed into me, palms pressing against my shoulder blades.

"I'm guessing it was the landlord. Probably rat poison. I don't know. I found him in the courtyard."

It took most of November, but I let myself be persuaded that he hadn't intended to punish me. I convinced myself he was just sad, waiting for me in the vestibule with a dead pet. We drove to Saugatuk, and he paid for an anniversary weekend at a cottage on Lake Michigan. We slept late, made love, and walked along the beach, despite the chill, which had me feeling mournful.

We stopped to watch a seagull pick at a fish carcass. "Did I ever tell you about the accident off of I-94?" he said.

"What accident?"

"Well, not exactly an accident." He stuffed his hands in his pockets. "It was fifteen years ago. I was in this band that was finally getting some attention. We actually opened for Buddy Guy once in Indiana. Anyway, we had this bus with all our equipment. We were on our way to New York, where we had a club date lined up. I knew it was going to be our big break."

He walked closer to the shoreline, picked up a flat stone, and wiped at the sand.

"So we're on I-94, and our drummer, Derrick, he decides he has to take a leak. He takes some spur and, instead of looking for a gas station, parks on the edge of the road, near this little lake. Here's a nice spot to take a leak, he says. Anyway, pretty soon everyone gets out. They're piss-ing in the woods and stretching and getting high. Nobody's at the van. Then suddenly we hear it—a horn, and then a crack."

Rennie lifted his eyes from the stone and fixed them on me.

"A big old refrigerator truck smacked into the bus, sent it right into the lake. All our equipment, gone. All our bags, gone. All our money, gone. My future, gone."

He tossed the stone into the water.

Fifteen years later, Rennie was still the kind of guy who spent all his money on musical equipment, and it showed in his closet. So, when we got back home, I bought him expensive pairs of pants and the blue cashmere sweater.

Then around Thanksgiving, just days before Brian and Jennifer's baby was due, Rennie and I threw them a shower. Not one of those luncheons with frilly tablecloths and pink pastries. Just a get-together for our friends, to gather provisions for "player," the baby to be named later. The baby bash was set for Rennie's apartment, which had a better parking situation than mine. We knew nobody wanted to lug big boxes of car seats and highchairs too far. Unfortunately, The Voodoo Farmers got a last minute job too good to pass up. Brian got a stand-in for his percussion, but Rennie was fronting the band, and Mona's voice was the draw. They were coming to the shower, but late.

So, I was hostessing alone in Rennie's apartment. Setting out his mismatched silverware, scrounging through his cupboards for glasses that weren't chipped or plastic. It was like being married—cleaning his whiskers from the bathroom sink and straightening his bed, where guests would likely throw their coats. Between that idea and the baby, I felt hopeful, romantic. I opened his blinds and cued up some Bonnie Raitt. Maybe someday, Rennie and I would be living together, expecting our own child. Maybe we could name it Luke.

I smoothed out the comforter and plumped up the pillows. And there, where it must have slipped out of a careless hand, was a guitar pick. It wasn't Rennie's guitar pick. It was Mona's. Nobody but her carried a white Pickboy with the grim reaper on the front, scythe in hand. It was her little fetish. She toyed with it while she sang; she scooped the grime out from under her nails with its pointed edge.

I felt nothing. I calculated it like a formula: Her Pick + His Bed = 2 Timing. I perched on the bed, waiting for jealousy to occur. I felt distant, cold, mathematical. Egyptian, I thought. I looked in Rennie's mirror. I wasn't pale; I looked fine. The bell rang. I answered it. An immense Jennifer waddled in, with Brian bringing up the rear. She was puffing, and her cheeks were flushed with the effort of climbing three flights. If anyone had something to complain about, it was her.

"The doctor says I'm fully effaced," she huffed. "I'm already dilating." I nodded at her medical jargon.

"Yep," said Brian. "She's locked and loaded. We might not make it through the party."

I steered them into the living room, and as guests arrived, I busied myself. When my thoughts strayed toward Rennie and *why Mona's fucking pick might be on his bed*, I refreshed drinks, served food, and stuffed shreds of balloon-festooned wrapping paper into oversized garbage bags. I drank more beer than an Egyptian slave and tried to laugh at the right places.

It was late when Rennie and Mona came. She was in a tight red velvet dress; he was wrapped in the amethyst sweater. I nodded hello and ducked into the kitchen, fighting the urge to compare my regular old self to dark, bewitching Mona. When the last guests left, Rennie found me scrubbing plates.

"What are you slaving away for?" he asked, face ablaze with some kind of ecstasy—a great gig, great sex.

I turned off the water and wiped my hands on a green checkered dishtowel. I hung it through the refrigerator handle. "Are you screwing Mona?" I asked.

"What? Mona? You're out of your mind," Rennie said.

I shook my head. "The funny thing is, Rennie, I can't feel anything. Jealousy, despair. So, maybe I am out of my mind."

He lunged at me and grabbed my shoulders. I pulled away. Then, more gently, he tilted my chin toward his face. "Look at me." I looked. "Julia, I love you," he said.

I scrutinized him, saw the refrigerator reflected in his eyes with its dangling green swath of dishtowel. "Maybe you do." His hands were clammy. I shrugged them off my body. "Maybe I love you, too. I don't know."

He pulled me tight to his chest. In his mind, the argument was over. "Julia, what can I do to make you sure?" He was murmuring against the top of my head, into my part.

I felt repelled. "Nothing, Rennie. Just let me go. I need some rest. This was a long party."

He stepped back, hands held high, as if I had pulled a gun. Like the night he'd tried to get me to quit work to play keyboards. "Okay, okay. So I wasn't here to help. Is that it?"

"This was on your pillow," I said. I handed him Mona's pick. "Like a hotel chocolate."

Rennie looked at the pick. It didn't carry the weight of a dead squirrel. "She lent it to me, you asshole."

I nodded. There was a remote chance he was telling the truth. Rennie was always losing, borrowing picks. Even if he was lying about fucking Mona. But I knew his motto: *Stand to play an electric.* As long as I'd known him, he'd practiced in the living or dining room. I strained to picture him plucking away on his bed, but couldn't.

I could more easily see Mona, cleaning out her fingernails on the edge of his mattress, while Rennie tugged at her fishnet stockings. It was his word against my suspicion.

"Fine," I said. "I'm going home."

"Stay. I'll give you a back rub." He nuzzled up to me, blue cashmere against my cheek. "I'll rub oil into your feet."

Images clicked away in my head like slides: Rennie swaying under the tyrannosaurus in a musical trance. Rennie against my sheets, the contrast of his dark pubic hair with his crop of peroxide locks. Peeking out between bunched marigolds. Miming a piano concert on that first wintry day.

I hate yellow, I thought. I hate mimes.

"Rennie, right now even sex sounds like a hassle."

I got my coat from his bed. I inventoried the room: a poster of John Lennon in a sleeveless, Give Peace a Chance T-shirt, a stack of blank sheet music on his dresser, incense cones resting on a square of plum porcelain on the nightstand. I pictured leaving for good.

Driving, I enumerated hidden parts. The pieces eluded me. Missing feelings, secrets between Rennie and Mona, Luke, the past. Kate, off in Peru, out of reach and sight. And other cutaways. The objects in a pantomime, water-eroded rock, dinosaur flesh, desert-swept empires, the absent sound in quiet. All these little deaths, hollowing me out.

I slogged up the stairs through weariness into the living room. The piano looked hostile. It was too big, too black, too shiny. I wanted to cradle something in my arms. I lifted Patsy Cline. She weighed more than I remembered. More than the slim Eye-Banana.

Again, I recalled Rennie's joking admonition, *Rule one, Julia. You always stand to play an electric guitar.* I sat on the couch in defiance and worked at a simple Robert Johnson tune that Luke had once taught me.

There was a specific pleasure in picking out some blues when nothing else consoled. It was a task; it commanded my attention. Patsy Cline articulated the ache even as I embraced her. I got a glimmer of what it was for Luke or Rennie to play guitar. Like holding a lover's sleek torso and making her purr or wail against your own.

Through December, I didn't press Rennie about Mona. I wasn't ready to break things off. I still desired him. And it wasn't just that. Without Rennie, who would bring me daffodils? Who would meet me for lunch at the Berghoff and take me to Koko Taylor? If not him, not Luke.

I couldn't bear letting the music go. There was such comfort in a *twang* and *wah wah* down the hall, muffled feedback through a wall. Rennie was Luke on the window seat and me on his bunk. I was infatuated with the guitarist part of him. It lent the universe an illusion that fate might right me a wrong, trade me Rennie for Luke.

We still behaved like people in love, exchanging gifts and kissing at midnight to bring in the New Year. But soon enough, Rennie was badgering me about quitting the Field. Maybe it was Brian getting scarce after Jennifer had Clark Addison (named for the location of Wrigley Field). Maybe he sensed me slipping away. I watched myself act more polite than familiar, or leave a gratuitous last name on his voicemail. I started to recede, to move out of reach, so he couldn't inflict more pain.

"What if we get more out-of-town gigs?" He was intent. "We won't have any time together. The keyboards would be easy for you. Just try."

I didn't say much. I had no interest in giving up a regular paycheck to stand by him. The Field didn't offer the same satisfaction it once did, but being The Voodoo Farmers' pianist, cook, and roadie didn't sound seductive either. I didn't want to back up Mona.

Maybe that spawned the press release incident. My intransigence. I was preoccupied, working late, preparing for the first new exhibit of the year: "Flies." We were calling the taxidermy demonstration "Flies at Work." This was the display plan: Cut the major meat and fat off some animal bones. Label them. Dump them in a glass case with a bunch of flesh-eating beetles and flies. Watch the bugs pick the bones clean. It was gruesome, yet cool—the two sides of science.

I called Midwestern travel journals, parenting magazines, local calendars, paper chains, and newswires. But I hadn't issued the release announcing the schedule of events. On Tuesday night, I taught two piano students, then Rennie rode over on the train for some fajitas. I drafted the release while he plucked at the Eye-Banana. By the time I emailed the release to work, he was hard asleep. I slept well, ready to broadcast the release to my fax list in the morning.

Wednesday was rainy, verging on sleet. Rennie left his blue sweater on my piano bench in favor of an old anorak. I gave him a lift to the train just as the deluge hit, and he made a quick choice between my umbrella and the Eye-Banana. More than anything, I don't think he wanted to slip and drop the guitar in the winter rain. He gave me a lingering kiss and said, "Don't forget—Lily's at ten."

I said, "I'll be there," and pulled away.

It took an ice age to inch down Lake Shore Drive. I parked and slung the Eye-Banana in the trunk, away from prying eyes and under the beach blankets, wiper fluid and folding chairs. By the time I shook the water off my coat and walked across the Great Hall, I was late. I swung into my cubicle and booted up. I spent the morning broadcasting the fax and taking calls. It was one-thirty before I took my lunch out of its sack.

I reached in and drew out the plastic bags. Leftover Mexican. Some chips. And some raisins? I never ate raisins. I looked closer. Flies. *A bag of dead flies.* A huge, thick bag with smeary insect secretion on the cellophane, scores of fly corpses in a sandwich bag.

My stomach clenched like a fist. I bolted up so fast that I knocked over my chair, which crashed into the wastebasket, which clanged against the cubicle's metal edge. Yesterday's half-empty Diet Pepsi can sprayed across my floor socket, shorting out the computer.

I cursed, shrilly, "Fuck you, Rennie."

LuAnn came running, shocked at my profanity, startled by the sparking outlet.

"You don't have a surge protector?" she said.

The rest of the day was computer hell. I tried to resurrect my press list on LuAnn's laptop. Working in her office, I didn't have the privacy to phone Rennie and dress him down. I worked over my gravelly wrath like a stone polisher while I typed. I redid the download, found an old backup, called a technician, unearthed the warranty, printed out lists. I nursed along the remaining faxes—too many phone numbers and area codes had changed for things to go nicely.

When I pulled out of the museum lot, it was dark. The rain had stopped, leaving a soft gleam everywhere. The night city reflected itself in small puddles along the curbs. I cracked my window to catch the cool, lakey scent, the *whish* of my tires through water pooling on concrete. I went home, ate, and crawled into bed with a musical sedative, the Brandenburg Concertos.

I had to face it: Rennie must have been collecting those flies for months, since those languid summer mornings on the back porch, baiting Bix with peanuts, wielding his turquoise swatter. This was beyond joking. It was a planned assault. On me, in the sanctity of my office. By a man who didn't have one. Of course "Eye-Banana" mortified him—he was a stock boy playing air guitar in his buddy's basement.

Why didn't I see it coming? I couldn't distinguish between teasing and cruelty because Luke had ambushed me with water balloons and poured hot sauce in my Coke? Or I just didn't want to admit the difference?

I tried to nap and imagined what Kate would say about loneliness, affection. She was gone, but I could still summon her chuckle: "Get a dog, Jules. Buy a vibrator." As the clock edged toward ten, I decided.

I called Lily's. Rennie picked up the phone at the front counter; I heard glasses scraping the bar, change jangling at the register. He was anxious, "Running late? Don't forget the Eye-Banana."

"Very late. I can't come," I said. "My car was broken into. In the lot, at work. I had to file a police report." I paused to whimper. "Oh, honey. I'm so sorry. The Eye-Banana. It's gone."

"Shit," he said. "Are you sure? Goddamnit. Okay, okay, okay. I can't believe it. I'll run home for my Fender. It's closer than you are. *That's* why you never leave a guitar anywhere. Ever. Shit. Do you have insurance?" His voice made a quick change from angry to factual.

"Yes, but it's got a deductible," I improvised, awed at the power of my fib.

"Anything else gone? Your CDs? Clothes?"

"Only the guitar. I'm so sorry." This lie was getting complicated.

"Okay. Shit. I gotta go. I've gotta get the Fender. I'll call you in the morning, okay?"

When I hung up, I pictured a distraught Rennie waving down a cab, frantically tuning the irritable Fender. I thought about my last theft—raspberry lip gloss in seventh grade. I was paranoid and agitated then, convinced that every set of eyes on the Old Orchard bus could see the contraband in my pocket. I was paranoid and agitated now, too. I thought revenge was supposed to be sweet. It wasn't. Whoever made that up, I wondered if they were really in love. I wondered if I was.

Rennie phoned the next morning. "Did the cops find the Ibanez?" he said.

I ignored the question.

"You have some nerve even asking, after those flies. What's wrong with you? You are one sick fuck. Mona can have you." I wanted to yell until my throat bled.

"It was just a prank, Julia. Don't overreact."

"No, Rennie. It wasn't a prank at all. It was sabotage. What was your point? What if I ate them?"

He actually laughed.

"I'm not laughing, Rennie," I shrieked. I wanted to burst his eardrum. "Do I sound like I'm laughing? This time, I'm not imagining things. Bix. Mona. I'm not waiting around to see what's next."

I told him not to bother calling again. That we were through. Jokes were one thing, viciousness was another. I'd send him a check if any insurance came through for the guitar.

But as good as it felt to scream, it was a letdown to hang up.

That was over a month ago, and I'm adjusting. I lost my sheen at the Field when my computer exploded. I get lonely. Rennie called, but I won't talk to him.

I *have* seen baby Clark Addison and Jennifer. She visited last weekend, lugging Clark in a fancy sling, blue bag of baby tricks over her shoulder. She burrowed into the sofa cushions to nurse him. He sucked away, eyes clamped shut in milky bliss, tiny hand resting on the side of her perfect swollen breast in a gesture that said, *Mine.* Clark laughed a sleepy baby laugh, and Jennifer extricated her moist, rosy nipple by poking a finger inside Clark's mouth, breaking their hermetic seal. Jennifer had that total lack of self-consciousness mothers have about their breasts when they transmute from erotica to sustenance. She shifted Clark to the other side and narrowed her eyes at me.

"You know, Julia, I love this baby more than I love Brian. More than I ever loved Brian. Maybe more than I'm capable of loving Brian. It's creepy. Clark here, he's basically a stranger, while I've known Brian for twelve years," she shuddered. "It's not what I expected, this baby business. It's not like we have a new member of the family. Clark's more like an occupying force. This incoherent, incontinent dictator. The weird thing is, I like it."

It was one of those bizarre confidences women make to their hairdressers or someone who borrows their lipstick in a bathroom between sets at a bar.

Jennifer shook her head as she placed Clark on her lap and tussled with the flaps on her nursing bra. "I have no idea how this happens. If it's hormonal brainwashing or what. Maybe motherhood's a kind of altered state."

I remembered my mom, howling through the heating chute, shrouded in Luke's cozy flannels and mourning him, the man she loved most.

Jennifer blushed a shade darker than her nipple. "I've become a bovine philosopher."

I smiled. She caught me up on Rennie: He's depressed; Mona fawns over him. I'm not interested in details. I can concoct them myself. I'm just crossing my fingers that he's not the most fascinating man I ever know. I'm banking on it.

I still have both guitars. Rennie never mastered the Gibson Les Paul single cutaway that Luke called Patsy Cline. There was something about the way Rennie held it—more like a rock than a jazz guitarist. He couldn't reach the highest frets as gracefully as he wanted. Maybe Rennie wanted his technique, like life, to be a little easier, to look effortless. Not a bad thing to want.

When I first snagged it, I considered dropping the Eye-Banana in the middle of Sheridan Road and watching the traffic grind it into yellow grit, but it seemed a waste of a good instrument. Luke would have loved it.

I'll probably keep the Eye-Banana. It's like preserving the best of Rennie—the musical part of him, the Luke part. Or arousing the dormant part of me. It sits out here, tempting me, and I can't help but sample it. I hold it. I strum. It *is* much easier to play a double cutaway. I don't care that it's not a collector's item like Patsy Cline.

I asked LuAnn if I could get hold of an extra sarcophagus. I'd love to store the Ibanez in one. I've heard that dead bodies decay in just weeks once you shut the limestone cover. Maybe it would cleanse the guitar of

Rennie's leftover skin cells. LuAnn squinted at me, as she does more lately. "Julia, it's not like we have extra coffins just lying around."

I finally mailed a letter to Kate. The Field is mounting an exhibit on Inca and Quechua culture, so I'm reading about the Andes. Maybe they need a music teacher in Lima. I could rent a piano and bring the guitars.

I still can't figure what to do with Rennie's sweater. I'm sitting here on the couch, cloaked inside it now. It has a lingering smell, like a pillow or soccer jersey would hold. I could unravel it and add it piece by piece to Hector's litter. Come spring, I could scatter the yarn on the fire escape and let the birds weave it into their nests. But right now, I'm chilly. It's thick and warm. And blue as a tranquil splash of water, however impotable, mirroring a clear Egyptian sky.

Decrepit

by Trinie Dalton

I'd want a range life
If I could settle down.
If I could settle down,
Then I would settle down.
—Pavement

We were performing a play about this maggot on our kitchen floor who grew until he was squishing out the windows, suffocating us and all those who came into the Ranch House. The maggot play was meant to be retro, like *Godzilla* or *King Kong*— one of those huge-creatures-dominating-humanity stories. But we were wasted on Xanax, dressed in red dresses and feather boas, so it had a New Wave feel.

"Don't eat me, you maggot," I said to the two-foot-long papier-mâché maggot lying on the floor.

"I vill crush you," said Heidi, in a low, Khrushchevian maggot/dictator voice from behind the door. "I am zee maggot."

That's the only part I remember. The script was pathetic.

Heidi, Annie, and I—roommates—renamed the Blue House, the Ranch House. It was a one-story, spread-out, casual Craftsman-style place.

Everything was decrepit: Termites ruined the walls, and vines grew in the windows. But it was gigantic, and there was space in the garden to grow pumpkins and watermelons. A skunk family lived in our ivy, so we got to see the babies. We spent our time learning Carter Family songs. Sara and Maybelle are easier to imitate than A.P.'s baritone parts. I can still play "Single Girl," "Wandering Boy," and "Wildwood Flower" on guitar. We had pie parties and sang to guys we invited over to eat elderberry pie hot out of the oven. The elderberries came from trees in Elysian Park because we had no money to buy grocery store ones. Countryfolk wannabes for sure.

My first night in that house, I raided the basement and found a shawl, rusty tools, and knitting equipment. I had a spooky meeting with the ghost of the old lady who died there. She was making the rooms cold. Drafts of winter air were leaking through sealed windowsills, even though it was summer. I told her to leave because three girls were moving in. I was alone and sensed her in the corner of the den, rocking in her invisible rocking chair. I heard the chair creaking and could smell the stale scent of the elderly. She'd died in the 1970s, and no one had lived there since, the Realtor told me. It made sense, then, that someone should tell her to beat it.

Back when I was nine, my aunt told me that to get rid of a poltergeist, I should be firm. It really works. The Ranch House Ghost departed that night. Our theory was that she'd been buried under the avocado tree in the backyard. It had years of leaf debris piled beneath it, and grew avocados the size of cantaloupes. We figured the human compost had beefed them up. Also, next to the tree was a defunct incinerator—convenient. Her son must have folded her up, shoved her in, fired up the stove, and burned her into an ashen pile, ideal for fertilizer. That's why our tree kicked ass.

There are a lot of ghosts and good avocado trees in The Echo Park. I didn't know there was a "the" before Echo Park until I went to the local liquor store, House of Spirits, to get tequila for our "ranch-warming" party. I was telling the lady behind the counter how I grew up in L.A. and had just moved back from New York. New York has too much cement. Even when I looked up, I saw buildings.

"Echo Park's the only place I feel at home," I said.

"So many kinds of people. Less old people now. They're all dying," she said.

I knew she meant the Echo Park Convalescent Home down the street, where heaps of old people roll around in wheelchairs and smell everything up. No one likes that haunted house.

The guys behind me in line started in.

"You went to live somewhere else?" one asked. He looked tight in his L.A. Dodgers cap, oversized white T-shirt, Dickies shorts, and Nike Cortez sneakers with white tube socks pulled up over his calves. Shaved head. All his friends looked the same.

"Yeah. But I missed stuff. Like kids setting off fireworks. And wild dogs," I said.

"You always come back to The Echo Park," he said. "You can't ever leave The Echo Park." He nodded his head at my tequila bottle.

I saw a dead body while I was living in the Ranch House. Not in the house, down a couple miles in the doughnut-store parking lot. I was walking by, and there was yellow tape all around, as if the cops thought people were going to poke the body or something. It was lying in a conspicuously contorted position, legs bent in wrong directions, neck turned too far over. Man, middle-aged. No blood. Almost like he'd been pushed out of the passenger seat by someone driving at high speed and rolled all the way into the parking lot. I associated the body with the doughnuts and haven't eaten there since. After all, Ms. Donut is right around the corner. It's the feminist doughnut shop.

"What kind of life would you have, if you could change yours?" Heidi asked me one afternoon while she washed potatoes in the sink.

I stood leaning on the doorjamb, loving the hugeness of our kitchen. "A range life," I said. That was my favorite song. I'd drink gin on the porch and listen to it. I'd gaze at the corn we planted where the lawn used to be and think about settling down. "Why?" I continued. "You sick of me?" I noticed the butter sitting out and put it back in the fridge. Heidi liked it out on the counter in a country-style butter dish. I hate soft, hot butter.

"Remember when the cats attacked that?" she asked. Her green gingham apron was spotted with potato bits.

It was Easter morning. We were out hunting colored eggs under the avocado tree. When we came back in and shooed the cats away, the butter was scalloped into a pyramid shape by lick marks. Land O'Lakes, unsalted—with the box where you can tear off the Indian princess and fold her knees into her chest area so she has major hooters.

There were two rules of the house: to wear clothes only when necessary, and to always burn candles and incense to appease spirits. Nudity made us feel closer to those in nether regions. Bare skin seemed more ghostly. We weren't trying to attract ghosts, but we respected them. The Old Lady Ghost was gone, but we still smelled her occasionally. I'd catch a whiff when I opened the medicine cabinet or stepped into the laundry room. She smelled like the nursing home, like musty sweaters and dirty flannel sheets. Ghosts smell pretty much the same as those about to die—which is totally separate from the way dead bodies smell. Ghosts aren't rotten, but there is a hint of putrefaction that makes me aware of their status: *not dead yet* or *already dead and separated from the physical body*. Why don't ghosts smell fresh and young? Maybe old people don't remember how they smelled as kids, so neither can ghosts.

There was another old lady next door, alive, but barely. She grew candy-striped beets and okra in her front yard. Yet she didn't smell like she was dying. She prided herself on her odorless house.

"I hate bad smells," she said as she gave the three of us a tour of her house one day. It was a Craftsman-style, too, stained dark wood inside, black velvet curtains over the windows. The bank was threatening to take it from her. They were a threat to everybody. "Your house smells," she added.

"Just that one time," I said. Some zucchinis in the crisper had gone bad. "Myrna, what can get candle wax out of carpet?" A votive candle had burned all night, tipped over, and run between the carpet hairs in our living room.

"An iron and a dish towel," she said. She showed us the method, making ironing movements in midair.

We fell asleep huddled on the floor around a candle because my mom called and was having visions of a murderer living next door to us, waiting to strike. My mom had psychic powers that we took pretty seriously, not seriously enough to move out that night as she had requested, but seriously enough to burn extra candles and incense, and to keep all the doors locked with the cats inside.

"Why is there so much spiritual drama here?" Annie asked that night. We listened to *Let It Bleed* by the Rolling Stones while locked in.

"Welcome to Echo Park," Heidi said. I thought again of that old folks' home down the block, and pictured their garden filled with car exhaust–coated agapanthus and weedy impatiens, barely tended to. Cars sped by their institutional garden, but who ever stopped to visit? Where were the relatives bringing flowers, or picking their grannies up for a drive down Sunset Boulevard?

"Do you two ever get a bad feeling when you walk past that convalescent hospital?" I asked. I kept thinking of that awful place. I took it as a sign, but I didn't know of what.

"No, except that everyone there's going to die," said Heidi.

"Maybe all their fears combine and rub off on you," Annie said.

That night I dreamt I was Sara Carter. I was dressed in raggedy clothes and holey leather shoes. The next day I tried to write a song about Echo Park, about how when I'm about to die, I hope people will bring me back and bury me . . . but not under an old willow tree. Where then? In Echo Park Lake, under the lotus flowers littered with McDonald's wrappers and devoured cobs of corn? Farther down Alvarado Street in MacArthur Park, where so many dead bodies are dredged out of the lake? Would I be buried under the aptly named House of Spirits? None of these places are worthy of my corpse, I thought. Just as in the old ballads, I wanted to be buried by the seashore, or under some significant tree.

We got evicted from the Ranch House when the bank bought it. Shortly before we got kicked out, our dog died, which was the first sign of things winding down. Then Myrna, our neighbor, declared bankruptcy and lost her house. The third sign was when our friend Melissa moved out of her house up the street because she kept hearing machine-gun noises on the ground floor. She found out that her house had been a gangster hideout during the bootlegging era—lots of people had died in it. My mom was hospitalized for hearing voices. A gardener chopped down our avocado tree.

I wanted to be buried under that tree, with the cremated Old Lady. It's the only place that comes to mind when I think of drafting a will. It's a place where my friends lived. I'd like to be charred in that very incinerator, but I don't think the guy who lives there now would allow it. I've driven by and seen him on several occasions, watering his lawn where our corn used to be.

The Carter Sisters are like ghosts, because they're dead, but I still listen to them sing about beautiful land. That land doesn't seem to include Los Angeles, though. I worry that I come from a place with so few legends, or, to be more accurate, legends that are speculative. Big deal—old ladies, gangsters, tequila, banks taking houses away from people, people getting killed in front of doughnut shops. There's no real way to know the other people who lived in these rented houses, apart from rummaging through what they left in basements, then concocting harebrained ghost stories about them.

On the nights I lie awake wondering where to be buried, I sometimes recall staring up at the Ranch House's stucco ceiling—the plaster sparkled with glitter. I'd wake up in the middle of the night, imagining it to be the night sky. A burning candle made it twinkle even more. It was disco and country at the same time—glam-rural—a combo that makes me realize the irony of a band called Pavement singing about "Range Life." I know I'll be an old lady ghost, because I lie in bed feeling young and old at the same time. Young in experience, but old because I wish to be part of some tradition. I crave a past, but don't want to live in it. Eras run into one ageless mess. Ghosts live in different times simultaneously. They yearn for what's lost. I haven't even lost anything, but I still find myself yearning for it. Not knowing where you come from is dumber than never wanting to leave.

Timing

by Tara Ison

They call her the Senator's Wife," he tells me.

"Oh. So . . . you still want to be a senator?" I ask.

"Well, yeah. Eventually."

"And that's what your friends call her? 'The Senator's Wife'?"

"Mm."

"She's supportive. Well-groomed. Law-abiding."

"Yeah." He shifts his weight, peeling himself away from me.

"She's beautiful."

"I think so," he says.

No. He doesn't need to affirm this; it is an objective analysis. She looks down on us from a cheap frame propped on a bookshelf, a shelf that still holds his adolescent and teenage books, here in his parents' house. I knew him in high school, but never came to this house. There would have been no reason to, then. Now he is back from law school, pre–his own apartment, and we are having sex beneath a photo of his by-any-standards-beautiful fiancée, left waiting with pearls and chignon back in Georgetown.

I hate that I have to ask. "So, what about me? Why are you here with me? What am I?" I am the Senator's Concubine, I'm dying to say, but that is too cute.

"You . . ." he says, tenderly stroking my sweaty hair, "are ambitious. You are going to achieve. You are going to do fucking amazing things, all on your own."

This is cruel, his faith in me. And inappropriate. At sixteen, he was gawky and spotty and too smart for his own good, hyperpolitical, a frenzied blur. Debating Club, Junior State, the ranting editorial section of the school paper. All the soft and nonthreatening civics of high school were mowed flat by his senatorial drive. I smiled indulgently, everyone did, then, at Chas's panting, socialist need to Do Something, at his angelic blond curls and beige corduroy slacks. I would have shunned a crush with cruel and condescending sweetness. I would have dismissed him thoroughly. I have now made the mistake of layering that memory onto this present man, reencountered five weeks ago in a bar I thought him too unhip for, and have wound up here, naked in bed with someone who is no longer who he was. Who now calls himself Chuck. Who has, in sneaking a new self past me, into me, lied.

"Can I kiss you?" he asks in a skilled whisper, like it is a meaningful thing. This man could, will, become a senator. He is well beyond me and in total control, cool and self-assured as a fascist.

"Yes," I whisper back, grateful and hating myself, hating him.

It is October. His wedding is scheduled for June. In January, a sweater for him half-knit (yes, I knit, you asshole, I think), my hatred frayed as used yarn, I pick up some other guy I truly don't know in the hip bar, have sex in his car, and later call Chas to tell him he's fucked, that I never want to see him again, and to please return my copy of *One Hundred Years of Solitude* some time when I'm not home. Because of this, I don't hear, a month later, of his engagement to the Senator's Wife abruptly ending when Chas decides he's just not ready to get married. She had moved here from Georgetown, bought the Vera Wang dress, registered at Williams-Sonoma. The cream-and-roses invitations had already gone out. I don't hear of it because Chas doesn't call me again for three years.

Somehow, then, we become friends. Once every eighteen months or so we wind up in bed, resulting in six months of revived snarl and separation, but we always work our way back to close-knit. He always has an excuse, and it is always Timing. He might have fallen in love with me, yes, but the timing was always wrong: He was engaged, I was seeing someone else, he was seeing someone else, I was being a lesbian, he was living in San Francisco, one of us moved and couldn't find the other's new address or phone number. To him, it would seem merely a matter of temporal misalignment. That we simply never fell into the solitude gaps in each other's lives. I think this is bullshit, but I let it stand; the truth doesn't flatter me. Years go by, and we go to the Frolic Room for drinks, to El Coyote for nachos, to the Nuart for Scorsese retrospectives. We applaud each other's successes and lacerate each other's antagonists. We riffle through other lovers. At some drunken point one evening, he concedes that if we ever were together, really tried being together, yes, we'd wind up wanting to kill each other, but no, we wouldn't ever be bored. This is a tiny victory, shallow and insignificant though it may be. I burrow into it like a hastily dug grave.

I finish the sweater I once started for him, and wear it myself. I wear it for years in front of him, carry it around, leave it lying in the hatchback of my car or draped over a chair, until, finally, one chilly night, we are sitting outside on the new balcony of my new condominium—he is cold, and I can offer it to him. A retroactive, conceptual offering. Hey, this is great, he says, fondling it. Did you make this? For you, I tell him. A long, long time ago. He looks surprised, then abruptly seems to remember a meaningful thing. He nods, puts the sweater on, admiring my skill. Zosia, my new little dog, nudges him. I named her after my grandmother; I'd finally decided I was saving the name for no reason. Chas picks her up, and nuzzles her in his lap. His fingers massage little circles in her fur; she closes her eyes blissfully, and I am uncomfortably reminded of his fingers once touching me like that, those same little massaging circles.

My new condo is beautiful, a result of my doing fucking amazing things, all on my own. High ceilings and hardwood floors. Stunning appointments, a desirable neighborhood south of the Boulevard in Sherman Oaks. I am the youngest person in the building, and the residents, many of them immigrants of forty and fifty years, still speaking with German and Polish and Yiddish accents, who came here with nothing and are now *comfortable,* treat me like a successful granddaughter and tell me they are happy the building has fresh blood. The next youngest are the two women who live next door, LouAnn and Bev, in their early forties, with Brooklyn accents and a lot of condo-oriented spirit; the three of us are elected president, vice president, and secretary of the Homeowner's Association Board, which entitles us to receive late-night, distraught, heavily accented calls about plumbing problems and being locked out. LouAnn and I post friendly, if slightly directive, notices on the lobby bulletin board, announcing, PLEASE NOTE: THE LOBBY FLOOR WILL BE WAXED THIS WEDNESDAY A.M.!, or PLEASE NOTE: RESIDENTS MUST PARK IN THEIR ASSIGNED SPACES—VISITOR PARKING IS FOR VISITORS ONLY! A gentlemen couple in their fifties sneak treats to Zosia, and insist I let them take her for walks; they tell me she is very ethereal, for a poodle. One time, I hear an old lady shrieking, "Fire!" across the hallway, and I race to her aid with a fire extinguisher; her teakettle, forgotten, has boiled out its water and the kettle's burning bottom is filling the kitchen with acrid black smoke. This sweet old lady, Mrs. Steinman, has a leg brace and a crumpled left arm, neither of which prevents her from taking out her own trash and doing all her own grocery shopping. In thanks for my blasting her kitchen with fire extinguisher foam, she leaves at my door three six-packs of Diet 7-Up, which she has wheeled upstairs to our floor in her little wire cart. She is from a tiny village in Poland, the same, we discover over 7-Up, as my grandmother Zosia. But my grandmother, daughter of the village rabbi, fled the Russian pogroms; Mrs. Steinman escaped as a limping twelve-year-old from the Germans. The village no longer exists. Her family no longer exists. I feel for her, having to live all on her own. I make it a point to engage with her in long chats when we meet.

One morning, LouAnn calls me early, distraught, to tell me a swastika has been carved into our most recent posted notice.

"A swastika?" I repeat. I have never seen an actual one, in my own actual life. "Who here's going to creep downstairs in the middle of the night and put up a swastika?"

"I don't know. Bev's totally freaked. You know about her grandparents, right?"

"Yeah . . . I can't believe this."

"And Mrs. Steinman saw it. She was hysterical. She started babbling in Polish."

"Oh, no."

"I'm going to call the cops, I'll call you back afterward." She hangs up.

Chas is in therapy. He is turning over a new leaf. He told me about this several months ago, sitting on the balcony of my new condo, wearing the sweater I once knit for him. He's ready to settle down, make a commitment. He has just been made the chief trial attorney for the Public Defender's office, and spends a lot of time in court, yelling at judges, Doing Something. He is interviewed on radio and television, his liberal dervish energy much in demand, and is earning one-fourth of what he used to make as a corporate litigator. He tells me about the new girl he is seeing, and uses the unfortunate metaphor of musical chairs to describe how he is now at a certain age, there is a certain point, there comes a time, something about the empty chair presented to you at the exact moment you feel compelled to sit down, how you take that chair. Like when the time comes, in life, to give up and buy yourself a condo. It is all about Timing.

She is bright and pretty, and her SAT scores were higher than his, he tells me, although he doesn't give me the actual number. She is trying to make it as an actress, and is really very, very talented. They have just found an apartment together—crappy, but with his pay cut, and, you know, her money situation, it's not too bad.

We are at the edge of the evening where we usually either turn to sex or we do not, and at this exact moment, he gets up to call her, to tell her he will be home soon. It's after two in the morning. Zosia looks at him, at me, hopefully, ignoring the impending implication of his empty chair. I pick her up. I'd always wanted a dog—this is the first home where I could have one. She has come into my life at just the right time.

"Chuck says you guys talked to the police?" Missy asks me in the kitchen; she has followed, helpfully, to help me pour the white wine.

"Yeah. After the fourth time, they finally came and took a report."

"Wow . . . and this is such a nice neighborhood."

"This place is fucking great!" Chas yells from the living room. Missy and I join him, Zosia trotting after us. "I told you this place was great," he says to Missy as she hands him his wine. "Thank you, sweetie."

"It really is. It's beautiful," she says to me.

"Thanks." We sit on my new couch, my new chair. Missy leans over to run her veinless, tendonless hand along the gleaming hardwood floor. Their ratty new apartment, I know, is in a lesser area of Santa Monica, and has shag chartreuse carpeting.

"Chuck says you looked at, what, like over a *hundred* condos?"

"Oh, thanks," I say to him. "Sure, make me look like that."

He shrugs. "You're selective. You're persistent. It paid off, you got the right place."

"Except for Nazi vandals."

"Dyslexic Nazi vandals," he says.

"Oh, yes," Missy says, "Chuck told me the swastikas are wrong?"

"They're backward. I want to post a notice that says, 'Learn to draw a proper swastika, you fascist prick.'"

"'You *stupid* fascist prick,'" he adds.

"Oh, come on. I can just hear you, pleading this guy's case. 'Your Honor, this isn't a Nazi swastika! This is the ancient Aztec symbol of peace!'" I tell him, and he laughs.

"Is that really what it means?" Missy asks him. He nods. Zosia pushes a ball toward her; Missy pats her gingerly, then looks like she wants to wash her lovely, lotuslike hands.

"We're installing a surveillance camera," I tell them. "In the lobby."

"Is that legal?" Missy asks Chas. He nods again. "Okay, doggy, go on."

"The cops suggested it to us."

"Sure, *they* don't have to pay for it," he says.

"It's going to cost us a few thousand dollars."

"Go on, doggy."

"Hey, come here, puppy . . ." Chas picks up Zosia, to distract her from Missy.

"It's worth it. The whole building's terrified. We're the Jewish Home for the Aged here."

"It *is* terrifying," Missy says.

"It's a felony," he tells her.

"Really?"

"Four felonies," I point out. "Each one's a separate charge. Hate Crime Unit took the report. Of course, the detective made a point of telling me he didn't believe in 'hate crime' legislation. 'Why should burning a black church be any worse than burning anyone's home?'"

"Cops . . ." Chas shakes his head.

"Excuse me, darling, you'd be the *first* to claim we violated the Nazi's civil rights by making the building too difficult to break into," I tell him.

"You're actually denying him freedom of speech. Freedom of expression."

"You'd get this guy off?"

"Nah. I want to fry the bastard." He rubs Zosia behind the ears. *"Woodja woodja woodja."*

"You're the voice of the downtrodden. The defender of the oppressed, the victimized, the unwashed masses."

"Oh, you guys," says Missy, smiling.

"Yeah, but *you're* a dear friend. You catch him on video, I say, screw the trial. Crucify him. *Howsat? Howsat feel?*" Zosia loves him madly. "I'd love to get a dog. Missy is not a dog person."

"Well . . ." she hedges, glancing at me. She is even more beautiful, I think, than Chas's earlier, dumped fiancée, in the looking-down-on-me photo. "This one's really cute, though," she says. "I could have one like this."

"There isn't another one like this," he tells her.

"That's very true. She's ethereal," I say.

"Terribly ethereal," he agrees.

"I'm knitting her a sweater," I announce.

"You are? That's so adorable!" Missy smiles at him, smiles at me. She is happy at becoming being dear friends with Chas's dear friend and her little dog.

Chas follows me into the kitchen for more chips, the entire basket of which he and I have devoured but Missy hasn't touched. He sits on the counter while I tear open a fresh bag.

"You know, the comps on this place have already gone up," I tell him. "It's already worth maybe thirty thousand more than I paid."

"The perfect time to buy," he says. "You are very wise. You made a fucking brilliant choice."

As I pass with the basket, he catches me within the V of his legs; I stop, and his knees tighten slightly at either side of my waist. I look down at the chips and he tugs me forward, rests his chin on top of my head. We stay this way for a moment, but I don't know what this is. Other than exactly a moment I wanted, and another thing to hate him for.

"Hey, you guys?" we hear Missy call. He takes his time releasing me, then lets me go ahead of him into the living room.

"Okay, so, the next thing, you gotta set the timer right," Cliff tells us. Cliff is our Surveillance Specialist. He has installed a fake fire detector—we had been given a choice of fake fire detector, fake briefcase, or fake teddy bear—in the lobby, its tiny hidden camera cued on the bulletin board, and he has wired this to a monitor and VCR hidden in the storage room. "It tells you the date and time, shows it right on the video. Important for when you go to court." LouAnn and I nod, take notes. "How many times this goon show up?"

"Fourteen," LouAnn tells him. "We have fourteen flyers slashed with swastikas." LouAnn is keeping a file of them, all the dates listed, just as the police instructed. Every time one is swastika'd, we immediately replace it, so all the residents coming on or off the elevator, collecting their mail, don't have to walk by it and get traumatized. Everyone is waiting, hoping, praying, they tell us, for this to end, for us to do something.

"He does it sometime between midnight and 6 A.M. Every third or fourth night," I say.

"We thought about staking out the lobby ourselves, but . . ."

"No, no, you ladies are doing the right thing." Cliff checks his watch, and programs in the correct date and time. "You don't want anyone getting hurt. You get him on camera, that's it, you got him. He's not getting away with shit."

LouAnn and I return to the lobby to post a brand new notice: PLEASE NOTE: DO NOT BUZZ ANYONE INTO THE BUILDING YOU DO NOT KNOW OR EXPECT PERSONALLY! WE MUST LOOK OUT FOR EACH OTHER! We stand for a moment, looking at the fake fire detector. She waves at it like a tourist.

"This is creepy," she says. "Every time we get on and off the elevator, we're being watched."

"I know. But I feel like I'm being watched, anyway. Every time I take Zosia for a walk at night, or just going into the garage. Who knows when this guy is hanging around or not? When he's going to show up next time?"

"How about what he's going to *do* next time? I keep waiting for it to get worse."

"Me, too," I say. "I'm not sleeping at night. I keep waking up, all the time. Every little noise . . . I feel like we're all so *vulnerable.*"

"We *are*," she says. The elevator opens, and we get in. "I mean, c'mon, we have a building full of dykes, kikes, fags, and cripples. This guy could have a field day."

"I'm only half kike," I remind her, and she laughs.

I want so badly to hate her; the best I can do is to feel bored. Despite the SAT scores, which I continue to be told were very, very high, her intelligence is responsive, the bright and supportive follow-ups in conversation. It doesn't matter. She is sweet and sincere, with Edwardian curls, birdlike bones, and healthy pink gums. She is delicate, sweatless. She answers the phone when I call him at home and keeps me there for long minutes, asking a vast range of personal questions, revealing private details, creating intimacy between us. Eventually, she stops turning the phone over to him at all, and goes ahead to make the plans herself, for the three of us. Eventually, I stop asking to speak to him at all, and succumb to the girl-friend chat. She is insultingly unthreatened.

The three of us go to dinner at El Coyote, where Chas and I each finish two double margaritas before our Numero 8 combo platters arrive. Missy delicately picks the canned green beans from her vegetarian tostada.

"So, you got him?" he asks, excited. "That's great, you got him. I love it."

"Yeah. Three different nights on tape. Two-thirty-three, 2:41, and 2:27 A.M."

"Nazis are very punctual."

"At one point, he actually stops, turns his head, looks right at the camera. LouAnn and I were sure he figured it out. But then he turns and carves a *second* one."

"Balls. Big, Nazi balls."

"Chuck said none of you recognize him, right?" asks Missy.

"Nope. He's some fat, schlubby, thick-necked guy. He's wearing the same T-shirt and shorts every time. And he's totally blasé about it, just strolls in . . ."

"That's so gross," Missy says.

"At least we're *doing* something about it. The video thing was brilliant."

"You're Simon Wiesenthal. You're Beata Klarsfeld," Chas pounds a fist on the table in tribute.

"And this schlubby guy . . . I'd always pictured some well-groomed, goose-stepping Aryan eating streusel and drinking Riesling."

"No, the Nazi from *Cabaret*," Chas says. "That beautiful, sweet, blond, angelic kid, who gets up in the tavern and sings, 'Tomorrow belongs, Tomorrow belongs—'"

"'Tomorrow belongs to *meeee!*' I join in singing, and the two of us raise our margarita glasses like beer steins. "Did we rent that, or what?"

"No, the Beverly Cinema."

"Oh, yeah, with the guy at the ticket window—"

"With the hair!"

"Yeah!"

"I saw that movie," says Missy, smiling. "It was really good."

We all smile and sip our drinks.

"So . . ." Chas says.

"So, anyway, tonight the cops are finally staking us out. They'll grab him in the act. LouAnn and I are going to wait up. I want to see this guy suffer."

"You know, even with the videos, they'll plead him down. You'll probably wind up with a few counts of vandalism, defacement of property, maybe a terrorism statute. Misdemeanors. He could even get off."

"Then we'll form a posse, track him down, and string him up by his hairy Nazi balls."

"You'll let me know, right? You'll call me tomorrow?"

"You don't want me to call at 2:47 A.M.?"

"Nah. I'm in court early." He gets up and heads to the bathroom. "Order me another, right?"

Missy and I smile at each other.

"Chuck told me how much he loved your book," she says to me.

"Really?" I ask, although he and I have already discussed it. He calls me every few days from his office. It is when we talk. I decide not to tell her this. I decide to spare her.

"Yeah," she says. "He told me he thought it was incredible. I can't wait to read it."

"I hope you like it."

"Oh, I know I will. Wow . . ." She sighs, takes a sip of her margarita. "I wish I could get it together. Maybe I should go to grad school. I don't know. I just think it's incredible, everything you're doing." She gazes toward the bathroom; Chas is on his way back to us. She leans a little closer to me. "I feel so insignificant," she says quietly.

I want to throw my drink in her face. No, I want to claw her first, so the alcohol burns.

"Hey, sweetie," Chas says to her.

"No, wait, I'm going next." She slides out of the booth. "Chuck, finish my margarita." She heads to the bathroom, calling back to me: "I'm *such* a lightweight!"

"How's Zosia?" Chas asks.

"She's delicious."

"I'm converting to Judaism," he tells me.

"You are?"

"Yeah."

"You are."

"Monday I begin instruction with the Janowsky family rabbi."

I suddenly get it. "You're getting married."

He nods. "Next August somethingth."

"You're a devout atheist."

"It means something to her. Kids and everything. It's okay. I like Jews."

"What does your therapist say?"

"He approves. Well, he *did.* I'm not seeing him anymore." He pours half of Missy's margarita into my glass and the rest into his. He raises his glass. *"L'chaim."*

We drink, and the salt burns my lips. Missy returns.

"Mazel tov," I tell her.

"Oh . . ." She slides in next to him, smiling, and slips her arm into his. "He told you. *I* wanted to tell you . . ." She playfully punches his arm. "I'm so excited. I can't wait."

"I bet . . . well, indeed, a big, fat, hairy *mazel tov.*"

"Thanks," they say together. He takes her lovely hand and she lifts her head to kiss him, perfectly on the lips, her white throat delicately arched. I think, unwelcomingly, of the last time I went down on him, my desperate, inelegant head-bobbing. Give me a chance, I want to say, one chance to do it over. I'll do it right this time, be everything you want, all of it, achieve everything, for you.

"Okay, are you ready for this?" LouAnn asks. She is calling from her office; she is just off the phone with the police. "Claudio Marcello Petrello, he's thirty-one, he's from Argentina, he's here illegally."

"You're kidding."

"No, wait. He's Italian, and they told me his parents, or maybe his grandparents, I don't remember, were fascists who fled Italy after the fall of Mussolini's regime."

"What? He told them that?"

"That's what the cops just said." Six hours earlier, at 2:57 A.M., we had awakened when a police helicopter, two black-and-whites, two squad cars, two plainclothes detectives, and four uniformed cops stormed our building. I'd grabbed Zosia, put on her little sweater, and taken her into LouAnn and Bev's place, to watch from their balcony overlooking the street. Other people in our building were on their balconies, too, in bathrobes and slippers, hiding their faces in curtains and shadows, still terrified. When they looked up and saw us, they'd waved, given us the thumbs-up. This morning, Mrs. Steinman posted a thank-you card on the bulletin board.

"Wait, you know how he got in the building? He had a fucking *key*. He's a delivery guy for the *Wall Street Journal*."

"A *paper* boy?"

"He's been here every night for five months, delivering the paper to Mr. Weiner on the second floor. And they asked him why he did it, right? He said he was mad the elevator wasn't working that one time. That we were too cheap to fix it."

"Oh, sure, that makes perfect sense."

"He's already out on bail. Fifty grand."

"I'd like to rip his throat open. Stone him to death. Something biblical."

"Me, too. Oh, and get this, the cops almost *missed* him. They were just going to wait until three o'clock, and then leave. He showed up just in time."

Chas answers the phone.

"Hi, it's me," I say.

"Hey," he says exuberantly. "So, so? What happened?"

"Is Missy home?"

There is something in my voice; his voice drops, subdues. "No, she's out. I can talk."

"Tell me you're madly in love. Tell me you're blissfully happy. Tell me she's everything you've ever wanted." I stop, awaiting a sentence.

He breathes, carefully. "Yes, I'm madly in love. And I'm blissfully happy. And no, she isn't everything I've ever wanted."

"What isn't she?"

"She isn't . . ."

"What? What? What *isn't* she? Tell me."

"It's not what she isn't. That's okay. What she *is* works. It'll work."

"It'll 'work.'"

"Yeah."

"I don't understand. I don't get how you can say you're madly in love, but she's not everything you want, and then wrap it up with, 'It'll work.'"

"I'm ready for it. What works for me is different now, I've changed a lot. It's the right time."

"You're sitting down, that's all."

"What?"

"The music's fucking stopped, and you're tired, and you just want to sit down."

"I have to go."

We both hang up.

Claudio Marcello Petrello, at his arraignment, hears the felony charges dropped to four counts of vandalism and four counts of defacement of property. They are all misdemeanors, with the slim possibility of a few months in county jail, or a few hundred dollars' fine, but, the city attorney whispers later to us, he will most likely receive a suspended sentence and probation. His bail is reduced to five thousand dollars, to the delight of his family members gathered in the courtroom, a schlubby, thick-necked mother and father and siblings. All of this is due to the fact that Claudio has no prior offenses, and there was no one-on-one threat of physical violence to anyone, and no permanent destruction to the building. It was all superficial, the damage. A trial date is set for next month. The Petrello family dances out of court; LouAnn and Bev, Mrs. Steinman, Mr. Weiner, some other residents, and I are seated in the back of the room, trying to be invisible. We still feel afraid. But Claudio does not even glance at us; it is entirely possible, we realize, entirely probable, that he has no idea who we are.

"This is it?" says Mrs. Steinman. "This is the worst that happens to this man?" She is furious, tearful.

"Well," says LouAnn, "at least we can start sleeping at night."

"Maybe we can get the *Wall Street Journal* to reimburse us for the video equipment," I say.

"I want an explanation for this," says Mrs. Steinman. "I want this man to look me in the face and tell me why. Why he would do such a thing. I don't understand."

LouAnn shrugs. "Maybe we'll hear it at the trial. Maybe it'll make more sense."

A few months later, Missy calls.

"Hi, honey," she says. "God, we haven't talked to you in so long! How is everything?"

"Fine," I say. "How are you doing?"

"Oh, Chuck's working crazy hours, you know. Oh, and he's running for city council, did we tell you that?"

"Ah. Great. Landslide. He's on his way. He'll rule the world."

"I know," she says proudly. "I'm trying to help him as much as I can. I'm working part-time at his office. *And* doing all the wedding stuff, you know. There's so much to do, it's great, it's keeping me busy. The invitations go out next month. Is there anybody you want to bring?"

"Zosia?"

"Oh, I wish. No dogs allowed," she says with a laugh. "It's going to be beautiful. It's going to be amazing."

"Oh, I bet."

"That's actually why I'm calling. I'm trying to decide what to get Chuck for a wedding present, and I figure you know him so well . . . I know you're really busy, but would you go looking with me? I have a couple of ideas . . ."

"Sure," I say. "Why not?"

"I was thinking maybe this Saturday. If you have time. Oh, I wanted to ask you, whatever happened to the Nazi guy? The one they caught?"

"He's gone. He never showed up for trial."

"Really?"

"He took off for Argentina. Well, he's gone, so that's what the cops think. They'll never find him."

"Wow . . . well, at least it's over. At least you can get on with your life."

"Right."

"So, anyway," she says, "come on, I need your brain. You should know. What would make him happy? What does Chuck really want?"

He's Not Here

by Gale R. Walden

T
he boy on the stage was bent over in the half-twist way of
someone cutting his toenails. He cradled his guitar as if it
were a baby, and sang a song about strings detaching themselves from the ocean and floating away where they could be viewed on
top of the water. He compared the solitary strings to sunken kites of
life. His voice, void of melody and melancholy, moved high, wafted between registers, caught, sustained itself, requited with future possibility.

Because her job was to critique literature for a magazine known for
its careful choice of stories, where the language of the story was the vehicle that propelled the story forward, she found herself inadvertently
moving toward an investigation of the lyrics. She noted the discrepancy
of using the words "floating" and "sunken" to describe the same object, and

then kindly noted that since the object was a kite, any location it maintained that wasn't in air could rightly be described as sunken, or at least failed. Satisfied, she turned away from the stage and toward the party.

It was a party at a convention where many people were editors and many people were publishers and many people sold books. It was a party where people who said they didn't smoke stood in line at the cigarette machine and paid seven dollars for cigarettes, and other people watching them understood that the cigarettes were only a function of the story insofar as it was a detail of character, which others would argue, at another convention, was the entire basis of the story. At another convention, one could arrange an entire pedagogical panel around the cigarette machine.

She was supposed to meet a woman who had been kind to her at a time in her life when few people showed kindness. The woman she was supposed to meet had curly long brown hair and looked vaguely European, but at this party, even from behind, there were none of her type. Many of the women had black matte hair or an unnatural gleaming red mane. Others were reflections of herself, a bob of brown. Some of the women were from the neighborhood, an old Ukrainian community recently invaded by artists, who accessorized their tiny black dresses with black clunky boots and silver chains. The women from the convention were distinguished from the neighborhood women because they accessorized with tiny gold chains and black pumps.

There were several types of men at the party, though at first glance, none really appealed to her. There were some men from the neighborhood standing around the bar looking as much like they weren't there as someone who was there could possibly look, accepting drinks as if they hadn't ordered them, money set on the bar, apart from any work they might have done to get it. These men had hair in various stages of sticking up, and chains affixed to at least one item of clothing. Then there were men her own age, whose presence was more pronounced. They had balding, ponytailed heads and touched their slightly pouching stomachs lightly against the bar, as they tried to make known who exactly was paying for the drinks. None of them looked like anybody she could love.

The place where the party was being held had been a small factory at one time. Hoses, previously connected to machines, were now braided onto the ceiling, and occasionally one dropped down like a vine. There was a series of rooms in the old factory; the only purpose of the first one seemed to be opening out into the street. It gathered the people coming in and held them until the moment for them to be embraced into the back room arrived, and also allowed the people leaving to pause before the bump into the street. When she was gathered into the room, it was early, and most of the people were arriving. Like them, she took the path of least resistance, moving with the crowd through the corridors of washrooms into the largest area, where the stage, the bar, and the cigarette machine took up portions of the room.

After she had watched the boy singing about the kite for a while, she walked back toward the cigarette machine. She'd quit smoking years before, but standing near a cigarette machine still seemed like a dangerous thing to do. A man next to her singled her out. He looked about her age, though he had foregone the ponytail. He was Italian, from Queens, lived in New Jersey now, and still loved poetry, he said right off the bat. She could tell he was trying to make her laugh, and she thought this kind of him, though she herself was not particularly kind and refused to laugh until he told her a story about meeting a retired Yankees player at the convention and how he had gone directly out to the hallway, called his father, and they both cried on the phone. After she laughed, he said that was a very good thing to see. He said she looked like someone who hadn't laughed for a while.

Since she didn't like that description of herself, she decided to try to make him laugh, too, so she told him about her cab ride. She didn't tell him how she could have gone to different parties, or how in front of the glass hotel, people she barely knew beckoned her into cabs and pretended like it was important that she come with them, but that in the earlier evening, on Navy Pier, watching the boats and the sun recede, smelling the particular smell of alewives, she'd sensed fate lurking someplace in the midst of the city lights and high trains, and how it was this party, off from the safety of the Loop lights, that she felt drawn toward.

She didn't tell him that she'd stood in front of the hotel talking to the bell-hops, trying to weigh the fear of going alone in a cab to an unknown part of the city before asking one of the bellhops how much it would cost to go out there. "Twenty dollars," he said. "It's a completely different part of the city. Why do you want to go there? Go to Park West. Good band." Just as the bellhop was advising this, a group of people revolved out the hotel, the women spinning in dresses of glittering rayon as they touched the sidewalk, while the men, boisterous in their suits, plotted how they were going to get another invitation for the party at Park West. She reached into her purse, pulled out the gold invitation, and held it out to the last man getting into the cab. He saluted her with the invitation, but didn't look surprised, as if he were a man accustomed to things com-ing through his window at the last moment. "Well, now you've really lim-ited your options," said the bellhop.

"I don't feel my fate is at Park West."

"Your fate?"

"Destiny might be a better word."

"Oh, brother. Oh, man. She's talking about destiny in front of the Hyatt. Get this." He gestured the doorman over.

"Did you need some help, madam?" The doorman was serious, and raised his eyes to the bellhop, signifying that this was the proper line of questioning for the situation.

"I already asked her that," the bellhop said defensively.

The doorman ignored him, which caused the bellhop to do a little plié. The doorman ignored the plié and turned all his attention back to her. "Ma'am?" he questioned again.

"He's helping me." She felt protective of the bellhop somehow.

"We're talking about fate," the bellhop injected.

The doorman scowled at him. "Is there something concrete we can do? Maybe call you a cab?"

"A cab might be involved," the bellhop confirmed.

"Twenty dollars. Not to mention getting back," she explained to the doorman.

"Some people don't think fate should have a price," the bellhop mused.

The doorman turned his attention to a shimmering couple revolving through one of the doors, and then walked over to a cab parked at the side. She stayed with the bellhop, watching the circling doors and cabs, as the bellhop occasionally inserted himself into the choreography, popping out to open a door of a waiting cab with a slight bow, and then straightening himself up again.

When the doorman returned, he informed them that the cab waiting at the side would take her to the party for ten dollars. "I didn't use the word 'fate,'" he clarified. "I used the word 'emergency.'"

None of that seemed safe to tell the man near the cigarette machine. So, she told him about the cab ride over, about how she was afraid of the driver at first because she was always afraid of cab drivers, and how the driver, speeding down the Congress Parkway, turned to her, smiled, and showed her a tooth capped with turquoise. He didn't let her discover it by herself; he pointed it out, with an accent that was deep and melodious and could have come from any number of countries she hadn't visited. "I've found people don't like it sneaking up on them," he said, "and yes, I can use regular toothpaste on it. My wife says she cherishes it, though of course she saw it before, when it was just a chip of a thing." Then they were on a rotunda getting onto the Eisenhower, which she wasn't sure was the right way. A man with a turquoise tooth could take you anywhere. "There's a lot of things you have to trust in the world," she said.

He turned and smiled, turquoise tooth flashing. "Like cab drivers," he said, "and passengers."

In the middle of the cab driver story, the man who had made her laugh was approached by a woman who put her hand on his arm and leaned her mouth into his ear. The woman had spiked red hair that stood up at different angles, but all the spikes shifted in agreement when she motioned her head toward the door. The man's shoulders slumped, but he said all right. The woman with the spikes turned her entire body toward the door, and the man from New Jersey started to follow her, but he turned back. "Wait here," he whispered, "I want to hear the end of the story."

She saw two women she had noticed earlier with the spiked-hair woman look over at her, and one of them put her mouth toward the other one's ear. It occurred to her, because the music had stopped and she was standing so far away from the two women, that she could never have heard them, that she was observing a visual whisper, an intended stance of secrecy. And because this countenance suggested something dramatic, she tried to decide if the man from New Jersey was the fate she had been searching for; she didn't want her fate to be in New Jersey. She decided that she wouldn't wait for him to return.

When she reached the stage, she noticed an alcove to the side of the stage containing bleachers and a sign that said, FROM THE REAL COMISKEY. The only people on the bleachers were a couple on the top row, necking. When she sat on the bottom bleacher, she felt a splinter of wood nudge her thigh. The boy had stopped the song about the kite, and she missed it. She had developed more questions about it while she was gone. Where, for example, had the strings come from in the first place? Were they literal? Seaweed could look like strings, but what about the substantial parts of the kite, the parts that looked like snakes and triangles? Were they in a hopeful location? Was it only by the severing of cords that something could float up toward God, or did the string just signify a severe tangling in an unseen tree of the other parts? When she thought back to the lyrics, she thought the boy hadn't even mentioned those parts, as if he were saying the kite itself was just the string floating. Which was just wrong.

The boy was of no help. He had moved on to another song about wobbly tops and Barbie-doll heads and knives, and though she was beginning to suspect he hadn't had a happy childhood, she was angry at the nonsense of his lyrics anyway, and wished he had at least put the knife in the song about the kite, alluding to a method of disengagement of string from kite.

When she got up from the bleachers, a part of the necking couple sighed, and she was careful not to look back. She started toward the corridor with the bathrooms, still halfheartedly looking for the kind, curly-haired woman at the same time she was thinking about how to get home. There were no taxis circulating in this area, and it wasn't a safe neighborhood in which to walk. When the cabbie with the turquoise tooth had dropped her off at the address she had been given, they were in front of a tavern named in neon, He's Not Here. The front door to the tavern was open, and from the cab, they could see an empty, oblong wooden bar. Though there were about thirty stools, there was only one man at the bar. He was stooped over his beer so completely that the bald spot of his head almost touched the bar top. The bartender stood at the far end of the bar looking up at what she guessed was a television, but she couldn't be sure from her vantage point. "They look like papier-mâché," she said to the cabbie.

"I hope he's not your emergency," the cabbie said back.

"I must have the wrong address."

"Listen," the cab driver said, "I have sympathy for mankind. I believe in God. I try to do my part, but this is as far as I go." The turquoise tooth flashed. "You can go back with me."

She couldn't go back. She paid the cab driver twelve dollars and entered He's Not Here. "Nobody is, I guess," she said to the bartender. The slumped-over man raised himself up and said he took offense, and then slumped over again. In his brief appearance, she could see that he was all eyebrow. "The party's on the next block," the bartender said. "Somebody gave out the wrong address."

It was a journey of an evening, she was thinking, squeezing out the bathroom corridor into the entry room, which should have led up to something more than being squeezed into a hallway with a bunch of strangers. At this point in the evening, there were equal parts people going in and coming out, causing traffic jams. Everyone seemed a little frantic, still searching for the potential of the evening; those who were leaving were off to other parties, while those who had been elsewhere laughed themselves into new rooms of possibility. The two groups avoided each other's eyes, protecting promise.

She was at the end of the corridor when she saw Him, not any new man who could make her laugh, but the one she followed through dreams and other passageways.

Lately, in the dreams, he was always standing at the archway of a door. He never entered the room. In the dreams, he always looked like himself, only different. Sometimes, in the dreams, he would take on other forms, and she would still know it was Him. When he was a dog in her dreams, she would think some form of loyalty was left. In real life, when she ran into Him, which happened more than once, in cities where neither of them lived, it took a moment for the molecules around them to adjust so that she recognized him as part of her former life. Once, on a subway in New York, she saw Him sitting on the other side of the car, while a guy with a boom box encouraged all the commuters to "Get Happy." She left the train without saying anything, but as she exited, saw a hand pressed against the window.

Tonight, all the molecules around Him were efficient, and it was as if he had appeared from a magician's cloud of smoke. As soon as she saw Him, the rest of the room stilled, but that was only true inside herself, because she was still moving along the path with the crowd, as was he, and when they got close, he saw her, broke into a smile, and reached out for her hand, which she didn't meet, because the juxtaposition of the stilled room along with the people moving around them rendered the rhythm in the room insufficient for the timing of a handshake.

They paused in front of each other, causing the lines behind them to stop also, and during their pause, she saw everything between them reflected in his eyes, the years together and apart, the bonds that kept them floating toward each other, and though she was grateful that their ties had not yet sunk into the ocean somewhere, she was angry at Him for pulling her here tonight. Her anger made the breath come back into the room. "You're smoking again," she said, pointing to the cigarette in his hand. She saw behind him a woman who was unattached and innocent. At that instant, the man who'd made her laugh came up to her and said he'd been looking all over for her and he was afraid she'd left and did she want to get out of this smoke hole, maybe they could go someplace else for a drink. Suddenly, the crowd moved with a force that pushed her through the room and out onto the street, and the man from New Jersey followed her.

Later, she thought the story of her seeing Him was part of a larger story. If only character weren't problematic, she could move the elements around to give shape to a story they would tell to each other as they watched their children fly their kites high into the sky. She can see the shapes now: the serpent, the dragon, the malformed dog with the long tail. Beneath the kites, on the ground, a boy and girl are forming also. Their legs are chubby and they run along edges of parks and deserts, holding tight to every thread that connects us to them, and we, in turn, follow the invisible strings, riding through a city with a coast of gold, our search through narrowed streets, warehouses, and ballparks justified, the story itself a string toward promise undenied.

Contributor Biographies

Emily Carter is author of the collection *Glory Goes and Gets Some*. She is a recipient of the prestigious Whiting Award for young writers and lives in Minneapolis.

Trinie Dalton lives in Los Angeles. Her first collection of stories was published in Akashic's Little House on the Bowery series, edited by Dennis Cooper. She works for Roman Coppola as his creative assistant. As well as stories, she also writes reviews of music, art, and books.

Calla Devlin is working on a collection of linked stories, one of which was awarded an honourable mention in *The Best American Nonrequired Reading 2003*, edited by Dave Eggers. Her literary interviews with Louise Erdrich, Dorothy Allison, and others have appeared in several Powell's Books publications.

Courtney Eldridge lives in New York City. She attended the Rhode Island School of Design. She has contributed fiction to *McSweeney's*, *Mississippi Review*, and Nerve.com. Her first collection of stories is called *Unkempt*.

Ariel Gore is author of the fictionalized memoir *Atlas of the Human Heart*. She is also creator and publisher of the cult parenting zine *Hip Mama*. She lives in Portland, Oregon.

Elizabeth Graver is the author of three novels: *Awake, The Honey Thief,* and *Unravelling.* Her short story collection, *Have You Seen Me?*, was awarded the 1991 Drue Heinz Literature Prize, judged by Richard Ford. Her stories have been anthologized in several editions of *The Best American Short Stories*, and in *Prize Stories: The O. Henry Awards.* She is the recipient of a fellowship from the National Endowment for the Arts. She lives in Lincoln, Massachusetts.

Janis Harper lives in Vancouver, Canada. She helped launch *The Republic* newspaper. Her prose has been published in several journals, including *Tessera*, the French-Canadian literary journal.

Amy Hempel is the author of four collections of stories, most recently *The Dog of the Marriage*. She lives in New York City.

Karen Herman was born in Philadelphia, but now lives in London. She worked as a journalist in the United States and South Africa before completing a Creative Writing MA at Goldsmiths College, University of London. She is working on a novel about rivers.

Tara Ison is author of the novel *A Child Out of Alcatraz*, a finalist for the Los Angeles Times Book Prizes. She has taught fiction and screen-writing at U.S. universities. Her short fiction has appeared in *Tin House, Mississippi Review,* and other journals.

Sara Jaffe is a writer and musician living in San Francisco. After four years of performing and touring with her band, Erase Errata, she is now working on solo music projects, writing short fiction, and releasing written and recorded projects through Inconvenient Press & Recordings.

Anna Sophie Loewenberg is a writer and filmmaker with a special interest in Chinese youth culture. Her career began in China, where she worked for the weekly magazine *Beijing Scene* during the late '90s. In 2003, her short documentary *China Pirates,* about pirated media and punk rock in Beijing, premiered at the San Diego Asian Film Festival.

Devika Mehra was born and raised in New Delhi, India. Her fiction has appeared in *Ploughshares* and *Best New American Voices 2004.* She is working on a novel.

Colette Paul was born in Glasgow, Scotland. She has published a short story collection, *Whoever You Choose to Love,* and is the recipient of a Scottish Arts Council Award to help her complete a first novel.

Gail Louise Siegel has published short fiction in *Zoetrope: All-Story Extra, StoryQuarterly,* and *Post Road* and another of her stories was nominated for a Pushcart Prize. She lives in Chicago, where she serves on MFA critique panels for the School of the Art Institute of Chicago.

Gale R. Walden lives in Chicago. Her stories have appeared in several literary magazines, including *Boston Review* and *Prairie Schooner.*

Acknowledgments

Love to everyone who helped, especially K

About the Editor

Amy Prior is a writer based in London. Her short fiction is regularly published in journals and anthologies, and her critically acclaimed collections have been published in both Britain and the United States. She is currently writing a book-length work of fiction set in London.

Selected Titles from Seal Press

For more than 25 years, Seal Press has published groundbreaking books. By women. For women. Visit our website at www.sealpress.com.

Inappropriate Random: Stories on Sex and Love edited by Amy Prior. $13.95, 1-58005-099-9. Established and emerging American and British women writers take a hard look at love, exposing its flaws with unflinching, often hilarious, candor.

Listen Up: Voices from the Next Feminist Generation edited by Barbara Findlen. $16.95, 1-58005-054-9. A revised and expanded edition of the Seal Press classic, this anthology features the voices of a new generation of women expressing the vibrancy and vitality of today's feminist movement.

Trace Elements of Random Tea Parties by Felicia Luna Lemus. $13.95, 1-58005-126-X. Leticia navigates the streets of Los Angeles as well as the twisting roads of her own sexuality in this crazy-beautiful narrative of love and *familia*.

Valencia by Michelle Tea. $13.00, 1-58005-035-2. This fast-paced account of one girl's search for love and high times abound in the drama-filled dyke world of San Francisco's Mission District.

I'll Know It When I See It: A Daughter's Search for Home in Ireland by Alice Carey. $14.95, 1-58005-132-4. This lyrically written memoir of a young New Yorker's ties to Ireland also chronicles her eventual move to the country as an adult.

Job Hopper: The Checkered Career of a Down-Market Dilettante by Ayun Halliday. $14.95, 1-58005-130-8. The author's hilarious misadventures in the working world—including stints as a lifeguard, artist's model, mime, mascot, and massage therapist—are chronicled in this entertaining collection.